OTHERWISE ENGAGED

LAURA YOUNG

SILVER DAGGER
MYSTERIES
An Imprint of The Overmountain Press
JOHNSON CITY, TENNESSEE

This book is a work of fiction. All names, characters, places, and events are either the product of the author's imagination or are used fictitiously. Any resemblance to actual events or persons, living or dead, is entirely coincidental and beyond the intent of either the author or the publisher.

Book design by Cherisse McGinty

Hardcover ISBN 1-57072-280-3
Trade Paper ISBN 1-57072-281-1
Copyright © 2004 by Laura Guetig
Printed in the United States of America
All Rights Reserved

1 2 3 4 5 6 7 8 9 0

For Alison

ACKNOWLEDGMENTS

A job ceases to be work when it becomes great fun. Spinning the tale of Kate Kelly's latest romp was made possible by the great folks at Silver Dagger Mysteries—Beth Wright, Sherry Lewis, and Karin O'Brien. It's a pleasure to work with you.

Ultimate thanks, as always, to Mom, for encouraging me, from the moment I could read, to pick up books and enjoy the adventures. You set me on this path.

Also, my enduring thanks to my "family" at WLKY, including Andrea Stahlman, for the book title. I know I can always count on the best minds in television to pop out the creative ideas.

For the best support and friendship ever, my thanks to Michelle and Mike Bottorff, Elaine Munsch, Robert Steurer, Rita Priddy, Molly Wolfram, Chris Vale, and Sher Stumler. Your support and creative ideas made telling this story fun.

And to "the girls," you never know how fascinated I am with your many stories—no telling where they'll end up someday!

And last, but certainly not least, this book would never have seen the light of day without the guidance and enthusiasm of Alison Shaw. Your unfailing support and insistence on meeting deadlines made this dream a reality. You are the best. Thank you!

C H A P ┇ E R · 1

"I NEED A FAVOR."

As I advance uneasily into old age, I am increasingly convinced that those are four of the most frightening words in the English language, or any language for that matter. While at first they appear innocent, devoid of any threat or vulgarity, these few words, when strung together, have the ability to instill a lingering, simmering fear akin to the churning stomach that accompanies the realization that a dental appointment looms the next day.

My name is Kate Kelly. I'm what's known as a travel writer, which basically means I travel here and there, covering interesting little towns and cozy tourist spots across the country. I visit my assigned locations, soak up the local culture, then pen what I hope is a delightfully entertaining article for *Travel Adventures*, the aptly named magazine I work for based in Washington, D.C.

And yes, contrary to the many snide remarks I've encountered over the years, it is a real job. I'm not sure what the exact definition of "real job" is anyway, other than something that is perceived as tougher than someone else's job. The circulation and advertising numbers are enough to prove that lots of people read the kind of magazine articles I write. Think of all the dog-eared magazines you see in waiting rooms across the country. It doesn't matter whether it's a doctor's office or a car repair shop, I can pretty much guarantee you that a glossy travel magazine beats *Popular Mechanics* any old day.

Like many jobs, it's not as glamorous as it sounds. Dealing with editors and publishers can be stressful enough to send a paratrooper into hiding. True, I'm not jackhammering concrete in sub-zero weather, but occasionally it has felt that difficult.

On the personal side, I'm single, on the cusp of thirty, have no kids, no major responsibilities, and no serious, heaving, soap opera relationships. On the whole, life is sweet.

While most of my high school chums are married and spawning offspring, I'm more or less a free spirit. I certainly hope to be married and be a mommy someday, but right now I'm having too much fun seeing the world and meeting all kinds of interesting people. I harbor a secret desire to collect all these stories and one day lock myself away and write the great American novel, but for now, simply collecting the stories chapter by chapter suits me fine.

Now that I think of it, one of the things I recently collected was a boyfriend, which is a strange thing to call a physician who routinely saves lives, including mine. His name is John Donovan. We met a few months ago when I ended up in the hospital while visiting my parents in Williamsburg, Virginia. Mind you, I wasn't hospitalized due to my parents, who are sweet, doting folks. On the contrary, I managed to become mixed up in a small-town murder, which landed me under John's care. I'm mended physically, but John and I still manage to play doctor regularly.

Unfortunately, thanks to his busy schedule and my many travels, we don't see that much of each other. When we do manage to get together, we have a great time, but recently, I've found myself wondering if this long-distance romance will work out. I worry and fret for a while, then invariably a girlfriend calls me and whines about her husband or obsessive lover, and I decide maybe what John and I have is actually the most healthy way to conduct a successful relationship.

Relationship—what a big, heavy word. Things must be getting serious with John, because I often find myself staring at a snapshot of him tacked to the gray fabric wall of my "office," a slightly enlarged cubicle at Patton Publishing, home of *Travel Adventures*. I exist in cubicle-land as opposed to officedom because, I assume, some highly paid, Brooks Brothers-suited consultant decided that writers who are gone on assignment love the outdoors so much, they don't mind sitting out in the middle of a windowless room with twenty or so of their closest friends.

But that issue could be debated forever.

It had been a relatively calm Wednesday—otherwise known as hump day, halfway round the bend to the weekend—when I got the unnerving request for a favor. I was busy at work, diligently contemplating the executive decision whether to head out to lunch or finish an article on holiday crowds and decorations at the Biltmore mansion in North Carolina. Even though I faced a two o'clock deadline and had thoroughly enjoyed visiting Biltmore for the article, I couldn't ignore the plaintive mating call of a double-decker turkey, ham, and Swiss from Deli Delights on Norton Street.

Food, work. Work, food. It certainly didn't take a college degree to guess the direction I was headed. To make matters worse, I also remembered that Wednesday was "Brownie or Bust" day at Deli Delights, so as far as I was concerned, my decision was complete.

My other decision was what to do about the awful request for a favor. I reached for a pen and pad of paper.

"Favors are mighty beasts," I answered to the voice on the phone.

"Aw, come on, Katemeister, you know you'd do anything for me," the voice purred. It belonged to Adam Kelly, my cousin and the closest thing I ever had to a big brother. Resolutely single, he traveled a lot, opening restaurants all over the place. "Meet me for lunch at twelve-thirty, at Chez Pierre on Seventh, near the Eastern Market on the Hill."

"That sounds a little upscale for me," I said. "Remember, I'm a lowly journalist, you're the highly paid restaurant consultant." I scribbled the address. "I still don't understand what you do. I think 'restaurant consultant' sounds suspiciously like a made-up position."

"And you can explain 'travel writer'?" he challenged. "Sounds more like vacation junkie to me. Look, you know what I do. I set up new restaurants, hire the cooks, the staffs, get them off the ground. My restaurants are my babies. Chez Pierre is just my latest adventure. It's not as fancy as it sounds, and lunch is on me, so you shouldn't complain. Come on, Kate, I haven't seen you since the big summer extravaganza your mom threw. I'm in town for a couple of days and would simply enjoy the pleasure of seeing my prettiest cousin." Maybe Adam should have become a chef instead, because he sure knew how to heap on the sugary goo.

"And there's also the matter of this favor you want," I pointed out.

He chuckled. "Well, yeah, that too. Please, Kate? You know I wouldn't ask if it wasn't important. Will I see you at the restaurant?"

I turned my computer screen off. "Yeah, yeah, you know me—I never turn down free food. I'll see you shortly."

The rest of my article could wait until after lunch. I grabbed my coat and tossed a dark green scarf around my head. November winds were hitting D.C. with a vengeance, which didn't bode well for the upcoming winter. I could have driven the half mile or so to the restaurant, but parking was always a nightmare in that area, and some inner demon reminded me that exercise was something I ignored too frequently.

As I navigated the crowded and narrow sidewalks, I thought about Adam. He grew up about a mile away from my family's home outside Williamsburg, where my dad was a tenured history professor at the College of William & Mary. An only child of working parents, I spent many hours at Adam's house and adopted him as a pseudo big brother. In fact, in high school, we convinced more than one teacher that we really were siblings. That always made life interesting on parent-teacher nights.

Though we'd had our share of scrapes over the years, I'd always adored Adam and would do anything for him. But I had a distinct feeling this favor might turn out to be something I'd regret.

I stared at the buildings down the street and spotted Chez Pierre, a tiny café tucked on the first floor of a row of law offices. The only thing that gave it away as a restaurant was a green-and-white-striped awning and a small sign hanging in the door. As I crossed the street, carefully scripting my suggestion to Adam for better signage, I realized my editorial comment wouldn't be necessary.

The joint, as they say, was jumping. Every table in the narrow restaurant was taken, and a row of nattily dressed, young, upwardly mobile Washingtonians lined the far wall like a living, breathing ad in the latest issue of *Town & Country*. They were packed together so tightly, I hardly realized there was a bar behind them. An impressive selection of antique mirrors and French theatrical posters covered every inch of wall space, and a hearty, deep-throated singer belted out a jazzy blend of French bistro music over the sound system.

As I pulled off my scarf and began working on my coat, a harried looking young girl in black pants, white shirt, and black bow tie scooted up to me, ready to practice what was left of her high school French. "*Bonjour,* welcome to Chez Pierre. I'm afraid there's about an hour's wait for a table."

"There's no wait for the great Kate," chimed a familiar voice behind me. Adam snatched my coat and scarf, and instead of kissing me on both cheeks in the traditional French style, he ruffled my hair, which no doubt improved its perpetually disheveled look. "Kate, I knew you'd come through for me."

"I thought you said Chez Pierre wasn't that fancy."

He shrugged his shoulders. "Well, to these people, it's not, and please don't call it trendy. I might have to slap you. Come on, I already have a table for us."

"One of the perks of being the boss, huh?"

We reached a table covered in starched white linen and set with crystal and delicate, yellow-flowered china. A basket of fresh, still-steaming baguettes sat next to a thin bud vase that nearly drowned under the weight of an enormous, milky-white calla lily.

"Calla lilies in November?" I observed. "Quite impressive, Adam."

"Hey, it's a touch of class. And I'm not the boss. I just come in here, suggest these wonderful ideas, then go my merry way. You should do a story about me, Kate. I could use the publicity. You could call me the fairy godfather of new restaurants."

I took my seat. "Okay, godfather, what's for lunch? I'm starved."

He crooked his finger in his best James Bond imitation, and two tuxedo-vested servers appeared on cue. One poured Chardonnay while the other placed artfully arranged salads in front of us.

Adam broke off a piece of the warm baguette. "I know your fondness for junk food. I thought a healthy lunch might do you some good for a change."

I looked up from my salad. "How thoughtful, I'll be sure to tell Ma and Pa you're taking care of me here in the big city. So, what's for dessert?"

He laughed. "I've missed you, Kate." He picked up his wineglass. "A toast—to family and the friends we've become along the way." It was a bit melodramatic, even for Adam, but we clinked glasses and downed the wine. "We need to get together more often, same as we used to do when we were kids," he added warmly.

He was leading up to something, but he was never very good at being serious for long. He put down his fork and stared at his plate. After a moment of indigestion, or maybe brilliance, he looked up at me, his blue eyes crinkling into a big grin. "About the favor. Now, before you say no, remember, it could be a lot of fun, and you'd be doing something wonderful for me, as well as something noble for a friend. A public service, if you will."

I raised an eyebrow. "Adam, that is no way to sell something before you've even said what it is. If it's so bad that you need a laundry list of qualifiers before you ask it, I probably have no choice but to say no."

The grin faded. "I forgot, you're a reporter and naturally suspicious of everything. Maybe this is a bit unorthodox, but it would mean a lot to me if you could give me a hand."

"Spill it, Adam. Just tell me what it is."

The grin flashed across his face again. He hesitated, then plunged ahead. "I have a friend who was engaged to this girl, but—"

I held up my hand. "Uh-uh. No blind dates. I stopped having those years ago. They're bad for my complexion. I usually turn green."

"No, no, it's not like that," he said quickly. "Well, not exactly. You know him from high school. Harrison Brentwood King."

The name scratched in the vaguest corners of my memory, but I couldn't produce a face. "You were three years ahead of me. I didn't know all your friends."

Adam leaned forward eagerly. "Sure, you remember him. He went by Brent, played soccer with me. Dark hair, blue eyes. His parents had a horse farm, raised Thoroughbreds. They moved to Kentucky senior year, so he didn't graduate with me."

A face popped into my mind, and I wasn't overly impressed. I saw a slightly pudgy, normal-looking kid with messy black hair and a shy grin. I remembered thinking that Adam and his friends were probably the only ones, other than horses, that Harrison Brentwood King conversed with on a regular basis. And what kind of a stuffy name was Harrison Brentwood King anyway? How could parents do that to an innocent baby?

"I think I remember him. So, what's the scoop on Harry boy?"

"The Kings are wealthy and move in all the equestrian social circles—dinners with the governor, boxes at the Kentucky Derby, the whole nine yards. Brent and his fiancée were supposed to announce their engagement at this big weekend house party that his mom arranged, but she's bolted."

"Mom bolted? Didn't like junior's girl?"

"Kate, please," Adam frowned. "No, the fiancée has disappeared, and they have to have this party. They have no choice."

"The show must go on, even without the main attraction? Isn't that a bit difficult?"

"Granted," Adam replied. "It's more complicated than that. His mom has . . . shall we say . . . a delicate problem. She has a slight mental condition, and they don't want to upset her after she planned this major party and invited all these socialites and important business leaders."

"And my role is what?" I asked.

"Well, someone needs to play the bride-to-be," he said simply.

I took a bite of my salad. "Oh, yeah, that sounds really fun to me—crazy mama and a bunch of stiff-upper-lip snobs, drinking French champagne and eating escargot. What a swell party."

From the look on Adam's face, I realized I'd said the wrong thing.

His eyes lit up. "I'm so glad to hear you say that. You'll make a great girlfriend for Brent. I knew you'd be willing to help. You're the greatest, Kate."

I shook my head so fiercely, my shoulder-length brown curls slapped my face. "No, Adam, I haven't agreed to anything. I was kidding. The party sounds like something out of an old 'Dynasty' rerun. I think Harrison, Brent—or whatever his name is—is taking you for a ride. Girlfriends don't just vanish into thin air unless they have a really good reason."

"Kate, you've got to help. This is serious. Brent's career is really taking off, and there will be people there he needs to impress. It goes without saying that it would be social suicide for his family if his mom's big shindig fell to pieces, and . . . well . . . if she, you know . . . went a little nuts."

"Oh, please, Adam," I interrupted. "This is just ridiculous. I am not an actress. And don't you think someone would notice I wasn't the real fiancée? If he's that serious about her, surely someone has met her before. Am I supposed to announce that I've been recovering from massive plastic surgery in the jungles of Africa or something? This would never work in a million years."

He leaned forward eagerly. "Of course it would. No one has met her. Brent's been working in New York for several months. He met her there, and he's never brought her home to Kentucky for a visit, but . . . well, I guess she disappeared."

"That should tell you something right there." I shoved a big fork-load of salad into my mouth. "So, what does Harrison boy do in New York?"

Adam's gaze shifted over my shoulder. He broke into a smile and waved his hand. "You'll see. He's here. I asked him to stop by so we could work out the details for this weekend."

I dropped my fork onto the plate. "Did you just assume I would—"

He grinned. "Yeah, Katemeister, I did. You're the greatest, remember that."

Unbelievable. I stared at Adam with a mix of righteous anger and hopeless amusement. We'd always gotten along famously as kids, so it was a good thing he was only my cousin and not my big brother. Sisterly responsibility would have dictated I kill him on the spot, or at least lob the bread basket in his direction. I sighed, swiped my napkin across my face, and turned in my chair to spy my first look at dear Harrison.

I looked, then looked again. I did, in fact, know Harrison Brentwood King. At least I was acquainted with his, um, intimate details. He was an underwear model for the Paragon Department Store. Not that I looked at their ads for just the pictures of beefy, beautiful men wearing the briefest of briefs and doing realistic things such as holding attaché cases on the subway or fishing poles in the great outdoors. No, not at all. It was just one of those things I happened to notice when reading the paper.

I'd learned to spot his photos nationwide during various travels. Harrison

Brentwood King didn't just model underwear. At least once a week I saw him staring back at me from the paper in a snazzy tailored suit or a rugged sweater and jeans.

So this was the geeky guy from high school? Thank heaven for puberty.

I wasn't the only one who recognized him. Female eyes throughout the café followed his every step toward our table. A few heads were bent in "Isn't that. . . ?" whispers, and waves of giggles erupted as soon as he acknowledged a leer here or there.

Adam leapt to his feet when Harrison reached us, and they indulged in a chummy back-slapping, hand-pumping display of testosterone. Once that was out of their system, Adam said, "You remember my cousin Kate, don't you?"

Harrison Brentwood King pivoted effortlessly toward me and, with a dazzling, practiced smile, gushed, "Kate, lovely as ever. It's so good to see you again. It's been way too long."

A tiny alarm sounded in the back of my mind. Although I knew he could have said that to any woman in the restaurant, if not for the ridiculous favor, he would have passed me by at warp speed. Still, some hormone was overtaking rational thought. Once I got past the perfect teeth, the aristocratic cheekbones, and the scent of expensive cologne, all I could see were eyes a vibrant shade of turquoise, flecked with little shavings of sea green that I could stare at for hours. Or days.

Ignoring years of journalistic toughness, I held out my hand and nearly whimpered, "Harrison, it's very good to meet you."

He pulled his chair close to mine and, wrapping both my hands in his, purred seductively, "Please, call me Brent. Only strangers call me Harrison."

"We *are* strangers," I blurted. "But Brent it is. You're looking . . . um, much different than I remember."

My choice of words didn't compute until I spotted the horrified look that spread across Adam's face. He quickly sat down and changed the topic. "You know, Brent, I was just telling Kate about the party this weekend. She thought it sounded like a good time."

I snapped back to reality and shot Adam a warning glance. I didn't think this was the time to remind him I was making a joke when I said it sounded like a fun party. In fact, I never agreed to play the happy girlfriend in his weird request. I sneaked a look at Brent again and decided it wouldn't be such a hardship to pretend for a little while. Maybe I was being too serious about the whole idea.

Brent's multiwatt smile grew. "That's great. Adam said you'd be good with this. You're a writer, right? You make up stuff all the time."

My eyebrows shot northward. "I'm a journalist. I don't make up stories. I report them as fact."

Brent's grin faltered a second. "Oh, sure, whatever. A journalist. That will work."

Adam quickly reached across the table and grabbed my elbow. He chuckled nervously, but his stare was intense and pleading. "Now, Kate, we all know you're a great reporter, just like your mom. Brent, Kate's mom—my aunt—is Helen Kelly, of the *Virginia Tribune*."

Brent looked blank. "Uh, I don't read the paper that much—just the sports page and comics, in between ad shoots. What paper did you say that was?"

Adam took a faltering breath. "It's not important, Brent. Now, a lot of fun people will be at the house this weekend, right?"

My rational side returned with a vengeance. Brent was beautiful, but I wondered if years of hair spray and basking under hot lights had fried his brain. Mom wasn't world famous, but anyone who read the *Tribune* knew very well who she was. Of course, he said he didn't read the paper, an offense I considered as bad as scraping nails down a chalkboard. Surely Brent had caught a story or two on the back of his clipped Paragon ads.

I stiffened, delivered a solid kick under the table to Adam's knee, and prepared to steadfastly ignore Brent's eyes while I told him I was not interested in attending his party. As I opened my mouth to speak, Brent slipped to the floor. At first, I thought he had dropped something, but instead, he was resting on one bended knee.

The restaurant grew uncomfortably silent as all eyes turned in our direction. Brent grabbed my hand and, in one swift motion, produced a tiny blue box and flipped the top open with his thumb, exposing a gumball-size diamond solitaire surrounded by a veritable army of smaller diamonds.

"Kate, darling, will you marry me?"

C H A P T E R · 2

"HUH?"

Like most red-blooded American girls, I'd waited all my life to hear that question, but somehow, this wasn't exactly how I'd pictured the magic moment. It was meant to sweep me off my feet, no doubt, but this particular proposal lacked a major ingredient—for example, say, the man of my dreams. Granted, Brent filled the bill on looks alone, but silly me, I wanted to at least be acquainted with my Prince Charming.

I'd always envisioned saying a resounding "Yes!" and then sharing my good news with everyone in sight. Though the crowd was there, the "Yes" was not. The breathless silence and prying eyes of the other diners made me want to slide under the table. Seconds ticked away like long, painful hours as I raced to say something intelligible.

Brent made matters worse. He slipped the enormous rock on my finger and reached up to touch my cheek. "Kate, make me the happiest man alive."

Oh, give me a break, Romeo.

A woman at the next table giggled. "Isn't that sweet, she's so surprised, she can't speak."

No kidding. "Brent, I don't know what to say," I began slowly.

Adam leapt to his feet. "We need champagne! Let's hear it for Brent and Kate!"

A deafening roar of applause, whistles, and old-fashioned foot-stomping blew through the tiny restaurant, and a waiter hustled past the well-wishers with a chilled bottle and two glasses. He popped the cork with an earsplitting bang, sending a foamy stream of champagne spurting from the mouth of the bottle, like molten lava erupting from a volcano. Champagne splattered onto the table and ran down the waiter's arm as he quickly poured two glasses.

Brent rose, handed me a glass, and raised the other. "To my beautiful bride, Kate, and my best man, Adam, who brought us together. Words just can't express how happy I am. And to everyone here, I'm so proud to share this moment with you all."

Applause erupted again. Brent tipped his glass to his adoring fans, downed a good chunk of the champagne in one swallow, then grabbed my hand and kissed it, to more cheers.

Adam surveyed the crowd with complete amazement, no doubt imagining his little restaurant as the new romance hub of the neighborhood. While he added up the PR points and dollar signs, I caught a glimpse of my reflection in one of the mirrors lining the wall. My face looked badly sunburned, my eyes were nearly bulging out of their sockets, and my mouth dropped open in an expression that, in other situations, would prompt medical personnel to call for the heart attack crash cart.

A demure, blushing bride I was not. In fact, I was so stunned, embarrassed, and furious that I wondered if I would indeed need that crash cart.

When the applause wound down to a dull roar and the diners slowly returned to what they should have been doing all along, Brent at last sat down and immediately poured another glass of champagne. "You haven't touched your glass yet, Kate."

He smiled. I didn't.

Adam's bravado dissolved, and his face morphed from glee to acute apprehension. He avoided my gaze. "Well, I guess you can't say no now, huh? I should check on things in the kitchen and let you two talk for a while."

I reached for Adam's sleeve and yanked him into his chair so hard, the jolt knocked over the salt shaker and caused the calla lily to shimmer in horror. "You're not going anywhere," I hissed. "Someone better start talking very fast, before I seriously hurt both of you."

Brent's grin resurfaced. "Feisty. I like that."

Adam quickly interrupted. "Okay, Kate, I'm sorry. We've gone a little overboard, I admit."

I nodded. "Keep talking, Adam."

"We thought you might get a kick out of this, but in retrospect, I realize we should have played it straight and asked for your help." He glanced at Brent. "And, Kate, you've *got* to help. It's only a weekend—a couple of days. It would mean so much to us. You won't have to do anything you're uncomfortable with."

"I'm uncomfortable with the entire situation," I retorted icily.

Adam sighed and reached for my glass of champagne. He raised it to his lips and emptied it. "I'll be there with you, and if anything goes wrong, or you feel strange about any part of it, we'll leave, no questions asked. Please, Kate? It will be fun, I promise."

Brent reached for my hand again. "I'm sorry if I embarrassed you, Kate. Let me make it up to you this weekend. My parents really do have a spectacular place, and I'm sure the party will be fun, regardless of the reason you're there. I won't embarrass you any further, and you have my word as a gentleman that I'll be on my best behavior."

I could have easily substituted two slobbering, glassy-eyed basset hounds for Adam and Brent at that moment. Both were nearly panting, and their mournful expressions were almost too much to bear. Adam had used the same tactic on me too many times over the years, and he knew I always fell for it. I didn't know what Brent's excuse could be, other than the fact that he had proven himself a fair actor. And his turquoise eyes were working overtime.

"I'll have to think this over and let you know," I replied slowly.

"But the tickets—" Brent began.

Adam cut him off. "Kate, what's to think about? No one there will know you. I'll be there the entire time, and, if anything, it'll be a free weekend at a private resort, of sorts. That's right up your alley." His face brightened substantially as he relaxed in his chair. "Make it useful. Everybody knows about horse farms in the spring and summer when they're busy racing, so why not show the world what happens during the colder months? Write an article on the year-round social whirl surrounding a famous Kentucky horse farm."

"There's plenty to write about," Brent added quickly. "I'd be glad to arrange interviews with some of our trainers and staff. That's a great idea, Adam. Oh, Kate, you can't turn us down now."

Leave it to Adam to come up with a viable excuse. "I'll have to discuss it with my editor," I said, regretting each word as it came out of my mouth. "Speaking of which, I need to get back to work. I have a deadline to meet, and something tells me it's going to be difficult to concentrate the rest of the day."

Adam grinned broadly. He knew he had cracked my shell. "We'll walk you back to your office and talk more on the way."

"I haven't agreed to anything," I warned as I rose from my chair.

"But the tickets," Brent said in a stage whisper to Adam.

"What do you mean?" I asked. "That's the second time you've said that."

Brent gently guided me into my chair again. "The arrangements . . . I mean . . . well, the airplane tickets to Kentucky are purchased. Everything is set. We leave in the morning. Adam hasn't told you yet?"

The grin faded, and Adam poured another glass of champagne. The bottle was nearly empty, and I had yet to have a sip. "No, not yet, Brent," he confessed. "We didn't get that far."

I shut my eyes and attempted to count to ten but made it only to four. "I have a job, guys. I have a life, too. Do you think just because I travel a lot, I can throw together a complete trip in an afternoon, not to mention fabricate an entirely new existence?"

"Well, sure," Brent replied. "Adam said you could do it with no problem. And, Kate, I'll make it worth your while."

I shot a look in his direction. I wasn't sure I understood what he meant by that, and I didn't think this was the time to ask for clarification. I also wasn't thrilled with Adam's broad assumption that I would be so eager to participate. The opportunity to have an instant article for my next assignment was tempting, but things were too neat, too clean, and too strange for my tastes. However, despite my many reservations, I was running out of excuses.

I stretched it pretty far. "I don't have anything to wear to a country estate and fancy party. When I work, it's in jeans, not sequins."

"You have a perfectly good black cocktail dress," Adam offered. "You wore it last Christmas. I remember it, short sleeves, short skirt. We're not talking Buckingham Palace, Kate. Just bring some sweaters, jeans, and a maybe a couple of skirts. I guarantee you can pack in an hour, right, Brent?"

"Oh, absolutely," Brent chimed in. "We're not that fancy, Kate. Adam's right, it will be a very casual weekend. Just one night where we need to put on the show."

I tried again. "I'm not an actress. Just how do you expect us to pull this off? Someone, somewhere, is bound to know I'm not your fiancée."

Brent flashed his photogenic smile and rubbed his finger on my new diamond cluster as if it were Aladdin's lamp. "Ah, but Kate, you *are* my fiancée, for now."

I snatched my hand away and buried it in my lap. "You aren't very torn up that your real fiancée is missing. Doesn't that bother you at all? Where is she, Brent?"

His face darkened. "I . . . I don't know. If I did, I could talk to her and then she wouldn't be missing."

Maybe she discovered too late how limited your reasoning skills are, I thought.

He sank against the chair and deflated like a shiny birthday balloon with a slow leak. "We weren't fighting or anything. We were happy, I thought." He gestured idly. "In my profession, I meet a lot of women. I guess they're drawn to me or something—you know, for my sex appeal. They call. Leave notes, candy, phone numbers, underwear."

Adam's jaw dropped. "Underwear? You're kidding, right?"

Brent looked surprised. "No. Hasn't that ever happened to you?"

It was Adam's turn to deflate. "Uh, no. So, how did you meet her?"

A faraway look clouded Brent's eyes. "We met at the grocery. Of all places, in the produce section. I said she had nice looking melons, and she slapped me, right there in broad daylight. It was great."

I sank my head into my hand and rubbed my temple. This was my dream fiancé?

Brent regained momentum. "You see, I really did mean she had nice melons—the food. You know, cantaloupe?"

For good measure, I delivered another kick under the table to Adam's knee.

He bolted up in his chair and fired an annoyed look my way. He cleared his throat. "Yeah, that's . . . that's a unique way to meet. I guess she thought you meant—"

Thankfully, Brent didn't let him finish. "Yeah, can you believe it? Paige has the best sense of humor. She's an artist, you know."

"Do tell," I mumbled.

"Yeah, she works out of her home, designing jewelry. She sells it to boutiques all over. Paige Kendall Designs. Have you seen them?"

Adam and I shook our heads. I looked at the diamond ring resting on my finger and asked, "How long did you date Paige before you got engaged?"

Brent shifted in his chair and, for the first time, looked uncomfortable. "About four weeks. But before you make another face, I want you both to know that we're serious about each other." He nodded furiously, as if to convince himself. "We're soul mates, bonded by destiny. That's what Paige's psychic told her."

Adam winced. "Did Paige break your engagement before she left?"

"No, that's what I don't understand," Brent said earnestly. "She woke up one morning, kissed me, and was gone."

"That's a little too poetic," I said. "What happened between the kiss and the disappearance?" I immediately regretted my phrasing when I saw the simpy smirk spread across his face.

"Well, I don't need to tell every detail, but let's just say things were normal."

He glanced at Adam and smiled. "Or, actually, pretty great. She said she was going back to her apartment to work on her jewelry and would be back that afternoon. I had an early shoot, but it lasted longer than I thought it would. When I got home, around seven that night, she was gone. History. Zippo. The weird thing is, she didn't take any of her stuff. She even left her toothbrush.

"I checked Paige's apartment and called her friends," he continued, anticipating my question. "It was the same thing. Her apartment was untouched, her closets full, suitcases under her bed. None of her friends have spoken to her, and her roommate has never returned my calls."

Adam jumped in. "She's been gone over a week now."

It appeared Paige needed breathing room. "She's an artist. Perhaps she took off for a few days to get new inspiration."

Brent shrugged his shoulders. "Maybe, but that doesn't sound like her. I guess I don't know her as well as I thought," he conceded. "I just hope she's okay."

I felt sorry for Brent. "Did you notify the police she was missing?"

His head shot up. "You think that's necessary? I mean, I just thought she split. Do you think she's in danger?"

Adam looked at me and said, "You never told me she just vaporized, Brent. You just said she left. Maybe you should file a missing persons report."

Brent's jaw tightened. He toyed with a fork on the table. "No. I don't want to. I can't risk the publicity. She'll surface; I know she will. Kate, I need your help. I have to have you at this party. You guys just don't understand what will happen if we don't show up there. Mom will . . . it won't be . . . I don't know what to do."

Staring at the table, he tapped the fork nervously against a plate. "No one wants to admit they might have been dumped. Usually, I do the dumping, so I guess I'm getting a taste of it now. I really do care for Paige, and I don't understand why she left. I was so excited about our engagement that I called home, and Mom set to arranging everything for this weekend."

He glanced at us uneasily. "My mom has some problems, okay? These big parties are therapy for her. I can't let her down. Please, Kate, help me. Go to this party with me, pretend you at least like me. When the weekend is up, we'll leave. I'll wait a couple of days, then call and say that on the way home we realized we made a mistake. I'll say we broke it off, and life will go on. You'll never have to see me again."

Brent, Adam, and I sat in silence. Brent did a great job of laying on the guilt trip. He might not have been the most suave or sophisticated suitor, but it was admirable how he was trying to help his mother. Plus, he was Adam's friend, and if I stretched my reasoning, that made it tolerable.

I still thought Paige simply wised up and realized there needed to be more to a relationship than a gorgeous face and body, but I also sympathized with Brent's position. It would be awful to face your family and friends and say, "Sorry, party's off. She realized I wasn't worth it."

And I needed an article for the magazine.

And it might be entertaining to play a society bride for a day.

I shut my eyes and took a breath. "I have to talk to my editor. She might not let me off until Friday. That might be the best I can do."

Brent practically jumped across the table. He sprang to life and wrapped me in an awkward hug. "Kate, thank you. Adam is right, you are a very special person."

Adam beamed like a proud new father. "Yes, you are, Kate. I owe you a big one."

I pushed away from Brent and stood up. "We'll discuss that later. I need to get back to work."

I extended my hand to him, but he rose quickly, wrapped his arms around my waist, and plopped a kiss on me that would have impressed Mae West.

He pulled away and nuzzled in my ear. "I can't shake your hand. We just got engaged, you know. Can't disappoint everyone in the restaurant."

I swallowed hard and tried to regain my composure. My goodness. This was not indicative of my usual lunch hour.

Adam helped me with my coat. "Sure you don't want us to walk you back, Kate? You look a little off balance. I overheard the waiter tell a customer that Brent just 'rocked her world.'"

"You're treading on thin ice, Adam," I said. "I'll talk to you later."

Ignoring the wink from Brent and the laughter from Adam, I quickly made my way to the door. I didn't even remember the walk back to work, where I spent the better part of the next hour staring blankly at my computer screen.

My gaze occasionally shifted to the ring. It was huge—stunning—and I couldn't fathom what it must have cost. The faceted, round, multicarat diamond solitaire was bolstered on either side by three slender, stacked rectangular diamonds. Smaller round diamonds formed connecting half moons across the top and bottom of the solitaire. I even stooped to counting the diamonds—fifteen in all, including the massive solitaire. I'd never seen anything quite like it.

"What in the hell is that growing on your hand?" came a familiar voice over the top of my cubicle.

It belonged to Alice Donard, my editor and best friend. My actual boss was Lou Woodson, the managing editor for *Travel Adventures*; Alice was the coordinating editor. Lou approved the stories and made final decisions on assignments and placements. Alice helped us loathsome writers with little things like verifying facts, checking grammar, and nudging us along when we slacked off—as I was doing at the time. Since Lou was out of the office for a couple of weeks, that bumped Alice up to reigning-boss status.

She swung around the cubicle wall and grabbed my hand. "Tell me you got this out of a candy machine. It can't be real. Look at that rock; you could give someone a concussion with it. Why didn't you tell me John was in town? I thought you were just complaining that you never saw him."

She slumped against the cubicle and pulled a cigarette out of her blazer pocket and shoved it between her teeth. "You can't get married. We're the last single women on earth. What am I going to do?"

"It's not what you think. I can explain, and I definitely need your advice." I reached in my desk drawer and tossed her a pack of matches. "You should give that up, it's a bad habit. But I have to admit, I almost took up smoking this afternoon."

"This must be serious," she said as she struck the match.

I spilled the entire story, ending two cigarettes later with the hope that Alice would tell me the idea was ridiculous and that she had me assigned to another story. In Fiji, if I was lucky.

I wasn't so lucky. She loved it.

"This is fabulous!" she enthused. She swept her hand through her long red hair. "It's Julia Roberts in *Pretty Woman*. No, it's Grace Kelly in *High Society*, only it's really Kate Kelly in *High Society Gone Nuts, Part Two*. What a hoot!"

"You don't really want me to go through with this, do you?" I pleaded.

"Of course I do. What a story. It's perfect. I don't care a whit about the horses; just write about the party. Kentucky Southern society at its most Southern—a hoity-toity engagement on a horse farm. I see well-dressed women, incredible recipes, guests sitting on the porch while horses graze in the background."

"It's November," I reminded her. "No one will be sitting on a porch watching horses graze in the distance."

Alice waved her hand in the air. "No matter. No one will care. I'll hire a freelance photographer and have him meet you at the airport." She grinned ear to ear. "You don't even have to write that you're the bride. The whole thing's a farce anyway, so just make up a bride and have the photographer take a picture of one of the women at the party."

"Alice, you're my friend. Don't make me do this."

"I'm also your boss when Lou is away. This is going to be a blast. Go home now and start packing. If you get the urge to stay all week, you've got my permission, and you've got an expense account. Go to it." She reached for my hand. "That is the biggest damn diamond I have ever seen in my life. Just promise me one thing."

"What's that?"

"If I'm your maid of honor, don't make me wear red or orange . . . or worse yet, a hoop skirt."

"I hate you, you know that," I shouted as Alice ran down the hall toward her office. "I'll make you wear taffeta polka dots," I added in defeat.

How did I get myself into such a mess? I slapped the rest of the Biltmore article together, turned it in, and reluctantly gathered a supply of notebooks, pens, and blank tapes for my microcassette recorder. I reminded myself that I loved my job and that I could have flatly refused to do this assignment. Neither argument made me feel any better. I also placed a call to Adam, who was thrilled that I'd made such a "wise" decision. He promised to call me at home later with our travel plans.

On the way home, I stopped at a bookstore and picked up a book on Kentucky, filled with pictures of fields of bluegrass, horses galloping around the track at Churchill Downs, and oodles of other photos and stories. I figured I could leaf through it on the plane and pick up pointers on social traditions of the horsey set. For good measure, I ran through the drive-up lane of a KFC for a three-piece, original recipe chicken dinner, complete with biscuits and gravy. I decided I might as well get in the spirit before I started packing.

I pulled into the underground parking garage of my apartment building and grumpily clomped up the two flights of stairs to my apartment. Located in a huge, blond-brick, 1920s-era building, with spacious rooms, tall ceilings, and Art Deco designs, the beautifully restored structure lacked the convenience of an elevator. I tried to ignore how winded I was as I reached my floor.

The more I thought about the impending trip, the less I wanted to go. Suddenly, all I wanted was to be alone for the weekend. I glanced down the hall and realized that wouldn't be possible. Sitting on the floor in front of my door was John Donovan.

He scrambled to his feet. "Surprise, Kate!" He met me halfway down the hall and took the boxed dinner off my hands. "We've got to work on your eating habits. I can't be a doctor who has a girlfriend who downs junk like this on a regular basis."

"Careful," I warned. "I know exactly where you keep your stash of Ho Hos and potato chips. What brings you here?"

"I missed you. Do you realize how long it's been since we saw each other?"

"Last weekend," I reminded him as I slid the key in the latch. I looked down and spotted the ring. I sucked in a breath and spun the diamond around to the other side of my hand so that only the band showed. Of course, the diamond was so big, I now had difficulty bending my ring finger. A quick side trip to ditch the ring in a drawer in my bedroom would be paramount.

"Is everything okay, Kate?" John asked as we entered the apartment. "You seem upset."

I slid my arms around his waist, trying to keep the ring out of sight. "I'm sorry, it's been a long day. You know there's nothing better than to see you sitting outside my door."

"I like to hear that," he replied.

For the second time in a day, I received a gold-medal kiss, but this one was much more welcome.

Then John reached behind his back and pulled my hands around to the front and said, "I have something I want to show—" He looked down at my hands. His thumb was planted firmly on top of the diamond. I felt the color drain from my cheeks as he twisted the ring around my finger and stared blankly at the cluster of gems. His brown eyes clouded. "Kate, what's going on?"

I watched him carefully and said soothingly, "John, let me explain. It's not what you think."

I had hoped to avoid mentioning the entire trip to him until it was long over and nothing more than a good story. I hadn't gambled on telling my boyfriend that, for the next few days, I was engaged to a male underwear model who'd invited me to a sensational society party among the rich and famous of the equine social set.

A brisk knock on the door gave me my first escape attempt, but John's grip tightened around my hand. "Don't answer that. We have to talk."

"Let me get rid of whoever it is, then I can explain everything. It's all right, trust me."

I stepped back and reached for the door, never once taking my eyes off

John's tortured expression. I swung the door open and almost slammed it shut immediately. I knew things were about to get worse.

Brent filled the doorway, along with a dozen long-stemmed red roses and yet another bottle of champagne. "Hi there, darlin'. I thought we could continue the celebration."

Oh, yeah, this had "long night" written all over it.

C H A P  E R · 3

OH, BOY.

Or should I say *oh, boy, squared*?

Brent completely blew past my train-wreck expression and sauntered through the doorway as if he'd been dropping by for months. He casually tossed the champagne bottle on my couch, ignoring at least three tables or other firm surfaces where he could have placed it upright. It landed softly on the cushions and didn't break open and shower my couch with the bubbly brew. He shoved the roses under his left arm and extended his hand in a friendly fashion to John. "Hi there, I'm Brent. And you would be?"

"Leaving," John clipped.

I leapt between the two men, one who seemed to be enjoying this entirely too much, and another one who looked ready to commit murder right there on my nice, shiny hardwood floor. I grabbed John by the shoulders and dug my fingers into the deep filling of his green ski jacket.

Satisfied I had him secured in one spot, I bore my eyes into his. "John, there is no reason to leave. This is Brent King, one of Adam's friends. I'm working on a story with him for the magazine."

I glanced at Brent before returning my gaze to John. "He obviously has an exaggerated way of thanking me for agreeing to do the story. It's a bit confusing, but I can explain everything as soon as he leaves."

Brent missed his cue entirely. Instead of disappearing, he shoved the roses at me and dug in his jacket pocket until he came up with an envelope. "Here's your plane ticket," he said brightly. "We'll pick you up around ten tomorrow morning. Since you weren't at your office, I thought I'd drop by here to see if you were packed yet. Need help with your suitcases?"

John's eyes widened. "Plane ticket? What kind of story is this, Kate? Plane tickets, rings, roses, champagne . . . it looks like you're going on a honeymoon."

I shut my eyes. What a choice of words.

"Hey, now," Brent began, and I opened one eyelid, praying he wasn't going to say something awful. "Don't go setting us off on a honeymoon yet, we just got engaged!"

So much for the power of prayer.

John's red-faced body trembled like a boiling tea kettle ready to blow. "You *what*?"

I dumped the roses on the floor, glared at Brent, and reached for John again. "He's joking, John. He wants us to pretend to be engaged for the story. It's about society weddings in Kentucky, and he gets off on wanting me to pretend to be the bride while I write my story."

"That's ridiculous, Kate," John hissed.

He was right. That didn't explain anything, and it sounded completely fictitious.

I looked into his eyes. "You know this isn't how I approach my stories, John. This is a favor for Adam, for which he will pay me back dearly. I'll only be gone through the weekend, and I certainly hope to have it finished by then. As for Brent, there is nothing between us. I just met him a couple of hours ago."

Brent nodded. "Yeah, she's just doing a favor. Don't get so bent out of shape."

I wondered if guys sized up other guys the same way women did other women when a beau was stolen. Would a man just react and fight for his girl, or would he think through the process? Most women I knew might have smiled politely, but underneath the facade, they were summing up the competition: flat chest, frizzy hair, big nose, and so forth. Once that was accomplished, the claws came out.

I surveyed the two gents in my apartment and saw that Brent was once again picture-perfect, still looking like a *GQ* magazine ad in his khaki pants, red sweater, and cracked leather jacket. However, in my estimation, John looked just as good in his jeans, rugby shirt, and Lands End ski jacket. He also had a mountain-load of charm, intelligence, and sexiness over the poster boy.

Despite my unwavering devotion, John didn't look convinced there was nothing between Brent and me. His eyes narrowed. "Do I know you?"

Brent grinned. "Well, maybe." He puffed his chest, cocked his chin in the air, and crossed his arms. He stood there, frozen in the bizarre pose, and I wondered if his mom's little "problem" was hereditary.

John broke the awkward silence. "What is that supposed to mean?"

Brent looked at the two cave dwellers in his presence. "Takeover." He struck the pose again. "You know, Takeover—the cologne for men who want to take over the company . . . or take over their women."

John stared incredulously at Brent as I sank wearily onto the couch, silently hoping it would swallow me up and transport me to that secret place where all loose change and crumbs hide. Instead, the champagne bottle rolled down the cushion and landed against my leg.

I briefly debated the merits of slinging the bottle at Brent. "Brent, what does that have to do with anything?"

"The ads. I did the ads. I'm the Takeover guy." He turned to John. "You look like the kind of guy who'd wear it. Didn't you recognize me?"

John ignored him and turned his sad eyes my way. "Kate. . . ."

He didn't have to finish. I stood and snatched the plane ticket out of Brent's hand. "If you want me to go anywhere with you, I suggest that you leave now."

John tugged at the zipper on his jacket. "I'm the one who should go." He brushed past me and headed for the door.

I lunged after him and grabbed his sleeve. "Stay, please. We need to talk. Stay."

I realized that sounded like commanding a pooch to stay, then glanced at the other man in the room and thought how much I wanted to command Brent to roll over and play dead.

"Kate," John said quietly. "I don't know what we could possibly say. I'll talk to you in a few days, when you get back from this so-called story." He pulled my hand from his sleeve and squeezed it tightly. His eyes were murky, like puddles of rain dotted with mud, and his voice held a low rumble. "I'll see you around." He pulled the door shut behind him with a resounding thud.

I knew it was useless to chase after him, so I decided to call him later, once he calmed down. I took a couple of deep breaths and faced Brent.

Before I could launch into his beefcake brain, he flopped onto the couch and said, "Man, he's a little intense. Did I interrupt something?"

I clenched my fists at my side. "I am about one second away from dumping this story and favor, unless you leave right now. I have a busy night ahead. I have to retrieve my sanity, fix a very important relationship, and pack for this weekend, where I am supposed to be madly in love with a person I am ready to annihilate at this very moment."

Brent stared at me, then slowly rose from the couch. He picked the roses up off the floor, smoothed them back into a semblance of their original bouquet, and pulled one out of the bunch. Handing it to me, he said, "I'm sorry, Kate. Please give me another chance. No more big scenes, I promise. Look, do you want me to call your friend?"

That was the absolute last thing I wanted. "No, Brent. Let me get my life in order tonight, okay? I'll see you in the morning."

"It's a deal," he said softly. He laid the rest of the roses on the coffee table and held out his hand. "Truce? Can we shake on it?"

I marched to the door and held it open. "Tomorrow, Brent."

"Well, okay." He rocked on his heels and looked around the room. "I guess I'll skip the good-night kiss and just see you in the morning, huh?"

I pushed the door open farther. "I think that would be a good idea."

Once Brent was safely out of the apartment, I locked my door and collapsed on the couch. The bottle of champagne slid my way again. This time I ripped the green foil off the top and, after a brief struggle, popped the cork. A sizzling fizz quickly foamed over the rim, so I sucked back the champagne. The bubbles tickled my nose and throat with a vengeance. I shuddered and fell into a choking fit and was rudely reminded why one is supposed to sip champagne. I recovered, stared at the bottle, and said aloud, "I don't even like champagne." Then I promptly gulped down more.

It dawned on me that a proper socialite bride shouldn't drink directly from the bottle, so I pulled myself off the couch and dragged the bottle into the kitchen, where I deposited more champagne into a juice glass. I shoved my cold chicken dinner into the microwave and left a message on John's machine, begging forgiveness.

I gnawed at the chicken but couldn't finish it. I dumped what was left in the trash, then headed to my room to pack for the weekend. I grabbed the phone and tried John again, left another message, then called Alice as I slung clothes in my suitcase.

She assured me John would recover, Brent would get better, and I'd enjoy writing the story. "Hang up, get some sleep, and call me tomorrow when you get to Southfork," she instructed.

"Southfork is in Dallas, I'm going to Kentucky," I grunted as I pulled the now-full suitcase off my bed. It landed on the floor dangerously close to my toes. I wondered if I could claim workers' comp.

"Whatever," Alice said. "Have a good time with your hubby, you hear? He's awfully cute. Cheer up."

I'd done enough damage for one day, so I called it a night. I hoped the champagne would lull me into a deep, restful sleep, but unfortunately, there were too many other things vying for attention in my confused brain. I tossed and turned all night. At one point, I got up, paced around the apartment a few times, reread the newspaper, then stood in front of the open refrigerator door and nibbled on a few pieces of cheddar cheese.

It was sad.

The next thing I knew, I was bouncing up with a jolt and slamming my hand on the alarm button to cease its infernal roar. *Roar* was not an exaggeration, because my head was playing a discordant symphony of its own and was backed up by a pretty mean rumba band in my stomach. I vowed never again to mix champagne and a box of greasy fried chicken, no matter whose "original recipe" it was.

I downed a couple of aspirin and hopped under a steamy shower with the hope it would restore me, but it only made me want to crawl back in bed. I barely had time to slap myself into reasonable shape before Adam came knocking at my door.

"You look like hell," he said in greeting. "We've got to work on you before you meet Brent's parents."

"Lovely to see you too, Adam," I growled as I pushed my suitcase into the hall and locked my apartment door. "Let me sleep on the plane, and I'll be just dandy. I can be perky with the best of them, I won't disappoint you. Where is my beloved, anyway?"

Adam picked up my suitcase. "He's in the cab. I think you put the fear of God in him last night. He was too nervous to come up."

Brent was leaning on the side of the taxi as Adam and I walked into the early morning sunshine. He quickly grabbed the suitcase from Adam and deposited it in the trunk. As we slid into the backseat, my tender senses were greeted with that peculiar cab perfume mixture of stale smoke, leftover fast food, and other sundry odors I preferred not to notice. The car lurched forward and dove into traffic, and I clamped my hand over my nose and leaned my head against the seat.

Brent spoke for the first time. "You okay, Kate? I'd say good morning, but it doesn't look much like one for you."

Adam patted my knee. "Oh, she'll be okay. She's not a morning person, right, Kate?"

"Yeah, whatever."

That set the tone for our ride to Reagan National Airport. We didn't talk much, thanks to our Cuban driver, who regaled us with an elaborate story about how he came to America and somehow lost the tips of two fingers, which he repeatedly turned around to show us. More than once, Adam nervously requested that the cabby concentrate on his freeway driving. His usual response was "America, land of the free." He'd turn around again and flash the stumpy fingers along with a stubbly, gap-toothed smile.

Despite the road adventure, we made it to our departure gate in one piece. I sank into a fuchsia plastic chair and tugged at Brent's jacket. "I just might agree to marry you if you get us some coffee."

He smiled and disappeared in a trot through the terminal.

Adam was eager to please as well. He shoved our carry-on totes into a pile. "I'm going to get a newspaper. I'll be right back."

While I waited for them to return, I dug in my purse to make sure I had remembered to bring my reporter's notebooks and a decent supply of cassette tapes. My story wouldn't go anywhere without those treasured tools, even though I sorely missed the convenience of a laptop computer. I wasn't able to coax one of those out of Alice, so I was forced to survive with the old-fashioned methods.

"Excuse me, are you Kate Kelly?"

I looked up to see a tall, rugged-looking guy in jeans and a khaki windbreaker towering over me. His scraggly blond hair fell to his shoulders, and his tanned skin stretched over structured cheekbones and a long narrow nose. A light shadow of unshaven blond beard edged his chiseled chin and outlined his jawbone, which looked strong enough to withstand several prize-fighting blows. He passed for Gunther, the Swiss skiing instructor, or one of those European rock stars who got by with one name. Given his tousled form and the big, square bag tossed over his shoulder, I had a pretty good idea who he was.

"Kate Kelly, that's me. I don't believe we've met."

He let the bulky bag holding his camera equipment slide off his shoulder, then extended his hand. "Hi, I'm Zach Tanner. Alice Donard hired me to shoot a wedding party with you this weekend. She didn't tell me a lot about it, other than you were traveling with the groom, so I hoped you could fill me in on the plane." He looked at my hand and the ever-glimmering diamond. "She didn't tell me you were the bride. It doesn't seem fair to make the bride write her own story."

"I'm not the bride," I interrupted quickly. "It's a mess, I'm afraid. It takes a little explanation."

Zach shrugged his broad shoulders and slipped into the seat next to me. "I'm all ears. You've got me for the weekend."

I postponed my story as Adam and Brent returned, coffee and newspaper in hand. Introductions were made all around, and I resumed an edited version of the reason we were gathered. I left out the part about Mrs. King's "problem" and some of the more colorful details about Brent and Paige's passionate relationship. I decided to let that information come out during any male bonding that might occur between my traveling companions.

Zach remained quiet and finally rubbed his hand across his stubbly chin. "Well, you're right, it's not your usual story shoot, but that's why I prefer freelance work. You never know what you're going to get." He looked at Brent with a practiced eye. "You're the Takeover guy, aren't you?"

Brent flashed a triumphant smile. "Yeah, I am. How'd you know?"

A muffled voice that sounded like Charlie Brown's unseen teacher announced our flight and rattled off an incomprehensible set of boarding instructions.

Zach reached for his camera bag. "I'm a photographer. I notice things."

Brent had already moved on to more-important matters. Two flight attendants recognized him and stopped the passenger line to plaster him with giggly compliments. He ate it up.

I flashed my ring and stroked his arm. "Come on, darling, you're holding up the line. It's not nice to keep your bride waiting."

The enamored flight attendants filed a look my way that said complimentary trail mix and mini bottles of Maker's Mark were banned from my consumption on this flight. Brent simply looked confused.

Our group arrived in our first-class seats almost immediately. While Adam, Zach, and I marveled at the rare prospect of traveling first class, Brent continued to hold court, smiling and even signing a couple of magazine covers as other passengers pushed their way toward the back of the plane.

Once we took off, I decided to postpone my nap. Zach, however, immediately slumped in the thick leather seat and promptly shut his blue eyes. Adam studied the *Washington Post*, and Brent flipped through a magazine. But I had work to do.

Reaching into my purse for my notebook, I turned to Brent. "Tell me what we're like as a couple. How did we meet? What do we like to do? What are your hobbies? What kind of food do you hate? Did you go to college?"

He immediately ditched the magazine and grinned broadly. I'd found a topic he could ramble on about forever—himself. "Gee, Kate, I didn't realize you were that interested."

Lest he be mistaken, I gently explained. "Brent, I'm supposed to be your fiancée. So, what will people assume I know about you?"

His eyebrows shot up like McDonald's golden arches. "Oh, you mean so we can fake it. I get it, that's cool." Nodding wisely, he proceeded to tell me his life story.

His early years were normal and uneventful. He loved soccer, hated carrots. His father was a highly successful dabbler in real estate, who funneled his pricier commissions into the purchase of the Bluegrass Winds horse farm in the late 1980s. The Virginia natives packed their bags and hoofed it over to Lexington, Kentucky, where Brent finished his last year of high school among the monied horsey set.

Landing his first modeling job when he was at the University of Kentucky, he never made it past sophomore year once the cameras called. Brent modeled regularly in Kentucky for a few years and then got his big break when he appeared in a regional commercial for a floating casino. He played a tuxedo-clad bon vivant and caught the eye of an agent in New York, who promptly moved him east to make him a star.

As for our "relationship," Brent figured we could pretty much make up anything, since no one had met Paige. He insisted that he had only said he'd met "a wonderful girl" and would tell everyone about her when he brought her home for a visit. When I pressed him about how to explain the name change from Paige to Kate, he stubbornly insisted that no one would remember if he had said his fiancée's name was Paige or Kate or even Bitsy.

"Not even your parents?" I argued. "Surely they'll remember."

Adam glanced over his paper. "She's got you there, buddy."

"No, really," Brent said. "It's not a problem. I've only talked to my mom, and she was so excited and distracted with planning the party that it'll be easy to convince her. And as for my dad, well, that's not a consideration. He won't be overly concerned. We'll just do it that way, it's very simple."

Zach stirred in his seat, his eyes still closed, and mumbled, "That'll be a neat trick."

Tricks were the last things I needed to ponder. Precious nap time was dwindling, so I gave up on my interrogation and, like Zach, assumed the position. I didn't expect to catch much sleep. Chalking it up to my writer's imagination, and ignoring my love of traveling, I knew I was one travel writer who wasn't a placid plane dweller. Granted, physics was never my favorite subject, but I found something pretty unnatural about thousands of pounds of metal flying through thin, thin air at hundreds of miles an hour.

I never unbuckled my seat belt, and I was one of the few loonies who actually listened intently to the flight attendant's litany of how to make your seat cushion a floatation device. Whenever I tried to sleep on a plane, I instantly became supersensitive to every bump and hiss that sought out my paranoid, overworked imagination.

However, I was also so exhausted at the time, I was pretty sure I could sleep through most anything, short of the plane crashing.

I didn't realize I was in for such a rude awakening.

C H A P T E R · 4

THE JOLT WAS FEROCIOUS. Everyone bolted to attention and nervously glanced out the windows as the wheels skidded and squealed below our seats and visions of every *Airport* movie played in our heads. We briefly ascended a few feet, then bounced down on the runway again, no less delicately than the first time.

We slowed to a stop in front of the Lexington Blue Grass Airport. As my fellow passengers and I exhaled, the pilot crackled over the intercom, "Well, folks, that sure was fun. Who wants to go up and land again? Welcome to Kentucky, where the horsepower is provided by the real thing. Thanks for flying with us."

I hated to tell the pilot, but this was one passenger who was looking forward to seeing terra firma immediately. In fact, I was close to adopting the Pope's tradition of kissing the ground once I was outside. I was unbuckled and out of my seat in no time flat and discovered that one of the perks of flying first-class meant I didn't have to hover in a half-bent-over position waiting to slither into the crowded aisle. Instead, we casually gathered our carry-ons and bid our daredevil pilot adieu, while the flight attendants formed a human shield in front of the riffraff.

Before long, we were schlepping our way through a crowded terminal, like salmon swimming their way upstream. Our chief salmon, Brent, led us confidently to the baggage claim area, where we smashed our way into the throng of bleary-eyed travelers fascinated by the revolving chain of bags slowly spewing out of the darkened tunnel against the wall.

I plucked my bag off the moving ramp just as the low rumble of a gravelly voice behind me announced, "Mr. King, welcome home. Your mother sent me to fetch you and your friends. I'd be most happy to assist you with your luggage, sir."

Brent bear-hugged the small, elderly man, who bore a haunting resemblance to Elmer Fudd. Brent beamed as if he were greeting his father, but we discovered that it was Mr. Tubbs, the family chauffeur.

Grabbing my hand, Brent dragged me in front of Mr. Tubbs. "I'd like you to meet Kate, my fiancée. How'd I do, Mr. Tubbs? Does she pass muster? Good bloodlines, great bones, huh?"

I struggled not to slug my dear fiancé. Pray, good folk, he didn't compare me to a summer's day. No, he compared me to a horse. I hoped the odds were on my side that his comment was not a typical Kentucky greeting but a warped attempt at humor on Brent's part.

A flash exploded in my face as Zach went to work with one of his cameras. "First meeting of the extended family," he explained with an impish grin. "Plus, I couldn't resist your expression."

Mr. Tubbs, pretending not to hear Zach, said, "Oh, she's mighty swell, sir. Your mother will be pleased. Welcome to the family, Miss Kate."

I swallowed hard. "Thank you. You can't imagine how I feel about being with Brent."

Three anxious male heads turned in my direction, but Mr. Tubbs let my comment sail through his large ears. Instead, he turned and headed for a black stretch limo outside the sliding glass doors. Brent trotted through the door behind him and dove into the back of the limo. Adam, Zach, and I hesitated.

"I haven't been in one of these since my senior prom," Zach mumbled.

"And I can't explain this sudden urge I have to start speaking with a British accent," Adam quipped. "Gee, Kate, once you're Mrs. King, will you have someone drive me around in one of these?"

I let loose the slug I'd restrained, and popped Adam on the shoulder. "Let's get this over with."

As we climbed into the cavernous limo, Zach leaned to my ear. "Cheer up, Kate, maybe there's a minibar inside. You look like you could use a drink."

There was indeed a minibar in the back, but we didn't utilize it. Adam and Zach were much too busy playing with the various electronic buttons and laughing like a couple of five-year-olds, as the windows, sunroof, and mood lights all switched on and off at a frenetic pace. For my part, I fought the urge to put on sunglasses and exercise my wrist with the royal wave.

Almost like a warning to behave, Brent cleared his throat. "Uh, it's not that far to our farm. We should be there in no time at all."

"Cool," Zach said, digging into his camera bag. "I want to wander around, shoot a lot of nature shots. I hope that's all right with you. I don't want to tango with any security guards or farmhands. I'm here to work, not interfere with farm life. You're a model, you should know how photogs work."

"Hey, no problem. Shoot anywhere, anytime. If anyone gives you trouble, just find me." Brent slid his hand on my knee and stroked his thumb across it. "I guess you'll want to shoot some pictures of Kate and me together, huh?"

I looked first at Brent's hand, then moved up to his face. His eyes were warm, and his smile lightly stretched across gleaming white teeth. My knee jerked involuntarily, and I felt Adam's big-brotherish stare without looking in his direction. Pictures of Brent and me together—as a couple. Plain, normal, little old me in the arms of a successful male model.

My face suddenly felt hot. I tried crossing my legs to force Brent to move his hand, but instead, he simply let it slide a little farther up my thigh. His grin grew as Adam and Zach zoomed in on his little unspoken statement. Since it was the focus of everyone's attention, mine in particular, I unceremoniously grabbed his hand and removed it from its resting place.

And, in what was surely a suave, silky manner, I turned to the window and blurted, "Nice hills out there, huh, guys? Pretty day for November. Lots of sun . . . lots of sun, no clouds."

Adam halfheartedly came to my rescue. "Yeah, it's really nice out there. Hills, lots of them."

We were driving along a stretch of interstate bordered on either side by softly rolling hills dotted with horses grazing lazily under the sunshine. For miles we passed a latticework of white wooden fencing that created a maze of rectangles and squares, which marked the boundaries of horse farms.

It was as if we were magically paging through a picture book of Kentucky and messing up the view by sticking a highway in the midst of all the natural beauty. Occasionally, the smooth green hills were interrupted by a lonely lake or a majestic-looking whitewashed building complete with red shutters and two spires emulating the famous twin spires of Louisville's Churchill Downs racetrack.

"Those are horse barns," Brent explained. "They're not just typical farm barns, either. They're heated and air-conditioned, and some have rooms where vets can work on-site. Those barns are huge, and I can assure you they cost just as much to build as some of the pricier homes in certain neighborhoods."

"Impressive use of big bucks," Zach mumbled. "I guess you have a fair share of similar barns on your property?"

"Of course," Brent replied, only belatedly catching the sarcasm edged in Zach's comment.

We exited the interstate and turned onto a narrow, two-lane road that wound in a dizzying pattern through groves of evergreens and wide patches of farmland bordered by stone fencing that had been erected decades earlier. Any thought of the highway vanished, and the view blended into one long, lush stretch of farmland.

I was ready to ask for some Dramamine from the effects of the hills and twists, when we came upon a set of massive wrought-iron gates heralding the entrance to Bluegrass Winds. Mr. Tubbs slowed to a crawl and moved through the gates onto a long, solitary drive. The house at the end of the road riveted my attention. It was almost a sacrilege to call it just a house, since its impressive expanse—a two-story Greek Revival white brick structure with tall, black-shuttered windows—dominated the landscape.

So, this was home? Not bad. Not bad at all. Scarlett was arriving at Tara. But my Rhett was a bit distracted.

Brent lurched forward and strained a look out the window. I glanced out and saw someone on horseback heading over a hill.

Instinctively, Zach swung his camera toward the window. "Who was that? You look like you've seen a ghost, buddy."

Indeed he did. Brent's tanned face paled a shade, and a muscle in his jaw twitched steadily. He slid back against the seat. "Nobody. I thought it was . . . um . . . no one, never mind."

He wasn't anxious to discuss it further, so the rest of us exchanged uneasy glances and let it drop. Mr. Tubbs parked in front of the house and, in an instant, opened our car doors.

Brent leapt out of the limo. "I have something I need to take care of, Mr. Tubbs. Please see that everyone gets to their rooms. I'll be back in a bit. Make yourselves at home."

"But, Brent," Adam said, "what are we supposed to do? Where do we go?"

Something itched Brent's underpants in the worst way. He was in no mood to play host. "Um, inside, I guess. Adam, you've met my mom. I'm sure she's in there somewhere. Talk to her, or grab one of the golf carts out back and drive around the farm. I don't care. I'll be back soon, all right? Just do that, okay?"

Mr. Tubbs, not the least bit distracted by Brent's sudden lack of hospitality, methodically unloaded Adam's and Zach's bags. He nodded toward the house. "The gentlemen will join the others in the west guest wing."

"And the lady?" I inquired politely.

He avoided my face. "Why, you and Mr. King are in the cottage. Mrs. King thought you might prefer the privacy."

Even though Brent had stepped away from us, he was close enough to hear Mr. Tubbs's comment. He snapped to attention and looked at me as if he'd been informed that the stock market had crashed. "What? The cottage won't be necessary. We should stay in the house."

"Yes," I added quickly, "the house is lovely."

Mr. Tubbs shook his head. "Oh, no, sir, it's quite all right. There's no need for modesty. Your parents are aware of how things are these days. There's no reason you shouldn't be together."

Of course there was. I could count any number of reasons, not the least of which was the fact that it put us in a highly compromised position. I supposed any other female, faced with spending a weekend in a cottage with someone of Brent's attributes, would be thrilled, but that was the farthest thing from my mind. Sorta.

Adam scooped up his bags. "This ought to be good. What do you say, Zach, shall we head for the west wing and leave these two alone?"

Zach grinned. "Why, sure, it's been a long trip. They'll want to rest a bit."

Brent shuffled back and forth. "Look, I need to go." He pointed to a small white cottage with red shutters that sat several feet behind the main house. "There's the cottage, Kate. We'll work things out later. Just get settled. I'll introduce you to everyone when I get back." Without another word, he took off in a run, down a narrow drive that wound around the left side of the main house.

Before we had time to gather our bags and follow Mr. Tubbs to our various rooms, the hum of a small motor broke through the air, and we spotted Brent bouncing into the distance on a golf cart.

"Where's he going, Mr. Tubbs?" I asked as the golf cart followed the road and disappeared into a grove of trees.

The chauffeur was equally perplexed. "I haven't the foggiest, miss, but if you'll wait here, I'll show the gentlemen to the house. I'll be back in a moment to drive you to the cottage."

I gazed at the cottage and calculated that it would take all of a minute or less to walk there. I ignored proper civility. "That's all right, I'll just walk." I reached into the trunk and plucked out my suitcase, a move that distressed Mr. Tubbs.

In a swift movement that belied his advancing years, he dropped Adam's and Zach's bags and yanked the suitcase out of my hand. "I simply can't let you carry that, Miss Kate. Please allow me."

He shuffled off toward the cottage, and Zach suggested, "Brent had a good idea about exploring on our own. Why don't we meet on the porch in fifteen minutes, find a golf cart, and see what we can see. Brent didn't sound like he'd be back anytime soon."

I shrugged. "Works for me."

Mr. Tubbs stopped, turned around, and gently ordered, "If you insist on walking, miss, it's this way, please."

"Keep the home fires burning, Katie," Adam said with a smirk.

He knew I hated that nickname. So, supremely mature person that I was, I stuck my tongue out at him and marched toward the cottage. By the time I reached my little home-away-from-home, Mr. Tubbs had deposited my bag inside the door.

"I hope you find everything to your satisfaction," he said. "If there are any problems, please see Mrs. Palmer, the housekeeper."

I thanked him and gingerly stepped into the cozy living room tastefully decorated in shades of cornflower blue, white, and gold. Matching blue-and-white-striped armchairs flanked the couch, and the coffee table held a smattering of artfully arranged magazines—*Traditional Home, Architectural Digest, Time*. And underneath a heavy issue of *Forbes* was a brand new *Brides*.

I stepped back as if I'd discovered an odorous pile. Very clever of the person who had decorated with my arrival in mind. No telling what the bedroom held.

To the right, through an arched doorway, were a tiny kitchenette and an even smaller powder room, both painted buttery yellow. I crossed through the living room and glanced at the narrow, white-carpeted staircase. I figured it was now or never, so I grabbed my bag and headed upstairs.

Just as I feared. The entire second floor consisted of one large loft bedroom and an adjoining bath. A king-size canopy bed anchored the center of the loft. Gauzy white linen crisscrossed the iron canopy frame and fell in a puddle of excess on the plush white carpet. My nose led me to the heavy white downy comforter sprinkled with bits of potpourri. Slender taper candles decorated nightstands on each side of the bed.

The cottage was truly charming. I was lost in the thought of a weekend away with John, but I snapped back to reality when I realized he was angry at me and I was stuck here with the poster boy.

What had I gotten myself into? I'd deal with it later—my headache was back.

I slipped into the bathroom and, splashing cool water on my face, tried to decide what to do about clothes. I'd slapped on a short black skirt and a thick green sweater that morning with an eye toward meeting the in-laws, but now that I was faced with exploring the farm in a golf cart, I heard the call of a comfortable pair of jeans.

The brilliant sun from earlier in the day was now taking a siesta behind a thick blanket of clouds, and the air was cloaked with a crisp chill scented by the November aroma of dried leaves rustling on the ground and smoke puffing out of chimneys in the area. It was the perfect afternoon to cuddle up in a big chair by the fireplace, not clomp through a horse farm in heels and a skirt.

But, knowing my luck, I figured the minute I pulled on my jeans, I'd probably run right into Mother King. My first big decision as an heiress-to-be. I stared blankly at my suitcase. Compromising, I ditched the skirt and heels for a pair of black slacks and leather flats—still presentable and, most importantly, warm.

"Oh, mistress of the manor," called Adam from downstairs. "Dost thou wish to join us?"

I tromped down the steps. "Don't you guys knock?"

"Nah," replied Zach, "we're in the country. No one locks their doors out here. We're all just one big happy family."

Zach and Adam had procured a standard-issue, four-seater golf cart. We hopped in, and Zach lurched toward the road Brent had taken.

"Do you have any idea where you're going?" I asked.

He shrugged. "Not really. I figured this road must lead somewhere. The farm can't be that large. How many horses can you keep in one location? Besides, if we get lost, we can hibernate in one of those big barns we passed on the highway."

"Where do you think Brent went?" I wondered aloud.

"He certainly was in hurry," Adam said.

Rounding a curve, we followed the fence line down a small incline and drove into a natural tunnel of evergreen trees. We emerged on a wide, hilly expanse of fenced paddocks holding several horses lazily munching on closely clipped grass. A few horses swung their heads toward us, and one whinnied either a "hello" or a "get lost" in our direction.

Zach stopped the golf cart, grabbed his camera, and jumped out. "Well, I really don't care where he went. I'm going to grab a few shots here. Why don't you guys go on?"

"We can wait," I offered, pulling my coat tighter around me and casting an eye toward the leaded gray skies.

"No, go on," Zach instructed. He dropped to his knees and crawled toward the paddock. "Too many of us will spook the horses, and I won't get the shots I want. I'll catch up with you later. Don't mind me, I'll explore some other time."

Adam scooted into the driver's seat. "Whatever. We'll circle around and come back in this direction to see if you want a ride back."

Zach waved us away and stretched out on the ground, his camera aimed straight up the nostrils of a chestnut Thoroughbred. Adam and I puttered away and followed the gravel road over a small hill. The scenery was lovely and quite peaceful, but the acres of white-fenced paddocks blended into a repetitive pattern that hinted of "seen one, seen them all."

I burrowed my hands in my pockets and wished I'd remembered to bring gloves. "Look, a barn. Let's check it out. Maybe there's heat inside," I said hopefully.

Adam grinned and parked the cart. We crunched up the gravel drive to the barn's massive wood door, which undoubtedly had seen the passing of many horses over the years. Closer inspection revealed that it was obviously not one of the high-tech horse hotels we'd spotted earlier. The wood, which was weathered a dark, splintery gray, sagged and bowed under the weight of the red-slate roof. The large handle on the door was rusted the color of the horses Zach was photographing, and we had to give a tag-team shove to push it open past clumps of hay bundled up on the other side.

We adjusted our eyes to the sudden murky darkness and inhaled the overpowering smell of musty hay, grain, and horse. The large and airy interior held six spacious stalls, carpeted in pads of straw and guarded by slatted wooden gates. Three horses were in residence. Two poked their heads out of the stalls to take in the intruders, while the third remained completely aloof. Adam scooped a handful of feed from a bucket and offered one horse a mid-day snack.

The second horse looked expectantly at me, but I passed on the slobbery snack and patted the black mare gently on the nose instead. "Adam will get you something next. I'm too nosy right now. I have to see what else is here."

The horse snorted its disapproval, so I moved on. A large loft, stacked with tightly bound bales of hay, hovered over the far end of the barn and provided the ceiling for two tack rooms, separated by a massive wood ladder. I walked over to the ladder and pulled myself up a couple of rungs.

I glanced down to the right and noticed the tack room door was ajar. I stepped down one rung and leaned over a little closer to peer inside. The door opened wide, and a large blur flew past. I was so startled, my foot slipped off the ladder and I slid to the floor with a thud.

The blur surged toward me and lifted me by my shoulders, spun me around, and shoved me against the ladder. "Who are you? What are you doing in here?" demanded a deep voice. A man with intense blue eyes, short, wavy blond hair, and a handsome, strong chin gripped me with big, thickly gloved hands.

I pushed him back and shook myself free. "I'm just looking around, I'm not hurting anything."

Adam ran up and took in my tango partner in one dismayed glance. Adam was athletic and quick, and played a mean game of soccer, but he was no match for the six-foot-plus guy towering over us.

"What's going on? Kate, are you okay?"

I brushed dirt off the front of my sweater. "Yeah, I'm fine." I looked at muscle man. "We're guests of Brent King. My name is Kate, and this is Adam. We weren't properly introduced. I didn't quite catch your name when you threw me against the ladder."

"Steve. Steve Mathias. I train the Kings' horses." He shuffled back a step and flexed his substantial shoulders. "I'm real protective of my horses. I don't like strangers bothering them. I'm sorry if I scared you." He flashed a tepid smile at me. "I heard there were a bunch of people coming to the house this weekend with Brent. You must be one of his model friends from New York."

"Hardly," Adam laughed.

I shot my cousin a look and smiled back at Steve. "We're friends of Brent's, but we're not models. Thanks anyway."

Adam pointed to Steve's jeans. "You okay? Is that blood on your pants leg?"

Steve's head shot down, and he quickly rubbed the dark red blotch with his glove. "Uh . . . it might be. One of the horses had a cut on its leg, and I was looking, and I guess—"

A deafening explosion rocked the air and interrupted Steve's tenuous explanation. The horses banged against their stalls and voiced frightened protests at the crashing boom.

Steve looked at us with wild eyes and forgot the bloodstained jeans. "I gotta go," he said.

The aftershock of the first rumble died away but was replaced with two smaller booms. I took off for the door, followed closely by Adam. We forgot about Steve and focused instead on a large column of dense black smoke rising from the bottom of a small hill a couple hundred yards away.

Adam and I raced across the field and stopped short when a wave of heat hit us. We shielded our faces from the cloud of smoke that swirled upwards, revealing the shell of a car engulfed in flames.

"What the hell is a car doing out here in the middle of nowhere?" Adam shouted over the fire's crackle and hiss.

There was nothing we could do. The barn and any hoses that might be inside were too far away to do any good. However, the commotion apparently had alerted someone near the house, because two pickups roared in our direction. Men in jeans and thick coats poured out of the trucks and tossed fire extinguishers at each other. They let loose a spew of foam that was too weak to douse the blaze, but strong enough to subdue it.

As the fire choked away in stubborn fits, one of the men squirted the side of the car again, then waved away a cloud of oily, black smoke.

He gingerly stepped closer, then screamed. "Oh, God, there's someone in here!"

C H A P T E R · 5

THERE WAS NO BETTER WAY to liven up a sleepy afternoon than to have a dead body arrive on the scene. Bluegrass Winds was a popular place within minutes of the explosion. The men armed with fire extinguishers were stable workers, trained from their first day on the job to pitch in at any puff of smoke. It made sense, given the thousands of dollars worth of horseflesh in residence.

While they attacked the fire with their woefully inadequate fire extinguishers, someone else dialed 911. The air was scented with a thick haze that burned our noses and throats. After the stable worker had discovered the body in the car, everyone emptied their extinguishers as quickly as possible, but it wasn't enough to put out the fire. There wasn't much left, other than a twisted, melted frame and flaming seats and upholstery that choked the air with a sickening odor.

Adam took a few tentative steps toward the car but quickly turned away, his face ashen. I sneaked a peek too, but it only made me want to shut my eyes and put my head between my knees until the trees stopped spinning.

Adam shook his head. "Let's get out of here. We'll find out the details later at the house. We need a change of scenery. There's nothing we can do now."

I was in full agreement but realized an escape wasn't in the cards. The fire engines arrived, followed by a police car with blue lights blazing. The young, uniformed officer leapt out of his car, grabbed a stable worker, and plastered him with questions. It took only a few seconds and one shaky finger pointed at the car before the officer ran toward the lingering flames. The firefighters simultaneously made their own gruesome discovery.

The officer yanked his radio microphone out the cruiser window and frantically called for backup. "Notify the coroner," he shouted. "We've got a body."

My attention was focused on him, so I didn't hear car doors slam behind me near the barn. Steve Mathias and a tall, silver-haired man tromped up and stopped just in front of Adam and me.

"What the hell?" the older man breathed to himself. He stared at the scene, then swung his gaze toward us. "Who are you?"

Steve answered, "They were in my barn right before the fire. They said they're guests of Brent's." Looking at us, he nodded toward the fire scene. "Is that your car?"

"No," Adam replied as I slowly pulled myself up and faced the two. "We were using a golf cart."

Never one to forget my inbred Southern manners, I extended my hand. "My name is Kate, and this is my cousin Adam."

The older man's eyebrows raised. "Kate? Brent's fiancée? I'm Douglas King, Brent's father. Where the hell is Brent?"

That, in fact, was a good question. Something awful made me glance toward the car. "I'm not sure. He dropped us off at the house and said he had something to do. He took off in this direction." My voice faltered.

We all stared at the car. I pulled my gaze away, looked at Douglas, and realized I was seeing an older version of Brent. Douglas had the same vibrant turquoise eyes as Brent, but his were even more startling, given his lightning-white hair. His tanned, handsome face announced that he was probably in his mid-sixties, and his tall, muscular physique was clad in expensive clothes that would be classified as "casual chic" in an L.L.Bean catalog.

If we hadn't been surrounded by the smoke and flames, I could have smelled money. I was fairly sure Douglas was as attractive to the country club ladies-who-lunch as Brent was to women of my generation. For that matter, what difference should age make? The King men certainly had very, *very* good genes.

"Who does that car belong to, Steve?" This time Douglas's tone wasn't curious, but accusatory. "It's parked near your barn."

Steve flexed his substantial shoulders. "I told you, I don't know. I've been with King's Ransom and Armstrong Bay all afternoon. I'm not the social director of the farm. I thought that was Brent's job."

Adam offered, "We came up to the barn from the far side. We never saw a car. Brent's on a golf cart, too, as far as I know."

"That's probably all he can handle," Douglas mumbled. He looked sharply at me. "Kate. . . . He never said your last name, not that I remember. What is it?"

I realized we'd never officially decided whether to fake it with Paige's last name or use my real name. Adam shrugged his shoulders slightly. That was helpful.

"It's Kelly," I replied, opting for the high road. "Kate Kelly."

"You don't look his type," Douglas snapped and walked away.

Welcome to the family. My cheeks grew pink in the sting of the cold air.

Steve took a step toward me. "Ignore him, that's what the rest of us do. No one ever said money made you polite. It's usually quite the opposite." He looked over my shoulder. "We've got company."

The officer's earlier radio call sparked a parade of cars that descended on Bluegrass Winds in short order. Another police cruiser led the contingent that included an unmarked car and an ambulance. Rounding the bend moments later were an evidence-gathering van and the coroner. I counted the assembled cars and hoped that nothing else dire was happening in Lexington at the moment.

Experience told me the assorted cars were normal for a major crime scene. However, it looked overly dramatic to me, especially since once everyone piled out of their respective cars, only a few appeared busy collecting clues.

Before I worked for *Travel Adventures*, I did a stint as a newspaper reporter for the *Virginia Tribune*, where my mom was recognized as one of the best investigative reporters in the region. I was constantly in her semi-famous shadow as I tried to go about being a normal city-beat reporter. Instead, I was always "Helen Kelly's kid," a title I really didn't mind, but one that made it hard to grill the police chief when he kept asking, "So, what's your mom up to these days, kid?"

I quickly learned that news could be a funny business. Not only did it grow under your skin the same as an itchy rash, it was also a great education. Where else would you be required to have a working knowledge of the court system, crime scenes, medical advances, city government, the entertainment world, election laws, weather disasters, and quirky holiday traditions? It was like playing Trivial Pursuit on amphetamines.

It helped also to be a master at judging people and their assorted motives and prejudices. I found out that when people heard you were a reporter, they either instantly feared you, hated you, or wanted to be your best friend. It didn't matter who you were or what your beat was, there was an odd veil around our noble profession that was probably of our own making. It was swathed in the journalistic tradition and enhanced by any number of pulp-fiction books, made-for-TV movies, and long-winded war stories.

My job offer for *Travel Adventures* actually came out of a story I helped my mom cover. The job was enticing and certainly a change from reporting on city council meetings and house fires. I looked at it as a welcome respite from the rigors of hard news. I often thought someday I might return to news reporting, but for now, I'd just stick to covering great travel locations.

I wrinkled my nose. I was covering both at the moment—a crime scene in a beautiful travel spot. However, I didn't think a burned car with a dead body was quite the same flambé Alice had in mind when she assigned me to this story.

I watched as members of the Evidence Technician Unit rolled out of their van and immediately began stringing the familiar yellow crime-scene tape. Another officer, armed with several cameras, shot pictures with the fervor of a fashion photographer hovering beside a Paris runway. They were oblivious to the cold weather and grisly scene, and all wore the same tired, grim face that said this was just another body, another day on the job, one hour closer to retirement.

The doors of the unmarked Camry swung open, and an Indian man, with thick black hair and a limber build, unfolded his long legs from the confines of the driver's seat. I pegged him as an LPD detective, in his late thirties. He wore blue jeans and a thinning, tweedy blazer that was probably left over from his college days. As he reached into his coat pocket to retrieve a notebook and pen, his shoulder holster slipped into view.

He was joined by an equally tall, thin woman with long, strawberry-blonde hair. She was wrapped in a bulky brown ski jacket that matched her dark brown pants and boots. The smattering of freckles that splashed across her nose and cheeks made it difficult to imagine her as a cop.

They silently took in the scene in a quick glance, then bent their heads together for a brief consult. The female detective used her teeth to pull off one glove as she rummaged for a notebook in the purse dangling from her shoulder. Mission accomplished, she tugged off the other glove, shoved the pair in her pockets, and stalked across the field toward the car. She looked impassively over the yellow tape, then joined Douglas and one of the officers.

Adam, Steve, and I were on the agenda of the remaining detective.

"Detective Jake Rami, Lexington Police Department," he said in greeting. "And that's my partner, Detective Terri Knight. Mind if I ask you some questions? Like who are you and why are you here?"

We told our feeble stories, which didn't impress Detective Rami. Beyond writing down our names, relationships, and reasons for being on the farm, there was woefully little for him to note.

He flipped his notebook shut and looked at me. "So, your boyfriend lives here. Why isn't he out here with you?"

I flinched. Not only did I realize I had just lied to the police, but there was something startling about hearing Brent referred to as my boyfriend.

Detective Knight walked up with Douglas and saved me from answering the question. Her soft voice was tinged with a slight Southern accent. "Excuse me, Detective Rami, this is Douglas King, the owner of the farm. He says it's too cold out here and he wants to continue this inside his house. I'll stay here, and you can shepherd these folks to warmer grounds."

Rami made a face and reached for his car keys. "Come on, you can all ride with me."

Douglas surveyed our group. "Mathias and I came up here in my car. We'll meet you at the house."

Rami raised an eyebrow and shook his head. "No, there's room for everyone in my car. It's cozy, but you're all family, more or less, aren't you? You'll ride with me."

His polite edict delivered, he marched to the Camry and opened the doors. Douglas promptly chose the front seat, so Adam, Steve, and I squeezed into the back.

Douglas glanced back at us, then assumed control. "Go down this road, turn right. It will take you directly to the house. You will take care of this matter, Detective. I trust it won't make the papers."

Rami stared stoically forward. "Yes, we hope to determine what happened, but I'll need your help, Mr. King. I'm afraid I can't control the press. You're on private property, so do what you must." He glanced at Douglas. "Within reason, of course."

We rounded the fence line, and the rocky pavement smoothed into the silky black asphalt of the main drive. Rami pulled in front of the house and parked. Steve, Adam, and I piled out the back like Silly String spilling from a can, while Douglas took his time exiting.

"Are you coming, Mr. King?" Rami asked.

Douglas rubbed his hand over his face. "My wife. I hadn't thought until now—this will upset her." He slammed the car door. "Shit, this is all I need."

I followed Rami's gaze to Steve, who was twirling his finger around the side of his head.

"Wacko," he mouthed to the detective, then bent to my ear. "Met your mother-in-law yet?" He let loose a smart-aleck chuckle, and I could feel his breath against my neck.

I looked straight ahead. "No, not yet. This isn't exactly how I pictured it."

"Well," he said as we walked to the door, "let's just say I hope you guys register for therapy sessions along with your china and silver collection. You'll need it." Steve sailed inside and left Adam and me on the steps.

I showed my displeasure. "Remember how you said we could leave at any point, Adam?"

He pushed me through the doorway. "I lied. Let's see what happens."

We were met by an elderly woman in a plain, institutional navy dress. She asked politely for our coats and took turns eyeing me with a curious grin and casting wary looks in Rami's direction. "Welcome to Bluegrass Winds. Mr. King will show you to the west parlor." She smiled at me. "It's nice to meet you, ma'am." She glanced at Rami, then turned back to me and added, "I hope you enjoy your stay, and that nothing gets in its way."

I mumbled a polite thank-you, but she had already gathered our coats and disappeared as quickly as she had appeared.

The entry hall was dramatically horsey, yet elegant. Deeply polished hardwood floors gleamed and caught the reflection of the massive crystal chandelier dangling far overhead from the second-floor ceiling. A dark cherry staircase on the left rose from the floor and twisted into a balcony leading to heaven-knows-what. The feeling was musky and masculine, with all the dark wood and burgundy walls that were home to several painted English country hunt scenes.

Douglas motioned us down a narrow hallway opposite the staircase. A life-size oil painting of a commanding Thoroughbred horse dominated the wall. The brass plate on the bottom of the large gold frame read: BAYOU FOLLY—BLUEGRASS WINDS.

Even as a casual follower of horse racing, I recognized that name. Bayou Folly had won several major races and was a strong contender in both the Kentucky Derby and Belmont Stakes a few years earlier. I was surprised that the Kings owned the famous horse.

"No wonder they've got so much money," Adam whispered.

The dollar-sign count would have to come later. Douglas ushered us into a large living room covered in a heavy rose-patterned wallpaper. Dark green couches and upholstered chairs picked up the green in the wallpaper's rose vines, and more paintings of horses decorated the room.

Brent, still in his jacket, decorated the fireplace mantel, and two women sat placidly on the couch. He glanced at us and broke into an uneasy smile. "There you are. I thought maybe you went home."

He whisked across the room and grabbed my hand. Even though he had been standing by the fire, his hand was deathly cold and swathed in clammy sweat. "Hello, Dad. I see you've met Kate and Adam." Brent looked at me and took a noticeable deep breath. "Darling, I'd like you to meet my mom and my sister, Meg. Um, this is Kate, my . . . uh . . . my fiancée." He choked on the last word.

I was as nervous as Brent. It was all a little too real, especially as I watched his mother stand and zoom her eye in on my clunky diamond ring. She also cast a doubtful eye on my slacks and bulky sweater. No telling what my hair looked like after all that time outside. I was pretty sure I wasn't what she had pictured for a daughter-in-law—real or imagined.

She was tall and appeared anorexic, with coal-black hair pulled into a tight bun at the nape of her neck. Her thinness accentuated her prominent, sharply angled cheekbones and long, narrow nose. She had thin lips penciled in with vivid red lipstick, and her large, dark eyes were shaded in dark brown with an abundance of eyeliner.

"Kate, I'm Jane King. It's nice to finally meet." She extended her hand and painted on an insincere smile. "We've heard so little about you, almost as if Brent was trying to hide you."

I took her icicle of a hand, returned the weak smile, and looked to Brent for help.

"Now, Mom, you know I wasn't hiding anything. It's just been such a whirlwind, and . . . uh . . . I just wanted our first meeting to be special."

"Oh, it's special all right," Douglas interjected. "Where have you been? What kind of man leaves his fiancée to ramble around the farm alone? What could have been so important that you just disappeared?"

Brent shrank under his father's wilting voice. The smile faded, and he stared at Douglas for a few painfully silent seconds. "Uh, nothing. I'm sorry. Um, you all remember Adam Kelly, Kate's cousin. Adam and I were in school together in Virginia."

Adam stepped up to the plate and cheerfully shook Jane's hand. He waved at Meg, who remained seated.

Jane glanced at Adam and sniffed, "No, I don't remember you."

Meg stirred on the couch. She had not inherited her father's looks. She wasn't ugly, just extraordinarily plain. She looked a few years older than Brent and had the Kings' long legs and thin build, but that was about it. Her short, straight brown hair, laced with strings of premature silver, was cupped demurely at her chin. Her skin was alabaster white, minus any hint of makeup, and she wore a white turtleneck and camel-colored slacks, which only added to her ghostly pallor.

She finally spoke, in a deep, expressionless tone. "We weren't anticipating such a crowd. I didn't think brides traveled with such an entourage these days. I thought that died with dowries and jousting matches."

"Meg, enough," Douglas clipped. He waved us to our seats. "We have something to discuss. I was out with Steve when I met Kate and Adam wandering on the farm. This is Detective Rami, from the Lexington Police Department. We need to talk about why he's joined us this afternoon."

That introduction garnered everyone's attention. Rami was used to it and merely reached for his notebook and pen, prepared to scribble as needed. Jane sank onto the couch and stiffened. Her eyes grew even larger, and she nervously picked at the red polish on her nails. Douglas, Brent, and Meg stared at her hands as if they were steeling themselves for some frightening outburst.

Douglas softened and placed his hand on his wife's arm. "Now, we don't need to get upset, but there's been an accident out near Mathias's barn."

Meg's gaze didn't leave Jane. "That's too bad, but does Mother need to be bothered with it? She has a lot to do for Brent's party tomorrow."

Steve had walked over to the window, but he turned around when Douglas pinned the location at his barn. He made a face to himself, then grinned slightly and mouthed "wacko" again in our direction.

Rami took note, then spoke to Jane. "Didn't you hear an explosion a while back? Or the fire trucks? A car in a field caught fire and blew up. There was a victim inside. We're trying to determine who it is and what happened. Did you have any visitors this afternoon?"

Jane stared straight at Rami with a glazed, eerily vacant expression. "I don't understand what you're saying. Make yourself clear, Detective. I have several guests coming soon. There will be lots of people here—important people. We're having an event. A party. My son is announcing his engagement to . . . to her."

Yikes, I'd been reduced to "her." I wished I had paid more attention to all those *Cosmo* and *Glamour* articles that taught you how to handle the in-laws.

Meg stood. "Several people have been in and out today—caterers, decorators, and such. You don't understand what my mother's parties are like.

We're also a working stud farm, Detective. This is a business, not just a home. I'm very sorry for whoever it is out there, but you must understand, it could be practically anyone. I suppose you ought to start with a head count of our staff." Her tone remained crisp and emotionless. "You've got your work cut out for you. Let's not bother Mother with this until you have more information. Now, Detective, can Mother and I be excused?"

Rami was flustered. "No, you can't. I have things to ask both of you. I understand you have a party to plan, but I have a burnt body outside that's my priority. Please have a seat."

Meg remained standing. The sheerest hint of pink flashed on her pale cheeks and quickly dissipated. She and Detective Rami indulged in a cool staring contest, before he gave up and jotted a note on his pad.

The tension eased a bit as the elderly housekeeper entered the room, clutching a cordless phone. She tentatively cleared her throat. "I'm sorry to disturb you, Mr. King, but there is an emergency call. It's Dr. Gerald."

Douglas took the phone and went into the hall. Steve followed, but before he could reach the door, Douglas shouted an anguished "What? How?" that caused Steve to sprint into the hall.

Rami questioned, "Dr. Gerald?"

Brent took a few steps toward the door. "Dr. Gerald is our chief veterinarian. There must be something wrong with one of the horses."

Meg put a hand to her mouth and joined her brother near the door. "Bayou Folly's at Churchill this week."

"As in Churchill Downs?" Adam asked. "Isn't it too cold in Louisville to be racing?"

"Fall meet," Brent said absently, his eyes still on the hall. "They race until the end of the month. You know, the Breeders' Cup Classic, the Churchill Downs Distaff, all the fall stakes races. We have several horses there."

Douglas came back into the room, his face as pale as Meg's. Looking like he'd been kicked in the stomach, he wandered aimlessly to a window and stared blankly outside. Tears escaped from his eyes.

Steve followed Douglas in, and he, too, had tears in his eyes. "Bayou Folly was put down. He broke his leg, kicked his stall. His cannon bone was fractured. They tried casting it, but it wouldn't hold. Surgery apparently wasn't an option. He's gone . . . so quickly."

The news hit the King family like a bomb blast. They were totally stunned and horrified. Douglas remained at the window, and Jane began to rock back and forth, murmuring a pained mantra of "No, no, no." Meg sank to the couch and buried her head in her lap, and Brent bit his lip and clenched his eyes shut.

It was too much for Steve, who ran out of the room. On the way, he nearly plowed over Zach and Detective Knight, who were being shown in by the housekeeper.

Knight looked at her partner. "Is there something I should know about the victim?"

Rami shook his head. "No, I haven't gotten that far. We had a horse die." He nodded to Zach. "Who's your friend here?"

Zach started to speak, but Knight flashed a manicured hand in his face and turned to me. "Miss, can you identify this man?"

"Yes, he's Zach Tanner. He's a photographer traveling with me. Is there a problem?"

"For starters," she said, "he showed up at the scene and started taking pictures. He doesn't have proper media credentials. So, you're saying he's supposed to be here?"

"Yes," Brent snapped. "He's with me, all right? Leave him alone. We have a major problem here, okay?" He looked disdainfully at Rami. "We didn't just have 'a horse' die. It was Bayou Folly. Surely you understand what that means."

Knight was genuinely surprised. "Bayou Folly? Wow, that's too bad. What a great horse. I'm sorry." She glanced at her stewing partner. "It's really sad about the horse, but, folks, we have a bigger problem. We've got a murder on our hands."

"What makes it a murder?" I asked.

Knight smoothed her unruly curls. "Several things we discovered, not the least of which is the presence of a highly flammable accelerant doused throughout the car. It didn't just blow up on its own. Someone gave it a nice helping hand. There was other physical evidence on the body as well, which we can discuss after the autopsy is complete."

Rami grimaced slightly. "Anything else?"

"Yep. One of the firefighters found a charred license plate blown several feet from the scene." She crossed her arms. "Anyone here know someone who lives in New York?"

C H A P T E R · 6

OF COURSE WE KNEW someone from New York. The problem was, the one who actually lived in New York didn't catch the significance. While we all zoomed in on Brent with dumbfounded looks, he innocently questioned Detective Knight. "So, you're saying it was a stranger, an out-of-towner, on the farm. We don't do tours or anything, so maybe it was someone looking to buy one of the horses? Did you have any appointments like that, Meg?"

"Brent," Meg stabbed acidly. "Think about it, baby brother. Where do you live now?"

His eyes grew, and a light bulb with minimum wattage turned on. "Oh. You're right. I guess I do live there." He swung his handsome head between the two detectives. "But I flew here. I don't have a car on the farm. I've never had a car with New York tags here, honest."

Jane rocked in her seat. "Bayou Folly, gone, gone, gone. We're ruined, finished." She stared straight ahead. Her husband and children unconsciously shifted closer to each other, forming an impenetrable human shield around her. It was a practiced move, full of an eerie awareness that an ugly or embarrassing scene was on the horizon.

Zach slipped away from Detective Knight's side and moved to the far side of the room. He nonchalantly placed his camera on a waist-high table and gently depressed the button as a perfectly timed cough covered the shutter's click. His action puzzled me until I followed the aim of the lens, which bull's-eyed to where Jane murmured to herself.

What would a picture like that accomplish for my magazine? I thought selfishly. Zach was here to shoot happy things, such as the party, the food, and all the pretty odds and ends surrounding a ritzy wedding. My ritzy wedding.

He wasn't supposed to document the rise and fall of the mental state of the mother of the groom. Or a murder scene, for that matter.

Granted, if he'd been a news photographer, I could picture him crawling all over the place, disturbing both the peace and the police. News photographers were trained to react to any spot news, whether it was their story or not. It was one of those nebulous unwritten rules of journalism: If it bleeds, it leads.

From what I'd gathered earlier on the plane, Zach didn't have a news bone in his body. He said he was strictly a product-and-fashion photog who hung around advertising shoots and glossy magazines, not cigarette-smoke-filled, obscenity-infested newsrooms. However, I wasn't being a snob about fashion mags. I worked for a glossy magazine, after all, and had a demented fondness for newsrooms like that. Zach's actions just didn't make sense.

Jane's unnerving trance caught Rami's eye. He made another note on his pad and turned to Brent. "So, you neglected to mention that you live in New York. Don't you think that's relevant?"

"Well, maybe." He stiffened. "I don't know. Why should I equate it with anything when I know that where I live has nothing to do with that car or whatever is in it?"

"*Who*ever," Detective Knight snapped. "There's a person in that car, not a thing. Do you have any idea who it could be, Mr. King?"

A flash of anger clouded Brent's face. "No, how should I know? New York is a big place. I can't possibly know everyone there. What do I look like, a genius?"

That was a stretch in anyone's book, family included. I momentarily forgot I was supposed to be blindly in love with Brent. I fought a smile and sneaked a look at Adam. He frowned a warning to behave.

"Well . . . I'm not, you know," Brent stammered. "A genius, that is. Very few of us are."

Knight's strawberry curls shimmied off the Richter scale, and she looked ready to whip out her handcuffs and haul Brent off for a little police-brutality session. His legendary charm wasn't working on the fair detective. I knew exactly how she felt.

I studied Detective Knight and wondered if there was something fundamentally wrong with us for not being blown away by the hunky underwear model. Surely not; we were both perfectly normal, hormonally crazed women, prone to our share of chocolate binges and leering looks at the opposite sex. I wasn't infatuated with Brent King because I had John Donovan. At least I hoped I still had John. I'd yet to hear from him after our little scene the night before, courtesy of Brent.

Rami nudged his partner's arm. "We'll get the ID as soon as possible, but it would be helpful if you all could put some thought into who the victim is."

Adam spoke up. "Maybe I shouldn't get involved, but could it be someone you know from New York who's coming to the party?"

Brent stared blankly, but Adam's eyes fell questioningly on mine, as if he might be trying to send me a message telepathically. It worked, and a nerve went haywire in my stomach.

Paige Kendall. Paige was missing in action, and she was from New York. Why wouldn't she head for Bluegrass Winds? Surely she knew about the party, and if she wanted to humiliate Brent in a big way, this was the perfect opportunity for her.

But if it was Paige, how did she end up blown to little pieces in that horrible fire? Why would someone want to kill her? If someone was after the bride, that certainly didn't bode well for my security. After all, everyone thought I was the real McCoy.

A flash of heat spread across the back of my neck, and little pools of beady sweat set up shop in the small of my back. How on earth would we explain this one to the police?

Jane snapped out of her tremor. "No," she spit. "There's no one else from New York. The only guests from out of town are from Louisville, Versailles, or. . . ."

"Florida and Virginia," Meg concluded.

"That's right," Jane said, quickly gaining momentum. "This is a local affair, a Southern event, a gracious evening with our friends. Brent and Kate can entertain their city people on their own time. Really, can't we discuss this later? There's so much to do for the party."

The change in Jane was startling. Talk of the party truly kicked her into gear. The color instantly returned to her cheeks, and the past few minutes of rocking and moaning dissipated like vapor.

Detective Knight spoke slowly and deliberately to Brent. "I understand you're engaged, Mr. King, but perhaps one of your former girlfriends is upset with your impending nuptials? Maybe she made an appearance and you didn't like it?"

There was the question, but it wasn't a former girlfriend I was concerned with—it was the real girlfriend. Adam, Zach, and I turned to Brent, and I almost missed Zach's subtle cough as another shot secretly advanced on his camera.

Reality hit Brent with a sharp intake of breath as it dawned on him. The game was up. I waited for him to tell the truth about who I was and why I was with him. *Get ready for some fireworks*, I thought stoically. He walked over to me, and I practiced my deep breathing for the coming explanation and, likely, the second explosion of the day.

Instead, Brent slid his arm around my shoulder. "I understand where you're coming from," he said coolly. "But that's not possible. Kate is the only one for me." His fingers dug into my shoulder, and he blazed his turquoise eyes into mine. "Right, darling? There's no one else, just us."

I searched his face and managed a bewildered, weak smile in response. Wasn't he concerned that it might be Paige? Why didn't Brent fess up to our charade? This was the prime time to do it—before the party, in his parents' presence, and before the police were more involved. I could pack my bags and return home posthaste and let the King family deal with the crispy critter in their pasture. What was I supposed to do—blurt out that it was all a ruse? Brent got me into this mess; I thought it only fair that he get us out of it.

"Detective Knight has a point, Brent," Adam began valiantly. "Could it be an old flame?"

"A flame? That's disgusting, considering the situation," Meg admonished.

Adam mumbled a contrite apology for his lack of eloquence, but he was cut off by an angry Douglas King.

"Enough of this. Come on, Meg, we have phone calls to make. There's a lot we have to do concerning Bayou Folly. I'll need your help." He turned to Brent. "Take care of your mother. Perhaps you could get her one of her snacks, to tide her over until dinner."

Brent and Meg exchanged knowing glances.

"I'll take care of it," Brent answered quietly.

Given the emphasis Douglas put on the word *snack*, I wondered if there was more involved than peanut butter and crackers. Like maybe a Prozac sandwich with a Valium chaser?

Jane stood quickly. "I'm not hungry."

Brent left my side and took his mother's hand. "Come on, Mom, we'll get a shake. It won't mess up your appetite, you'll enjoy it." He glanced back at me. "I can tell you all about Kate and me. We'll have a nice chance to talk before dinner."

I debated joining them so I could learn all the gory details about our so-called romance, but Brent dragged her out of the room before I could follow. Besides, Meg had other plans.

She looked at her watch. "Dad, I'll meet you in the office. I'll get the paperwork started and pull the phone numbers. Dinner isn't for a while yet. That should give us time to get things rolling." She ran her eyes up and down me like a high-tech X-ray machine. "You should all plan on meeting back here by seven-thirty. Kate, that should give you time to shower and change for dinner. You *were* planning to dress for dinner, weren't you?"

"Of course," I whimpered, keenly aware of all the eyes falling on me like a ton of fashion magazines.

Douglas instructed, "Detectives, do what you need out there, then leave your card with someone. I'll contact you Monday morning."

Rami's eyes grew. "*We'll* contact *you* when we want. That could be Monday or it could be later tonight. We'll make those decisions, Mr. King."

Color rose above Douglas's collar. "Try to get finished as soon as possible. We have important business matters to rectify." He marched down the hallway with Meg in tow.

Knight flew to the door and made a fist in frustration. "These people are freakin' unbelievable."

Rami nodded. "They're horse people." He turned to Adam, Zach, and me. "I trust you three will keep us advised of your whereabouts. And if you decide to return home, or think of anything I should know, please give me a call." He handed me a card with his office phone, pager, and what I assumed was a cell phone number. He joined his partner. "I'd appreciate any help you guys could provide. We're going back to the scene for a while. We'll be in touch."

Once they were down the hall, I threw my hands on my hips. "I want out. Now."

"But things are just getting interesting," Zach protested.

"Kate, Kate, calm down," Adam soothed. "Surely, by tomorrow, Brent will explain everything to his family. I know things are weird right now, but we promised."

"Promised nothing, Adam," I replied. "And it's gone beyond weird. We're dealing with a dead body and the damned Addams Family. What is with them? Was I the only one who noticed that no one cared about whoever was in that fire?"

Zach unscrewed a lens from his camera and zipped it in his coat pocket. "Well, did you see all that stuff with the horse? All the trophies, the race photos? Bayou Folly must've been worth a fortune. It's no wonder they're acting this way. That's a meal ticket gone *poof,* folks."

"I don't care about the horse," I argued. "Adam, what about Paige? Why didn't Brent say anything about her? Don't you think it's strange that she's missing and we've got a body in a car with New York tags outside? Did that just slip from his mind?"

He rubbed his forehead. "Yeah, I know. I thought that was odd. Maybe he's got some plan in mind."

"Like what?" I challenged. "Adam, he's your friend, go talk to him. Get us out of this mess. I want to go home."

He sighed. "Okay, I'll try to find him. But we'll have to at least stay through dinner, and I doubt we could get a flight tonight. Will you settle for tomorrow? Give me that, at least. I'm hungry. I want to see what dinner is like when it's prepared by servants, okay? Compromise?"

I studied the ceiling. "Fine. I'll see you at dinner."

Zach grinned. "Yeah, I guess we better get ready. After all, we need to dress. You better head over to the cottage, Kate. It takes a while to put on a tiara."

While the boys made do with the mansion, I settled for the cottage. The door was still unlocked, so I entered and poked my head around for any visitors. City girl that I was, I locked the front door before I headed for the shower. If someone wanted to get in, he could get a key or break a window. In any event, I hoped to be out of the shower by the time it took to accomplish either mode of entry.

Just to be safe, I also locked the bathroom door. After all, there was a killer out there on the loose. I had no intention of meeting my end in the bathroom. How undignified for someone with a diamond the size of Montana on her hand.

The hot steamy water was a welcome relief. By no means had this been a simple, fun weekend. I'd really goofed by agreeing to help Adam, but that had always been my problem since day one. I frequently wound up saying yes to things I knew would get me in trouble.

Like the time when I was a kid, and fat bully Cathy Agusta convinced me that since I was so scrawny, I was the perfect person to fit through the window of an abandoned trailer the neighborhood kids used as a secret hideout. The door was jammed, and some precious doll or game of Cathy's was inside, and her girth just wouldn't make it through the window. So guess who climbed over several bricks and boxes, squirmed through precisely half of the window, and couldn't go any farther?

My front dangled over the smelly, damp, dark inside of the trailer, while my posterior smiled to the heavens and every neighborhood kid who gathered and giggled, then mobilized to shove me through the rest of the way. I never forgot the thud of landing headfirst into a moldy bean bag chair that was missing most of its beans, and it took all my powers of sneakiness to hide my scraped and bruised stomach from my mother for days after the escapade.

I realized Adam had been there for that mess, too. He probably laughed the loudest.

And you know, I thought as I dried off with thick, white Ralph Lauren towels monogrammed with a big gold K, *I don't think Cathy Agusta ever thanked me for retrieving her toy.*

"This time," I said aloud to the bathroom mirror, "Brent King will thank me. Adam Kelly will thank me. The whole stupid state of Kentucky will thank me."

C H A P T E R · 7

SINCE I WASN'T QUITE SURE what "dressing for dinner" included, I opted for a black velvet turtleneck and a long, plaid wool skirt. I snapped on my very fake JCPenney pearl earrings and necklace, hoping to satisfy the "dressed" requirement. I shoved my tennis-shoe-loving feet into a pair of heels, thinking again how much I would rather be draped in thick sweats and socks, scarfing down a pizza on my couch in front of the TV.

No chance. I glanced at the clock and realized I was late. I smeared on some lipstick and blush, ran a brush through my damp curls one more time, and grabbed my coat. The sun had long since said good-night, and the moon dozed in and out of thick clouds. I focused my eyes to the darkness and hiked up my skirt as I ran across the yard toward the house, praying I wouldn't trip over something and fall flat on my face.

Brent met me at the door. "You look great. Smell good too." He took my coat and tossed it on a chair, presumably for some servant to retrieve later. "Everyone's in the dining room. We got started a little early, skipped the drinks, since, uh, Mom had her snack."

"Did her snack include something that you shouldn't mix with alcohol?"

He ran his hand through his hair. He'd changed into gray tweed pants and a thick, gray cardigan. A crisp white shirt and burgundy tie peeked out from the sweater. The only thing missing was the pipe and glass of cognac. "Yeah, it's one of Dad's old tricks. When she gets that upset, she fights her medication. We mix it into something sweet and call it a snack. Meg or I usually are tapped to give it to her. We've done it since we were kids. I can't believe she's never caught on to what we're doing."

His eyes lost a bit of luster. "This has been a hell of a day, Kate. I'm very sorry. We could all use a drink, I'm sure. There will be wine at dinner. We'll put nonalcoholic wine in Mom's glass."

"Another family secret?"

"You're learning," he replied.

Though he sounded tired, he flashed his winning smile as we entered the dining room, where the Kings, Adam, and Zach were already seated. Suits and skirts were the norm, and I sighed, relieved that my velvet top and faux pearls worked fine for this crowd.

Brent turned to his family. "We saved the best for last. Look what a beautiful treasure I found on the steps. Isn't she great? Let's all enjoy dinner."

The massive dining room was painted a soft dusty rose and edged with deep, ivory crown molding and ivory-framed windows. An antique mahogany table that seated a dozen-plus sat in front of an Italian marble mantel that hovered protectively over a softly crackling fire. The scent of roses, pine, and vanilla candles filled the room.

After Brent helped me into my chair, he settled next to me, with Adam on his other side. Meg and Zach faced us across the way, and Jane commandeered the end of the table, directly across from her husband at the head. I gave apologies for being late and received no response.

That was a precursor for the rest of the dinner. Brent made a few attempts at light conversation, and Adam offered several compliments on the food, but no one else was in a chatty mood. Meg glumly attacked her salad and main course of roast beef, steamed vegetables draped in a spicy white sauce, and delicately whipped potatoes enhanced with flecks of spice. She barely looked up from her plate. Douglas consulted his watch every time he took a bite, and Jane was unusually quiet, perhaps in deference to her afternoon snack.

Two plump women in gray uniforms removed the dishes from the table as a man appeared in the doorway. He was middle-aged, with a large nose and even larger middle section that stretched the seams of a black knit sweater with leather patches on the elbows. Most noticeable was his thick and unusually dark brown hair, which probably came directly from a bottle of Just For Men hair color.

He lumbered into the room, his arms swinging at his side as if they were loose in their sockets. "Douglas, I'm back. Let's go, we've got a lot to cover."

Douglas put down his fork and glared at the intruder. "Can't you see I'm busy, Larry? Go get something in the kitchen. I'll talk to you later."

Larry didn't budge. "Food can wait. Bayou Folly can't."

Douglas threw his napkin on the table. "Damn it, Larry." He stood so quickly, his leg caught the end of the table.

Wine swished in crystal glasses, the candles teetered, and a salt shaker tumped over. None of the Kings moved. No one spoke or looked at each other.

Douglas stomped away and led Larry out the door. "Let's get this over with, I've had enough today."

Brent finally looked up from his plate. "Dr. Gerald, our vet. He was at Churchill when Bayou Folly had his accident."

"I should be with them," Meg announced. She rose quickly, dumped her napkin firmly in the center of her plate, and stalked out.

Jane was next. She scooted her chair back and said, "This will not do. Does that man have any manners at all? This day has been a disaster, a complete disaster." She shot a look in my direction. "It all began when you arrived."

Great, just great. I was on my mother-in-law's list, and we hadn't even set a wedding date yet. I kept my head down and twisted my diamond around my finger to keep myself occupied.

Brent made a fist in his lap. "Mom, don't be that way. I agree, it's been a long day, but we've got a big day ahead of us tomorrow, so maybe in light of everything, we should all get some rest."

Adam rose. "That's a good idea. If you'll excuse me, Mrs. King, I'm tired. I think I'll call it a night."

The scent of something wonderful tickled my nose. A slightly bewildered server carted little dessert cups to the table. I nearly whimpered with delight when I saw that the cups contained fresh crème brûlée. Adam changed his mind and settled into his chair again.

"Take it away," Jane ordered. "We're finished here. No one wants our company tonight, so we'll consider dinner complete." She motioned us out of the room, as if we were guilty little children. "Out. Go to your rooms, go to sleep."

My heart plunged as I watched the server silently back out of the room with the little caramelized custard delights.

Jane looked at us and repeated, "I said, we're finished. Good night."

Brent mumbled, "I'm sorry, guys. Let's just give up. We'll see you in the morning."

Zach shrugged his shoulders. "I'm going to take a walk. Anyone want to join me?"

Adam begged off. "No, I really am beat. I'm going to turn in early."

Brent turned and took my hand. "Good idea, I think we'll do the same."

Adam's sudden grin hit me. We—Brent and I—were heading back to "our" cozy little cottage. As Brent guided me toward the door, Adam whispered, "Behave, or I'll tell your mom."

Brent helped me into my coat before I could protest. He grabbed my hand, and we were out the door, leaving my grinning cousin and the photographer behind.

I pulled my hand free as we walked down the sidewalk. "Look, Brent, we've never discussed how we're going to handle this."

He smiled. "Handle what, Kate?"

Despite the arctic breeze, a flash of heat lit my cheeks. Little puffs of breath smoked out of my mouth. "You know what I mean. The cottage. Where we'll sleep. There's only one bed."

"I can count, Kate."

A cold wind whipped my hair into a frenzy. "I have a boyfriend."

He shoved a wayward piece of hair from my face. "And I have a girlfriend."

I stared at him for a second, then stomped across the yard. I passed a large bush and came to a sharp halt as angry voices sliced through the night air. Brent ran up behind me and wrapped a protective arm around my waist as we froze in our spot and tried to determine the direction of the voices.

I recognized Steve's voice. "It's all your fault. You did it, you asshole. You ruined me."

"You're drunk and stupid," shouted the other voice. "If you know what's good for you, you'll keep your mouth shut. No one would believe you anyway."

"Dr. Gerald," Brent whispered.

The voices moved closer, but there was no place for us to hide. We stood like very obvious statues in the middle of the yard.

"You know what I'm gonna do," Steve growled. "I'm gonna call one of those investigative reporters at the TV stations. When they start poking around your practice, they're gonna find themselves knee-deep in horse shit, and it won't be from any of your horses. You've got plenty of that on your own."

"Nobody threatens Larry Gerald, you hear me, Mathias?" He flew past the bush and stopped in front of us.

Steve stumbled from behind the bush and nearly crashed into Dr. Gerald. They both stared at us like deer caught in the headlights of an oncoming truck. Steve had a nearly empty bottle of Jack Daniel's in his hand and was missing a coat.

He pointed the bottle at us. "What are you doing here, kids, makin' love in the moonlight?"

Brent reached for the bottle but missed. "Mathias, leave us alone. You need to take this somewhere else." He turned to Dr. Gerald. "I thought you were with my father and Meg."

Dr. Gerald stared at me, then slowly turned his attention back to what Brent was saying. "I'm going back there. I had to talk to the stable boy, there, but as you can see, he's too drunk to make any sense. I thought you had rules for your employees, Brent. Your father wouldn't approve."

Steve halfheartedly swung the bottle at Dr. Gerald and missed by several inches. "Piss off, old man."

Dr. Gerald ignored him and leered at me. "Who's the doll, Brent? Aren't you going to introduce us?"

"This doll's name is Kate," I clipped. I wanted to add it was none of his fat, big-nosed business, but I didn't want to give him the satisfaction of knowing how revolted I was.

Dr. Gerald leaned forward, his roving eyes mentally undressing me. I pulled my coat tighter and was glad I had on a turtleneck. This guy defined creepy.

"So pleased to meet you, Kate. You pick 'em, boy."

Brent's arm grew tighter around my waist, and he pushed me forward. "We've got to go. I suggest you find my father. Mathias, you need to go back to your cabin. We'll see you later."

I hadn't thought it possible, but I was quite pleased to have Brent escort me the few feet to the cottage. Dr. Gerald and Steve stared after us as we jumped through the unlocked door and flipped on a light.

"What jerks," Brent grumbled, shrugging off his coat.

I gazed at the door. "I thought I locked that when I left earlier."

Brent was unconcerned. "We never lock it, there's no need."

"I'm sure that I did," I repeated and opened the door. I peeked out into the darkness. There was no sign of Steve or Dr. Gerald. They had quickly moved on to drunken battles elsewhere. "What's the story with those two?" I asked as I shut the door again and took off my coat.

Brent hung our coats in a small closet, walked back to me, and stood uncomfortably close. "Who knows? Dr. Gerald is a first-class sleaze, and Steve is just a big, dumb jock."

Spoken like a big, dumb male model, I thought. "What was all that about keeping quiet and getting a reporter interested in something?"

"Kate, I don't know. It's too late for you to play reporter. Office hours are over. Let's get back to our other conversation." He was unbearably close and positively reeked of expensive aftershave, hormones, and heat.

I backed up a step and banged into a small table. Brent cornered me and reached his hand into my hair. His fingers worked their way through my curls. He was awfully close; so close, those darn eyes seemed bluer than ever. So he wasn't Einstein. Who needed a dissertation when you looked like that?

He bent his head toward my face and gazed at me for an eternal second. "You want me on the couch tonight, don't you? It's all right, I understand. It will be our secret. I'll get a blanket and extra pillow out of the cabinet upstairs, then I'll leave you alone. Is that fair?"

I tried to speak, but all the air was locked in my lungs. I swallowed and squeaked a desperately weak, "Okay, that's fine."

He smiled and backed away a step. He took my hand and led me upstairs to the bedroom loft. My throat tightened again when the big canopy bed appeared in all its glory, but Brent was true to his word.

He headed for the bathroom. "I'll just be a second. Can you grab the pillow and blanket from that armoire?"

I numbly followed his instructions and pulled out a sheet, thick red blanket, and two big pillows. He was out of the bathroom in a flash and stuffed the pillows and blankets in his arms.

"Can I help you with that?" I asked.

"Nah, I've got it all. I'll be down here if you need anything. Sweet dreams, Kate. Get some rest." He winked his good-night and slipped down the steps without another word.

I stood in the center of the bedroom for a minute, then rummaged in my suitcase for my nightgown, a decidedly unromantic, long-sleeved, ankle-length flannel job. It came from Victoria's Secret, so it had a ruffled, plunging neckline, but the style was definitely not a hot, satin thingamajig that barely covered all those important parts. Instead, it was more suited to a single girl's cold winter night.

I clumped into the bathroom and washed my face and brushed my teeth, not sure whether I was imitating an old maid or one half of an old married couple. I stared at my reflection in the mirror, wondering if I had an abbreviated form of jet lag. Could you get it from a two-hour flight?

Maybe starting the day with a hangover sped up the effects of jet lag so it could hit without traveling cross-country. Of course, most people wouldn't add the afternoon and evening I'd had. That was enough to make anyone wave a white flag in defeat. I pulled back the skin around my eyes, but that only made me look like a tired, big-haired, old sack of bones.

I shuffled into the bedroom and listened for signs of an amorous attack from Brent. The light was off downstairs, and not a sound danced on the airwaves. It looked as if he really was asleep on the couch. No panty raids tonight. A tiny part of me was a shade disappointed with Brent's promise to remain a gentleman. He certainly gave up easily. Was I that unattractive? That forbidding?

I rumbled those thoughts out my ears. What was I thinking? Diamonds, crazy families, male models with hormonal overloads, dead horses, dead bodies, drunken shadows that go bump in the night. Whatever possessed me to agree to this stupid favor and then seal my fate by mentioning it to Alice? I had to be crazy—certifiable even. Just like my dear old mother-in-law-to-be. Poor Jane. I was pretty sure she was harmless.

I brushed the potpourri scattered on the fluffy white comforter into my hand and deposited it in a neat little pile on the nightstand. Next came the assortment of white throw pillows that I sent airborne with perfect little Frisbee tosses to the floor.

"It's all just make-believe," I whispered. "A goofy little story that will probably never hit print once everything is said and done. It's almost over. Enjoy this nice, big comfortable bed," I told myself as I yanked back the comforter. "One day down, only two hopefully uneventful days to go."

Maybe, maybe not.

I wasn't alone.

I jumped back and let the comforter land in a thick pile at the foot of the bed. In the center of the mattress, near the pillows, lay a Barbie and Ken dressed as bride and groom. I think it was Ken and Barbie. I couldn't be positive, since their heads were missing. A toy horse was placed next to the pair.

There was more. The miniature lace dress and the little black tux were spattered with something red, and the horse's right front leg was broken. A piece of ivory parchment stationery rested under the dolls.

I gently pulled it out from underneath the gruesome bride and groom and bit my lip as I read the words that had been printed out in a flowing, Gothic font:

Something old, something new,
Something borrowed, something blue.
One body's turned up dead, it's true.
Who will be next? Will it be you?

C H A P T E R · 8

MY MIND SCREAMED, *For cryin' out loud!* My voice took its own cue. "Brent! Come up here! Now!"

There was no response from below.

I walked to the top of the stairs. "Brent! Come up here! This isn't funny; you need to see this!"

Silence.

I stared into the darkness that swallowed the bottom of the staircase and filled the cottage's big room—the room where Brent was supposed to be slumbering peacefully. Why didn't he answer? My flannel nightgown grew uncomfortably hot and itchy, and my hands melted into the clammy consistency of raw meat fresh out of the butcher's case. The stillness was complete, except for the impatient tap of wind-driven bare branches on the windowpane and the irregular whap of my pulse against my skin.

I stood deathly still, but my mind raced. It wasn't as if we were wings apart in the mansion—Brent was just one room away . . . in a tiny dark cottage that was home to a bloody Barbie doll meant for me . . . on a farm with a psychotic woman, a drunk horse trainer, and a creepy vet, not to mention whatever remained of a dead body in a field nearby. Just because every Alfred Hitchcock movie I'd ever seen was playing in full Technicolor in front of my eyes was no reason for undue alarm.

I squeaked out a weaker call. "Brent? Where are you?" I took a halting step down and brilliantly announced to any serial killers or werewolves below, "I'm coming down there . . . down the stairs. Right now. I am."

'Twas the peril of twenty-first-century heroines, I thought as I crept down the staircase. I had the flowing, Victorian granny gown, but like any good, soon-

to-be-frightened-out-of-her-skull victim, I didn't have a blazing candlestick to lead me down the stairs to my doom. Instead, I scraped my hand along the wall, searching in vain for a light switch.

I reached the bottom and squinted, until I made out the faint outline of a light switch on the wall. I waited for the boogeyman to jump from the shadows, but to my great relief, nothing happened. I lunged for the switch and flipped it on, illuminating the once cavernously dark room.

The peaceful blues and yellows bathing the room laughed at my paranoid mind. The room was untouched. There were no bloody, dismembered bodies heaped on the floor, no psycho killers hiding behind plants.

There was also no Brent.

The blanket on the couch was bundled in a hastily tossed ball, and the cushions and pillow showed dented evidence of someone's prior presence.

This was the second time he'd pulled a disappearing act, and it was already getting old. I poked my head into the kitchenette. Nothing. I peeked out the windows but didn't see anything of interest. I stopped at the front door, and an icy breeze slapped my ankle. The door was ajar.

I pushed it open and peered into the darkness. *Maybe Brent ran up to the main house to get a warm pair of jammies*, I thought. As logical as that sounded, I doubted it was true. I shut the door and, grumbling, opened the closet door just inside the entry. I pulled out my coat and discovered a pair of large, well-used boots in the corner.

In the interest of time and necessity, I shoved my size-7 feet into the much larger boots and wrapped up in my coat. I was engaged to a model, so I figured he could be the "better half," thereby freeing me up to get away with the massive fashion faux pas. I also discovered a riding whip in the closet, which I held on to for added security. My combination wool coat, flannel nightgown, large boots, and riding whip probably wouldn't subdue an intruder, I thought, but the sight just might scare him away.

I ventured outside and crunched over crisp leaves scattered in the grass, announcing yet again that I was out in the middle of the big, wide world, ready to meet any rabid killers. I crept around the side of the cottage, whip in hand, and discovered how difficult it was to sneak anywhere in rubber boots several sizes too big. I'd be a goner for sure if I had to run in the opposite direction, I thought. I'd fall flat on my face after the first sprint.

A bush in front of me shivered to life, and I swung my little whip wildly in the direction of the big, dark blur that emerged.

"Hey! Kate! Stop that!" Brent screeched. "What are you doing?"

Roughly gripping my wrist, he yanked my arm and mighty whip aside. "What the hell are you doing with that?" He snapped the whip out of my hand, then paused long enough to take in my sexy outfit. A delighted grin exploded on his face. "What are you doing out here like that? It's freezing. You should be upstairs in bed."

"As you should, too," I argued. "Inside, I mean. On the couch." I noticed he was still wearing the same clothes from earlier, missing his tie and coat. "You should be the one who's freezing. Where's your coat?"

"It's inside. I just stepped out here for a second. I didn't expect to find you out here too. I didn't want to alarm you, but I thought I heard someone messing around the bushes. I was afraid it might be a prowler, and with everything that's gone on today, I decided I'd better take a look."

I studied the outline of Brent's face in the darkness. "Well, did you find anyone?"

"No," he replied. "I guess it was just the wind."

"I don't think so," I said. "Come inside and see what I found upstairs. Unless you have a really warped sense of humor, we did have a visitor tonight."

He reached for my arm. "What are you talking about?"

A blinding flash illuminated the darkness, and since it was the middle of November, I ruled out any sudden thunderstorms. Brent instinctively smashed me to his chest and dragged me toward the bush. He missed, losing his balance, and together we fell smack into the prickly, spiny branches of the big evergreen.

Another blue-white flash illuminated our tangled predicament, and a laugh sliced through the air. "I'm saving these for my blackmail files," said Zach. "What is this—some kind of kinky Kentucky engagement ritual?"

Brent scrambled to his feet, leaving me behind to hoist myself free from the branches that took an instant liking to my wool-and-flannel ensemble. He stormed over to Zach and yanked the camera away. "What's wrong with you? What do you think you're doing out here?"

Zach held up his hands. "Hey, calm down. Give me my camera. I was just having some fun. I won't do anything with those pictures; they probably won't even turn out. I was taking a walk before I turned in, that's all. I didn't expect to run into anyone, especially not the two of you."

I clomped over to Zach and Brent. "Do you always carry your camera in the dead of night? Does it help you fight insomnia or something?"

Zach grinned and pulled a leaf from my hair. "Great outfit, Kate. Love the boots. The whip's a nice touch, too."

I thought of a few things I'd like to do with the whip, and they had nothing to do with horses but plenty with a horse's ass. "I don't want to hear it, Zach. Why are you out here in the middle of the night, prowling around the cottage with your camera?"

"Would you two calm down?" he said. "I told you, I was just getting some fresh air. No offense, Brent, but it was so oppressive in there tonight that I thought I'd suffocate. I enjoy the outdoors; I could easily camp out here tonight. I don't think it's that cold." He took the camera back from Brent. "As for my camera, I carry it everywhere. It's my job. I'm a photographer, remember?" He held open his oversize, weather-beaten jacket. "As a reporter and a model, you two should recognize this jacket. All these little zippered pockets aren't a fashion statement. They hold lenses, film, and cameras. You know that; it's no big surprise."

So he was right. We gave him that one.

But Brent wasn't completely satisfied. "Were you looking in our windows just now?"

"No, no, no. I was taking a walk. Period. I saw you both out here, doing whatever it is you were doing in the bushes, and I thought I'd have a little fun. No big deal." He swept a look around the darkness. "I'm not the only one who's prowling around the woods tonight, okay? You're not the first people I ran into in the last few minutes."

I pulled my coat a little tighter and tried to ignore my frozen bare feet inside the rubber boots. "Who else have you seen?"

Zach nodded toward Brent. "Your sister, for one. She was over by that first barn, the real nice one. She and that vet were exchanging papers of some kind. They were having a huge conversation."

Brent shrugged his shoulders. "So what? It was probably a meeting about Bayou Folly. Dr. Gerald was at Churchill when the accident happened. I'm sure they were just going over the paperwork. Didn't you listen to anything that went on tonight?"

Zach zipped the camera into one of his jacket pockets. "Well, yeah, I guess you're right, but she sure wasn't thrilled to see me walk past. I thought I was interrupting something important."

Brent chuckled uneasily. "Meg is never very happy to see most people. Don't take it personally. She's just that way. Dad's passing most of the business end of the farm off to her, since I've got my modeling career in New York." His voice dropped slightly. "I guess I've never been good enough for the family biz, but to tell the truth, it doesn't interest me at all. Let Meg deal with all the insurance, vet bills, stud fees, and all that crap. I'm not the one with the business degree. She can have it."

I wondered if Zach had caught up with Dr. Gerald before or after Brent and I had our little encounter with the good doctor and Steve by the cottage. "Did you see Steve Mathias anywhere? Was he at the barn, too?"

"Who?" Zach said.

"The horse trainer," I answered. "He was at the house earlier."

Zach shook his head. "Nah, I didn't see him at all. Why?"

Brent took a step closer and gripped my elbow. "No reason, right?"

I glanced at Brent. Answering for me now, was he? "I just wondered if he was with them, or if you saw him anywhere around the cottage."

Zach smiled. "This place is turning out to have quite a night life. No, I haven't seen Steve."

Brent pushed me forward. "I think we've all had too much night life. I'm cold, let's go inside." He shoved me so hard, I almost fell over the tops of my boots. He steadied me, and we clomped around the side of the cottage.

Zach followed us to the front porch. Brent forgot his manners and plowed through the open door first, leaving me behind.

"You better get inside, Kate," Zach said. "You're turning blue. Or is that just part of that old bride's saying—you know, something borrowed, something blue? You can do better than that."

I froze on the threshold.

Zach grinned. "Sleep tight. Pleasant dreams."

He turned and lazily walked toward the main house. I stared after him, all the while hearing "something borrowed, something blue" as it sloshed from my ear to my brain.

Brent materialized at my side. "What's wrong, Kate? Come on in, close the door, it's cold. What's this sick joke you want to show me?"

I peered outside into the darkness, but Zach was gone. "Something borrowed and something blue," I said quietly.

Brent reached over my shoulder and pushed the door shut. "I don't get it, what do you mean?"

I slid out of my coat and yanked off the rubber boots. "Come upstairs, and I think you'll understand in no time flat."

"All righty then," he said, just a little too eagerly.

I started up the steps, Brent right behind me. So he wouldn't think it was an invitation of some kind, I stopped at the top of the loft and pointed to the bed. "Go over there and look at what I found under the covers."

He grinned as he passed me, but the grin slid right off his face the minute he spotted the dolls. He studied them as if they were Fabergé eggs, then slowly reached for the note. He read it to himself a couple of times before he turned a blank face my way. "I don't get it. Who would do this? I certainly didn't put these here. This isn't funny, Kate."

"No kidding."

"This is just gross. Someone is really messing with us. Do you think it's the killer?" he asked with wide-eyed innocence.

Of course it was the killer. Who else did he think it was, the Welcome Wagon? "Who would do this, Brent? Who'd be so upset about your engagement that they'd want to scare us?" I took a leap. "Could it be Paige?"

He tossed the dolls on the bed. "No way. She's missing, remember? How would she know? I mean, she knew about the party and everything, but she didn't know you were involved. And besides, what if . . . what if . . . she's the one who . . . was in . . . you know, the car?"

"Do you think that's possible? Why didn't you say anything to the police when they were here? We all heard about the New York tags. Why didn't you just tell the truth about me then? What if it *is* Paige? Who would want to kill her, Brent?" I promptly ignored the section of my brain reminding me that Brent was the only one who knew enough about Paige to have a motive to kill her.

Apparently I hit the overload buzzer on his question capacity with that barrage. His face grew crimson, and his forehead shrunk into a mass of little furrowed lines.

He swept past me and started downstairs. "I don't know. I just don't know. This is all going too fast for me. It can't be her, I know it in my heart. This was supposed to be very simple, and it's just exploded."

"Literally," I added.

He stopped midway down the steps. "I'm sorry, Kate. I don't know what to tell you. Look, are you too scared to sleep alone tonight? I can keep you company, or if you don't want to be up here, we could concoct something on the floor with the couch cushions and some blankets." His expression softened, and his *GQ* face appeared. "I can tell when a woman needs me. You don't have to be shy."

My eyebrows arched. "No, Brent, I'm just dandy up here alone. We'll have to show these dolls to the detectives tomorrow if they come out again. We can't do anything until then. Go downstairs, go to sleep, and don't go for any late-night strolls without telling me first. Is that fair?"

He stared at me, obviously struggling with yet another rejection. "If that's what you want. But if you change your mind. . . ."

Poor guy. "Good night, Brent," I said firmly.

I stood there until he made it to the bottom of the steps and turned toward the couch. Still not satisfied, I waited a couple of minutes while he banged around the room and finally turned off the light. Next I dealt with my friends on the bed. I carefully placed the dolls and letter on the floor, out of sight, lest I wake up in the middle of the night, forget where I was, and come face-to-face with a bloody, beheaded Barbie.

Just in case our killer decided to get in some climbing practice, I double-checked the locks on the windows in the bathroom and the bedroom. Then I shook the comforter in the air and looked under the sheets to make sure there were no more surprises waiting. Since everything was relatively peaceful, I turned off the light and burrowed beneath the covers.

Despite my exhaustion, I lay there with my eyes wide open for an eternity. I played the day's events over and over in my brain, trying to block out the ghastly vision of the burnt body. What did it all mean, and how had I managed to get involved in it? Brent was right—it was certainly a much more complicated weekend than what was anticipated.

What if the body was Paige? How would we explain that, and why on earth wasn't Brent overly concerned about the possibility? I didn't like knowing that someone was getting his or her jollies trying to scare me.

And Zach's little comment about "something borrowed, something blue" hit way too close to home at the worst possible time. What did I know about Zach? He was a freelancer I'd never worked with, for Pete's sake.

For that matter, what did I know about any of these people on the farm, other than Adam?

I scooted farther down the mattress, pulled the comforter to my chin, and forced myself to close my eyes. There was nothing I could solve now, other than a bad case of sleep deprivation.

I fell into a restless sleep. My dreams were disjointed and plodding, jumbling into a confused batch of visions holding indecipherable meanings.

In one dream, I felt very still, very heavy, unable to respond to a far-off voice calling my name. Someone was shouting "Kate! Kate!" but it was so far away, shrouded by a dense fog that drugged me into a deeper sleep. I wanted to answer the caller, but all I could do was bury myself deeper into the warmth of the covers. I rolled over, but the voice kept yelling my name.

The dream, I thought semiconsciously, had lost its luster. It was time to move on, so I rolled over again and this time opened my eyes to check the clock.

It took a second of comprehension, but I realized the voice frantically calling my name was, in fact, real. It belonged to Brent. I sat bolt upright as reality shot through my nose and throat, then took up unwelcome residence in my lungs.

The room was filled with dense, black smoke.

C H A P T E R · 9

STOP, DROP, ROLL. STOP, DROP, ROLL. Bless the brilliant PR person who developed that simple little catchphrase. Like a shot from my childhood, I heard the familiar fire-safety chant in my head, but I remained frozen on the bed. I'd stopped all right, but I wasn't sure I was brave enough to drop, and I certainly didn't know where I was supposed to roll.

Brent helped make up my mind. "Kate! Come help me!"

I focused my eyes on the stinging, noxious smoke and realized I didn't see flames. That was a good start. However, the smoke was billowing up from the staircase, so that didn't bode well for bounding downstairs. I ripped a pillowcase from the bed and ran into the bathroom and doused it with cold water. I smashed it against my face and crawled across the floor.

"Brent! Where are you?" I choked out to a thick, black wall covering the staircase. "Where's the fire?"

I heard him cough. "Here. Right at the bottom, but it's not on the steps."

The rest of his answer was consumed by a thick cough, so I scooted down the steps. Brent was frantically beating at flames crawling up the curtain in the front window. The front door was open, and a pile of something just inside the doorway burned brightly.

The smoke channeled up the steps and left only a gray haze in the rest of the living room, so I ran to the kitchen and grabbed the first bowl I could find. I filled it with water and ran back to the door and dumped it on the burning heap. It subdued the flames with a noisy, extinguishing swish, giving me time to run back for a quick refill. I sloshed the water onto what was left of the flames, then threw the pillowcase on top of that, trying to smother the rest.

In the meantime, Brent successfully snuffed out the curtains with the blanket he'd used on the couch. He threw the blanket outside, then with one hard tug, yanked the curtains off the rod and sent them through the doorway. He flopped outside and collapsed on his knees, wheezing and coughing up the hairball of the year.

I stumbled out behind him, adding my own contribution to the hacking contest. We were oblivious to the brisk, cold November air that flew in our noses, clearing our lungs and sinuses. The cold, harsh air was a shock, but it was a much better alternative to where we'd been seconds before.

Brent rubbed his eyes with his sleeve, forgetting that his shirt was saturated with smoke and soot. "Damn, damn, damn," he squealed. He sat back on his heels and shook his head as if he were trying to empty it. "What was that? I can't believe it. How did that happen?"

"You're asking me?" I coughed. I realized how churlish that sounded, despite the fact that I wasn't used to waking up to a burning house. I added more softly, "Are you okay, Brent? How did you discover the fire?"

A vacant look clouded his eyes. His black hair stuck out in wild directions, and sweat and black smudges smeared across his $1,000-a-day face. He looked like a linebacker with an attitude or a kid who'd played with one too many tubes of eyeliner.

"You're barefoot," he said. "And I'm cold."

I knelt beside him. "You're barefoot, too. Brent, are you sure you're okay? Are you hurt? Can you breathe?" I wanted to ask if he was thinking clearly, but he didn't do that well on a good day, much less after a wake-up call like the one we'd had.

His eyes cleared a bit, and he pierced a look my way. "I was sleeping and heard this thud, and then some kind of poofing sound."

"Poofing?"

"Yeah," he continued. "A swish and a poof. I was tired and didn't think much about it, and then after a few minutes, I heard a crackling noise and felt really cold all of a sudden." The words spilled out of his mouth like a head of foam sloshing over the rim of a beer mug. "I woke up and sorta noticed all at once that the front door was wide open and that's why I was cold . . . and then there were these flames . . . and all this black smoke. I couldn't believe it. By the time I got up and ran over there, the curtains had caught fire."

"You didn't see anyone?" I asked.

"No," he snapped. "I was a little busy, you know, trying to put out the fire and keep us from dying."

"I'm sorry," I mumbled, feeling about the size of a bug's rump. I also realized how blasted cold I was. I glanced back at the cottage. "Let's go back inside and get into some warm clothes. We'll need to open the windows and let the smoke out, not to mention that we'll have a lot of explaining to do before breakfast."

Brent stood slowly and coughed a few more times. "I don't even want to think about explaining anything. What time is it, anyway? The sun's starting to come out, so it's at least six-thirty or seven. Kate, this is going too far. We've not even been here a full day. I promised you a nice weekend, and look what's happened."

I could have added any smart-aleck comment, or snapped any manner of "I told you so," but I didn't. I was tired, cold, and more than a little scared. I actually felt sorry for Brent.

"Let's go inside," I prompted gently.

We walked to the porch, and Brent paused to looked at the charred heap just inside the doorway.

"What is that?" he grumbled. "Some kind of newspapers or something?"

I bent down and examined what was left of the smelly, smoky, black mound. It couldn't be. I broke a small branch off a bush and poked at the mass, confirming my fear. Our little incendiary device was a nifty stack of magazines. I gazed inside the doorway. The reading material that had earlier decorated the coffee table was gone—including the issue of *Brides*.

"It's all the magazines that were in the cottage," I said. "Are you sure you didn't hear anyone walking around inside?"

Brent shook his head. "No, I was sleeping pretty good, but I would have heard someone moving around the room. Maybe whoever got inside earlier and put those dolls upstairs took the magazines for future use."

"Probably," I agreed. "But that also means all this stuff is premeditated. Someone doesn't want us around. Who is that, Brent?"

He crossed into the room and flopped on the couch. He fumbled inside his suitcase and retrieved a pair of socks. "Look, I told you once already, I have no idea who it is. I'm not the most popular person around here, with either my family or the staff. I guess someone's pranks are starting to go bad. Let's air this place out, take showers, and get some clean clothes on before we go up to the house. You go first. I'll clean up the mess down here."

It would take more than a dust rag and some lemon-fresh Pledge to clean the cottage. The room was in dire need of a new paint job, curtains, and a few heavy-duty fans. I hated the smell of paint. I couldn't sew buttons on a blouse, much less whip up a pair of curtains. And I certainly didn't know where to get industrial-strength fans. I decided to let Brent ferret that out on his own. Domestication 101 was one of those courses I skipped in college.

"All right, I'll go," I agreed. "But don't let anyone come up and get me, okay?"

A gentle smile broke across his face. "Does that include me?"

"It definitely includes you," I replied. I smiled back, a little unsure why I had hesitated ever so slightly before I answered him. Before I could process that further, I sprinted upstairs to the bathroom.

I emerged later, squeaky clean and smelling fresh. I put on a pair of navy pants and a dark emerald pullover, but I soon realized that my clothes reeked from the smoke, which had invaded my suitcase.

Though I'd made sure the bathroom was amply steamy and warm, Brent had opened every window wide, and the cottage felt like the inside of a deep freeze. I shivered as I slipped into a pair of trouser socks and leather flats, then headed downstairs, where I found Brent and Steve scrubbing the floor with some astringent liquid that was probably doing more damage to the wood floor than the fire did.

Steve looked up and grinned. "Morning, Kate. I see you and Brent have been roasting marshmallows. Aren't you supposed to do that over a fireplace?"

I stepped around the two. "Do you think you should scrub the floor? You're destroying the evidence."

Steve's grin dissolved. "Evidence? That sounds pretty ominous. It's too early for that kind of talk. It was a stack of magazines that left a mess, that's all." Before I could ask why he was at the cottage, he added, "While I was out for an early morning ride, I saw Brent here playing maid. Quite a night you two had."

I glanced out the open door and saw a chestnut Thoroughbred waiting placidly outside, his reins tied lightly around a thick tree branch. Steve may have been out for some early exercise, but I wondered if he'd ever gone to bed. Dark circles shaded his blue eyes, and a stubbly shadow of a beard hugged his chin. His jeans and hooded sweatshirt were battered with wrinkles and brown smudges that were either mud or leftover Jack Daniel's. Regardless, I didn't get too close.

"How are you doing this morning?" I asked. "From what we saw last night, I'd say you're the one who had quite a night. You could probably use a couple pots of coffee. Or don't you remember?"

He dropped his wet towel into the ammonia-filled bucket. He stared coolly at me. "I was upset about Bayou Folly last night. That's not typical. I'm sorry you had to see that." He backed out the door. "I should go, I need to tend to my horses. Look, whatever is going on here, I hope you work it out. I'll see you around."

As Steve mounted the horse and galloped off, Brent picked up the bucket. "He was only trying to help, Kate. I guess you're right, we shouldn't have cleaned the floor, but Steve thought it was really important to do that first."

I glanced at Brent. "Why did that matter so much? And what did you do with the magazines?"

He nodded outside. "I shoved them onto the porch. I didn't destroy them, if you're wondering." He disappeared into the kitchen and returned quickly, sans bucket and towels. "Look, I think I've done as much as I can right now. I'll get some of the staff in here to help, and we probably should send the rest of our clothes to the house laundry. I'll take care of that after I shower. You go ahead to the house; I'll catch up with you for breakfast. Try not to get into too much trouble."

I looked toward the house. "I really don't want to go up there alone. Why don't I wait for you?"

"No, go ahead, I'll be there shortly. I'm a master at quick changes."

I retrieved my coat, but only for a second, before I dropped the smoke-encrusted jacket onto a chair. "It's not that chilly, I guess. I'll leave this for the laundry. I won't freeze running to the house."

"Doubtful," Brent said. "I'll be there soon."

Plunging my hands into my pockets, I jogged across the lawn to the house. A familiar dark Camry was parked in front. I passed it and bounded up the porch steps. The front door to the house was slightly open, so I stepped inside. Detective Rami stood in the entry hall, staring intently at the huge portrait of Bayou Folly.

"You're here awfully early," I said in greeting.

He walked over to me and extended his hand. "Good morning, Ms. Kelly. You're up pretty early, as well. Unfortunately, we're not on vacation as you are. We've got a lot of work to do. I trust your first night here went more smoothly than your afternoon?"

"Hardly," I snorted instantly, and then caught his surprised expression. "I think you'll find my evening and, in fact, my morning quite interesting. It hasn't exactly been restful. Interested?"

"By all means," he replied. "Let's go in here where we can talk in private. Maybe we can find someone to get us a cup of coffee."

We ducked into the side parlor, where we had gathered the day before. The room was empty, but a warm, welcoming fire already crackled in the fireplace, and Rami's sought-after pot of coffee waited on a table near the door.

"Beautiful," he mumbled as he filled a cup. "So, now, tell me everything."

I passed on the coffee for the time being and sank into a pink upholstered armchair that probably cost more than my car. "Have you ID'd the body yet?" I asked.

He raised his eyebrows. "You'll be the first to know. Now, your story?"

So much for that. Good little soldier that I was, I began with Dr. Gerald's blustery arrival, then moved on to the seamier details of the dolls and the fire. Somehow, in the opulence and safety of the mansion, the previous night's disjointed events were strangely detached, almost like a story I'd read in a novel. The dumbfounded look on Rami's face made me smile.

He finished his coffee in a quick gulp. "Well, I know now where we'll begin today. What do you make of this, Ms. Kelly?"

"Please, call me Kate. You make me feel like my grandmother. Quite frankly, I don't know what to think. I think I want to go home," I added truthfully.

He swallowed a quiet laugh, then changed the subject abruptly. "So, what do you think about Bayou Folly?"

"I think it's sad."

"That's all—just sad?" He walked over to the fireplace, keeping his back to me.

"Well, it's obviously a tragedy for the family, but I'm not that versed in the horse business. I'm not aware of all the implications, other than the fact they probably lost a lot of money yesterday with the horse's death."

"So you're not looking into anything in particular, then?"

I wrinkled my nose. "What are you talking about? Yesterday was the first time I'd heard of Bayou Folly. I'm here for a party. That's all."

Rami smiled slightly. "Oh, that's right. The big engagement. You know, it's kind of odd that you're engaged to such a horsey family, yet you say you don't know the first thing about horses."

Oh, lord. I had to defend my lie to a police officer again. Phrases such as *obstruction of justice, perjury,* and *withholding evidence* danced before my eyes like the flashing lights migraine sufferers see before the big one hits.

"I'm not engaged to the family, I'm engaged to Brent. And he doesn't fool much with the horse business." It was half true, half false. I wasn't under oath, after all. I was satisfied. Sort of.

I walked over to the coffeepot and doctored up a cup, heavy on the cream, even heavier on the sugar.

Rami turned toward me, leaned against the fireplace, and crossed his arms. "You know, I just have a really hard time picturing you engaged to Brent King. You strike me as someone who'd go for a guy a little more . . . I don't know . . . intellectual? I hate to sound ridiculous, but what's a nice girl like you doing with a guy like him? How did you two meet?"

My breathing increased and my throat swelled to uncomfortable proportions. I stared at the coffee cup and knew I couldn't drink it if I tried. I took a deep breath and returned his stare. "Fate brought us together."

His grin grew as he counted aloud on his fingers. "Is that so? D.C. reporter, with family in Virginia, meets New York model from Kentucky. Happens all the time, every day, I guess. I must be doing something wrong, not getting out enough. That must be why I'm not married. Maybe I should get some pointers from the two of you."

The orange glow of the fire flickered against his dark skin as he turned into the wonder cop once more. "You know, it's part of my job, particularly in a murder investigation, to check out all my suspects. I did a search on you, but I have to admit it was a bit difficult."

My throat clamped shut. I was a suspect? I felt more like a victim.

Rami noticed my discomfort. "Put in the name 'Kelly,' and a lot of stuff comes up, particularly in the press."

"Well, yeah, you know, that happens all the time," I threw back. "People always mistake me for Grace Kelly. All that press attention is something else."

"Very cute. I think you know I meant it brings up a lot about your mother and yourself. Both reporters. I understand your mother has quite an investigative streak."

I rearranged a couple of candy dishes on an end table while I searched for a reply. Rami remained against the fireplace. I glanced at him and thought he had to be hot, given his thick, slate-gray sweater that soaked up the heat rolling off the fireplace. I thought it was warm, and I was on the opposite end of the room.

"She's good at her job," I said slowly. "What does that have to do with anything?"

"It seems you've inherited some of those qualities." He shrugged. "The town of Woodbury, Virginia, appeared in the search a few times. Interesting stuff. I read it and thought I'd place a courtesy call to my counterpart in Woodbury."

Wonderful. Woodbury was not only where I'd met John Donovan a few months back, but it was also where I'd become involved in a nasty little murder and learned I was no favorite of the Woodbury Police Department. And now I was involved in another murder investigation, where I couldn't explain the real reason I was in Kentucky. This was great, just super.

I sank onto the arm of the couch and tried to look completely relaxed and natural. I, of course, looked totally stressed and completely unnatural.

"I talked to the sheriff there," he continued. "It sounded like he really had to dust off his badge when you came roaring through his sleepy little town. Not that I'm lazy or anything, but I hope I don't have to do the same."

"I don't think that will be necessary," I said, gaining a little momentum. "Just what is your point, Detective?"

He stared into the fireplace. "I just can't place you as the bride."

Big surprise, Sherlock, neither can I.

"I think it's odd that you arrive," he continued, "and we get a dead body and a dead horse in one day, not to mention all the things that happened last night and this morning. It makes me think it's all connected." His gaze hardened. "What are you investigating, Ms. Kelly?"

That one threw me. "What? I'm not investigating anything. I'm here to announce an engagement."

"Uh-huh, so I've heard," he said indifferently.

"What would I be investigating? Something to do with Bayou Folly? You're wrong there." *But,* my mind argued back, *what's to investigate about a dead racehorse?* The reporter in me surfaced. "Is there something I should know about Bayou Folly?"

Rami's eyebrows twitched. "No, and remember that *I* ask the questions." He ran his hand over his face. "I assume you're saying you're above it."

"Above what?"

"Doing it all for your story. Going in for the kill."

His "Dragnet" imitation didn't work on me.

Picking up on my puzzled expression, he said, "I'll cut to the chase trading sex for information. You're a nice-looking young woman who happens to be a reporter; Brent's obviously a handsome guy who probably thinks more with alternate parts of his anatomy than with his brain. Put the two together, and there's no telling what secrets will come out in moments of passion. You got anything to share with me?"

I leapt to my feet, firing on all cylinders. "What on earth are you implying? I'm not trading anything for . . . for anything else," I sputtered.

Ghostly visions of flannel nighties and dusty boots played in my mind. Rami didn't know how true that was.

He raised his hands in defense. "Hey, calm down, I just asked a question."

"Well, I don't appreciate what you're implying. No matter what you may think of my profession, I do have ethics. I would never compromise a story by sleeping with a source. And for that matter, who I choose to sleep with is absolutely none of your business."

"Brent's your fiancé, isn't he?" Rami prodded. "I just assumed you were intimate. As upset as you are, it's almost like I'm accusing you of something horrible, being with the man you love. Of course, if you don't really love him, I guess an assumption like that might raise your blood pressure some. In that case, I could see why you'd be angry." He locked eyeballs with me. "But you've got that pretty ring there, so I guess that means you don't have ulterior motives of any sort. He's your lover, not a source, right?"

Motives? What did he want me to say? It scared me to death that he sensed our engagement wasn't completely legitimate, but it frightened me more that he was using the words *suspects* and *motives* and *dead bodies* in relation to me. With all that churning in my gray matter, I didn't have time to stomach his question of Brent and me as lovers. Little hairs stood at attention on my arms and the back of my neck.

I turned away from Rami and walked over to the window. A brilliant sunrise had deposited splashes of bright sunlight that, from the inside, made it look like June or July outside. The only things that gave away the truth were the bare branches and people bundled in thick coats and hats.

I focused in on one couple in particular. Brent was walking away from the cottage with Detective Knight. Well, well, what an interesting pair.

Turning back toward Rami, I asked, "So, where's your better half?"

He shrugged and pretended to study a framed photo of a horse bedecked in a winning blanket of flowers. "Why do you ask? Do I make you nervous?"

He made me very nervous, but he didn't have to know it.

I crossed my arms and lied. "No, you don't. I just wondered if she was having this same conversation with Brent right now. You know, so you two could compare notes later at the doughnut shop."

Rami glanced at me from under heavy eyelids. "It's a possibility, I suppose, but I don't keep track of her every move." He placed the framed picture back on the table. "And besides, she doesn't do doughnuts. She prefers bagels. Tragedy, really, but she'll learn eventually."

Oh, yeah. He knew exactly what she was doing—and with whom. Detective Rami was a hard read, which meant he was good at his job. I thought I was good at my job as a reporter, as well, and I'd watched my fair share of "Columbo" movies, so I tried to play his game. Tit for tat. Question to question.

"So, tell me, is this the good cop, bad cop routine?"

He stared at me with impassive, soulless brown eyes; no answer was forthcoming.

"I thought so," I replied. "Which one are you? Bad cop or good cop? Should I be scared of you, or totally trusting, while you try to trip me up?"

"You tell me," he answered.

CHAPTER · 10

"YOU WERE NOT ANNOUNCED."

Saved by the sister. I was pretty good at avoiding questions from law enforcement, but this time I gave credit to Meg. Her chilly declaration at the door sliced past Detective Rami's little challenge and hung in the air, with all the sweetness of three-week-old leftovers.

"I didn't know that was necessary," Rami said coolly.

"Do you always burst into someone's home unannounced?"

"I tend to, when I'm investigating a murder," he shot back. He'd held his patience with me, but his welcome mat dissolved with Meg. "Besides, Ms. King, I've already been here a while, talked to some of your staff. And as you can see, Kate and I were getting to know each other better. Do you have a problem with that?"

Meg would have a problem with the Salvation Army bell ringers at Christmas. All that racket, after all.

She was dressed the part of the Thoroughbred farm manager, in worn leather boots, light brown riding pants, and a thick, white fisherman's knit sweater.

She peeled off dusty white gloves and threw them on a nearby chair. "Look, Detective, I am responsible for most of this farm's management. I am up very early every day with the horses, before I get to work running this place. As you know, my time is consumed right now with Bayou Folly. This car-death thing is on your agenda, not mine."

Her beady brown eyes then lasered through me. "Additionally, I am not the social coordinator, and I have no intention of being one. Your problems are causing enough disruption, not counting this party. I don't have time to play hostess, but I am accustomed to at least a modicum of civility, even from people like you."

She was such a sweet little Southern belle. I assumed she'd ditched her charm classes and cotillions for horseback-riding lessons and mucking out smelly stalls. I was no debutante, but I thought her little comment about the "car-death thing" was a tad much.

Rami agreed. "You'd better make this 'car death' your priority, Ms. King. We will not simply ignore this, whether your family likes it or not."

"You can say that again," added Detective Knight, who appeared with Brent and brushed past Meg.

Brent cast a worried glance at his sister, then, almost as an afterthought, tapped my forehead with a practiced, light kiss. "Everything all right? Everyone getting along?"

Meg's eyes flew heavenward.

"Have you told him?" he asked me, gesturing toward Rami. "I've talked to Detective Knight."

Meg's features froze, and she moved closer to Brent. "Told him what? What are you talking about?"

"Things went on last night," he began slowly.

"What? What things?" she demanded. "Speak clearly, I don't have time for this. What is that crap in the front of the cottage? I saw it piled out there when I rode past earlier. What did you do in there?"

Knight finished loading a cup of black coffee. "That crap is part of the cottage that caught on fire when someone tried to pass along a threat to your brother and his fiancée this morning."

Any warm and mushy thought about our safety sailed through Meg's ears. "Fire? For heaven's sake, Brent, can't you take care of anything? What will guests say when they see the cottage all messed up? You never think ahead, do you?"

"Meg," Brent sputtered indignantly, "we didn't plan—"

She threw her hand in the air, like the crossing guard from hell. "Fix it before tonight." Turning to the detectives, she ordered, "And get your investigation wrapped up as soon as possible. There's work to be done here." She stalked out into the hall.

A few seconds later, the front door slammed. Stony silence filled the room. Just me, my beloved, and the cops. How cozy.

For lack of conversation, Brent suggested we sit down for breakfast, but Detective Knight KO'd the offer.

"No, thanks," she said. "You've given us plenty to do this morning. We'll be around. Don't go too far."

Rami followed his partner out the door. "Watch yourselves," he said. "It wouldn't hurt to be supersensitive to the people around you. We'll be here for a while, and you know where to reach us if needed."

That was a comforting thought. *Have a nice day, don't get yourself killed.*

Brent rubbed his face until his cheeks glowed. "It's not even nine o'clock yet, but I feel like I've been up for hours and hours. Let's get something to eat." He pointed toward the hallway. "It's set up in the breakfast nook, just down here to the left. I'm sure Cook has prepared something decent."

Breakfast nook? A person named Cook? My usual breakfast nook was my car as I navigated traffic and tried not to wreck while I munched on a Pop-Tart—chocolate on a good day, apple-cinnamon when I wanted to do "healthy."

I stared briefly at my engagement ring for inspiration, then followed Brent down the paneled hallway. I caught up with him and tugged his red sweater. "Meg doesn't like me, does she?"

His hands landed on my shoulders as he turned around. He smiled gently. "No, I doubt she does. But I wouldn't take it personally. Meg and I have never seen eye-to-eye on most things. She's too serious for me and—quite frankly, I think—a little jealous. It's only worse now that I'm engaged. I've had it easy, in a lot of ways, and she . . . well, she's never learned how to relax."

He straightened and pulled a sour face that mirrored Meg pretty well. "Even in school, you know, I'd get prom king, and she'd stay home from dances. She always said she didn't have time for such stuff, but the truth is, no one ever asked her out."

"And that should make her mad at me?"

"No, it's not you, Kate. She's always so centered on her work and the horses. She doesn't make time for herself, which is her own fault, but believe me, she'll be the first to grump that I'm having fun or moving ahead. Getting married and having this party only brings it out into the limelight that the baby's got it all, while the one everyone assumed would be married is most definitely not."

"Then wouldn't this be a good time to tell her you're not really getting married?" I suggested. It sounded good to me.

Brent, however, had other plans. "Absolutely not. We've got to get through this weekend. Then, like we planned, I'll break up with you, well away from here. See, in a way, that's even better because, once again, I'll be the screw-up."

Shrugging his shoulders in defeat, he started down the hall again. "Don't let her get to you, Kate. That's what she wants. Just ignore her."

I followed Brent into the "nook," which was actually a large room flushed with sunlight from the combination of a windowed wall and an adjoining set of French doors leading onto a brick patio. A speckled, glass-top table, surrounded by twelve chairs, dominated the room and was flanked by tall potted trees.

Jane and Adam shared one corner of the table, which was loaded with platters of steaming scrambled eggs, hash brown potatoes, bacon, assorted Danish, fluffy biscuits the size of small pizzas, and a tureen of thick, white gravy speckled with brown blobs I hoped were pieces of sausage. The goop, which was the consistency of kindergarten paste, smelled peppery enough to clear my sinuses and coat my stomach sufficiently so I could ingest lighter fluid with no ill effects.

It was a long way from Pop-Tarts and Diet Pepsi.

Adam rose. "Morning, guys. Have a seat and help us plow through this. There's enough for a small army here."

I walked over to Jane. "Good morning, Mrs. King."

Her narrow nose shot up in the air. "Kate, do you smoke? Brent, you never said she smoked. She smells."

I pasted a tight smile on my face and dropped into the chair next to Adam.

Brent let loose a controlled sigh. "No, Mom, Kate doesn't smoke. We had a little trouble in the cottage this morning. Her clothes, and mine, will air out soon. When we get the rest cleaned, we'll change."

Frowning her disapproval, she swept a chunk of biscuit through the hot glue on her plate. "Well, I hope that's the case. We can't have you smelling so awful all day."

"Forget to open the fireplace flue?" Adam queried.

I reached for a plate and flopped eggs and hash browns in neighboring towers until they covered the pink flowers on the china. "Something like that. Brent can tell you all about it."

Jane pushed her plate aside and reached for a notebook that sat at her feet. She plucked a pair of bifocals out of her skirt pocket and flipped open the book. "There is an enormous amount to do today. There will be no time for interruptions. Meg has already eaten and has gone to meet Dr. Gerald, that vile man. I don't know where your father is, so I'll need you to help herd the caterers and decorators around. Your friend Adam, here, told me about his restaurant business, so I'm delegating the caterers to him."

Adam's eyes grew three sizes, and he struggled to swallow the piece of bacon midway down his throat.

Brent jumped in. "Mom, Adam is my guest. I'm not putting him to work."

Jane's black eyes glistened through her glasses. "I require the assistance," she clipped. "You don't mind, do you, Adam?"

Adam darted anxious looks past each of us. "Why, no, I'd be happy to take a glance at your plans."

Jane stood and snapped the notebook shut. "Good. Meet me in the kitchen in fifteen minutes sharp. My next task is the florist, and then I have to tackle the RSVP list once more. Brent, darling, the least you could do is show the list to your fiancée and explain the significance of some of our guests."

She walked past the table and toward the hall. "Kate, I do hope you're familiar with moving in the circles we do. I have very important people coming tonight; I hope you'll make our family proud."

I was caught with a mouthful of scrambled eggs. Oh, how I wanted to go home. I quickly swallowed, grabbed a sip of orange juice, and smiled. "I don't think you'll be disappointed, Mrs. King."

"See that I'm not," she decreed, then pointed to Adam. "Fifteen minutes. Please be on time."

She disappeared into the bowels of the house and left us to our biscuits and eggs. Brent immediately took out his frustration on his plate, which was packed so high with comfort food, I was sure a 98-pound New York fitness trainer somewhere would have a stroke on the spot if he saw a certain model's current calorie intake.

I looked at my plate and tried Brent's scoop-and-swallow technique. As we inhaled our breakfast, Adam surveyed us with trepidation.

"Are you guys going to tell me what's going on?" he asked. "Either you had a hell of a workout last night, or you're avoiding talking. And for the record, you both *do* smell awful. What gives?"

Brent and I exchanged glances. Brent chewed a few times and mumbled, "You tell him. I've already done it today."

And I hadn't? I pushed my fork away and spilled the entire story for what felt like the millionth time.

Adam gripped his coffee mug like a vise and drank nearly the entire cup in one swallow. "Brent, this is too much. You told me this weekend would be easy."

Brent exploded. "I didn't plan for any of this to happen. How many times do I have to say it?"

"Say what?" ordered a deep voice.

Douglas King strode into the room and reached for a large linen napkin, which he immediately filled with several Danish. He tied the napkin into a high-class take-out package and remained standing. He was dressed in a dark gray suit topped with a long black wool coat. An expensive leather briefcase, covered with enough security clasps to satisfy Fort Knox, sat in the doorway.

Brent's cheeks flushed. "Good morning. I was just talking about . . . um . . . things that . . . um . . . you should probably know."

His father frowned. "It better be worth it. I have too much to worry about from yesterday, without adding anything new. Follow me over to the main office, Brent. You should be in my meeting with Meg this morning."

Brent squirmed in his seat. That was the last thing he wanted on his party agenda. "Dad, I really don't have time to—"

Douglas interrupted. "Make time. You can join Kate and . . . and. . . ."

"I'm Adam, Kate's cousin," Adam offered.

Douglas's face darkened. "I knew that. Brent, follow me. You can join them later."

Brent cursed under his breath and stalked out the door behind his father.

Adam consulted his watch. "I better get to the kitchen before she sends out a posse. You gonna be okay by yourself?"

"Just swell," I answered glumly.

He stood. "Look, I'm beginning to agree with you. We should get out of here. I'll play happy host with the caterer, then we can find Brent and tell him we're gone. Forget this party. It's too weird."

"Thanks, Adam. I'm glad to hear that. I'll finish up here and try to track down my clothes so I can pack them and leave. This engagement is for the birds."

He winked. "See you in a bit."

I quickly ate my breakfast, rationalizing that after the morning I'd endured, I deserved no less than about a billion calories of fried food and sweets. I cleaned my plate, then headed out the door, where I bumped into Zach. We backed off each other and exchanged mumbled pardons.

"You're a little late for breakfast," I said. "Everyone else has eaten, more or less. Good luck finding anything."

I looked a little closer at him and thought what wonders a bath, shave, and new set of unwrinkled clothes would accomplish. To top off his disheveled ensemble, he still wore his bulky photo jacket. I doubted any safaris were leaving anytime soon, but a quick once-over of Zach's outfit might convince someone otherwise. I wondered if the jacket was surgically attached.

"Rough night?" I asked. "Did your walk keep you out past your bedtime?"

"My walk was nice—and eventful, as you know intimately." His eyes scanned me up and down. "You look more comfortable today. Sleep well?"

"Not really." I decided to let the gossip mill fill him in on our overnight adventures.

"Well, I guess that makes two of us," he said. "I was up early, trying to catch some shots of the sunrise and junk. You know, like the words to that song: 'The sun shines bright on my old Kentucky home.' I thought you'd probably write something similar to that, and good Boy Scout that I am, I thought I'd be prepared."

"I don't write with clichés," I answered, "but thanks for the thought."

Zach apparently thought himself the comedian, but I wasn't in the mood. I followed him into the sunroom and watched him grimace at the near-empty platters. He piled a few broken pieces of Danish in his hand.

"Just how early were you out?" I asked.

He brushed crumbs off his chin and lazily filled a glass with overly pulpy orange juice. "Early. It was dark, then it was light. Cold, too. Kinda biblical, don't you think? Why all the questions, Kate?"

I reached for my own chunk of peach-filled Danish. "I just wondered if you saw anyone or anything strange?" *Like a pile of burning magazines, or the cottage on fire.*

"Nope, not really. I saw several horsey types hosing down the horses and mending fences. You know, all the usual farm stuff. It's not something I see every day, so I don't know how strange that is. Did I miss something?"

I decided not to relate our story. My gut told me he already had a pretty good idea what had transpired. "I suppose we should get to work on this story so we can all go home."

Zach finished his juice. "Whatever you say, although I've already been working hard the past twenty-four hours. Which means I'm really, really tired. I'm going to crash for a while. What are your plans later today? I want to shoot you and Brent this afternoon."

"I hope you mean with a camera."

He squinted his eyes. "How else would I mean it?"

"Nothing. Just kidding. See you later."

I wandered into the hall and left Zach contemplating cold scrambled eggs.

Everyone had pulled a disappearing act, which left me with nothing to do but snoop around. Unfortunately, I didn't know what to snoop for, so I gave up on that and settled for the darkly paneled den, where I found a big, over-stuffed red leather couch; a nice, warm fire; a big-screen television; and a remote control that delivered my daily dose of CNN.

A short time later, satisfied that Wolf Blitzer had saved the world for another day, I reached for the phone on a side table. It was time to give John another try. I had also told Alice I would call as soon as we arrived, but with everything that happened, time had slipped away.

I dialed John's number, knowing he was probably at the hospital. I wasn't a bit surprised when I got his machine. I left a cheery message and promised to call again. Without looking at the keypad, I then dialed Alice's number and took a deep breath, prepared to spurt my damsel-in-distress tale.

"It's me," I began innocently enough.

"I am so furious with you," she shouted through the phone.

"What? I'm sorry, I know I promised to call yesterday, but—"

Alice interrupted, her voice still shrill. "I have left messages for you every-where. You never returned my calls. And there were many, *many* calls. I've dialed the number you left me over and over. Who is Meg King? I've practi-cally filled her voice mail. I'm sure she's tired of hearing my voice."

I blinked. Meg never mentioned any messages for me. "Meg is Brent's sister. She never passed on your messages, honest. And I'm sure she's checked her voice mail. I know she's been in her office, because there's a lot going on, which I want to tell you."

Alice wouldn't relent. "No, I don't have time for that. What the hell is wrong with you? I know you don't want to do this story, but you've never pur-posely tried to sabotage an assignment before. I can't believe you would do that, and especially to me." She sounded like a wounded puppy. "I was teas-ing you about Brent, you know that. You're my best friend—teasing is in the rules. But I can't believe you'd try to mess up an assignment. It's not just *your* job, Kate, it's my job too."

Knowing that Alice chain smoked when she was upset, I figured she was probably already on her second pack when I heard her take a long drag on a cigarette and loudly blow the smoke out. I used the opportunity to jump in. "I'm the one who's confused. Why don't you tell me exactly what I've done that's so horrible?"

"You left your photographer at home, that's what," she screeched. "Were you just going to say that you collected his film and, oops, dropped it in the river or something? Do you think I'm that naive? Kate, I can't believe you'd lie to me."

My knuckles grew white around the phone. "I've never lied to you. I didn't leave my photographer at home. Zach is right here. And has been—all day, all night."

"Oh, really?" she shot back. "Then why did he call me and say that he never found you at the airport? I'd told him you would track him down at the gate, and when you didn't, he thought the story was canceled and no one bothered to tell him. He's not happy, Kate. He rearranged another shoot in order to do this, which means I'm going to get stuck with a bill for services not rendered."

"Are you sure about this?" I asked stupidly, trying to comprehend what she was saying.

"Of course I'm sure. I'm the one who left the message for him in the first place. He called me back, I hired him over the phone, gave him instructions, and sent him on his way. This same guy spent the better part of yesterday afternoon making my life a living hell and threatening all kinds of breach-of-contract shit." Her voice took on the "Don't forget I'm also your boss" edge. "You wanna explain what's going on?"

A tympani symphony kicked in with a vengeance between my eyes. Rubbing my forehead in frantic little circles, I spoke slowly. "A guy who said he's Zach Tanner met us at the airport, got on the plane with us, and has been shooting pictures of everything in sight since we set foot in Kentucky. That couldn't have been him on the phone with you yesterday, because I was with him almost all day."

There was silence on the other end while Alice considered my argument. "Well, if we were both with him more or less at the same time yesterday, then who is the real Zach Tanner? I hate to pull rank, but I'm pretty sure my guy is the bona fide photog." She paused, then asked the same question dripping from my lips. "Are you going to tell me you have an impostor traveling with you?"

C H A P T E R · 11

I ALWAYS THOUGHT that I was an intuitive, intelligent person, able to uncover deceptions and BS in a single bound. At least, I often told myself that. On more than one occasion, I'd convinced myself that as a reporter, I possessed that sixth sense, that almost psychic way of knowing all.

It was painfully obvious that I'd goofed big-time on this one, but I wasn't eager to give in to Alice right away. "Why should I think Zach is an impostor?" I asked. "He acts like a photog, dresses like one, and shoots pictures like one. He also knew to find us at the airport, and he said Alice Donard hired him. What was I supposed to think? I have no reason to doubt him, other than what you just said." I added gently, "Maybe you're wrong, or maybe, just maybe, he really is the same person and is just trying to scam more money out of you."

I smiled at the phone, delighted with that sudden inspiration. *Watch out, Sherlock Holmes, Kate Kelly's on the job.*

Watson, however, was not convinced. "Not a chance," Alice snapped.

I rolled my eyes. "Okay, then at least consider that option for a while. How did you get his name in the first place?"

"From our files," Alice stammered. "I've never hired him before . . . but Lou used him a while back for a story."

She exhaled heavily, and I pictured the swirl of cigarette smoke encircling her head like a dusky halo.

"Hold on a minute," she ordered, dropping the phone with a thud that probably permanently damaged my hearing. She banged around, clanging drawers and pawing through papers. She returned to the phone, out of breath, either from exertion or the smoke slamming her lungs shut. "Okay, I've got it now, March '98 issue. 'Spring Gardens in Georgetown' was the lead feature. There are nice little mug shots crediting Taylor Rightson, copy, and Zach Tanner, photography." Alice cleared her throat. "Okay, ready? Answer yes to the following, Kate. Zach Tanner is a heavyset black man in his mid-to-late forties, balding on top, nice smile, looks like someone's dad or cuddly big brother."

My multi-calorie breakfast did a somersault in my stomach. Zach Tanner most certainly did not possess any of the aforementioned qualities. I burrowed deeper into the couch until I could smell its cracked leather.

"Oh, my," I breathed.

"Oh, my, what," Alice replied. "Kate, what's wrong? That's not your photographer? Who is he, Kate, and why do you sound so scared?"

I stared at the door, suddenly paranoid that someone was perched outside, planning any manner of hideous ways to do me in the minute I got off the phone. I licked my lips and kept my eye on the door. "Didn't you do any background checks or anything?" I whispered hoarsely.

"Kate, you're overreacting. I was hiring a photographer, not an altar boy. What was I supposed to do? His name is in our photog file, which said we've used him, with good results, in the past. As you well know, we had to do this in a hurry. It's not my fault," she whimpered in defense. "What is going on? You don't sound right."

I stood and stretched the phone cord as close to the hallway as it would go. "Hold on a second." I peeped into the hall. No one was around that I could see, so I sprinted over to the couch again and, in an urgent whisper, spit out my entire tale of life on the farm.

After Alice's incredulous "A dead body?" she let me continue without comment until I finished.

"Oh, Kate, I'm sorry, I should never have insisted you do this story. Grab Adam and get the hell out of there."

I studied a painting of a horse. I'd had enough of horse country for one lifetime. "My thoughts exactly," I agreed. "Engagements and marriages are highly overrated. Why don't I come back and do a story on after-the-divorce destinations?"

"You got it," Alice said. "Look, you be careful, and call me later today when you're leaving. In the meantime, I'm going to dig around and find out who your Zach Tanner is."

"How are you going to do that?"

"I'll figure something out," she answered. "Just stay away from that guy and everyone else on that farm who isn't your real-life flesh and blood. Is that a promise?"

"Scout's honor," I said and hung up the phone.

"Scout's honor?" came a voice from behind me. "Isn't that reserved for the Boy Scouts? Equality is one thing, but you Girl Scouts are stealing all our best phrases."

I spun around to find Zach, or whoever he was, standing in the doorway, camera in hand. I tried to ignore my muscles constricting into tiny, tightly coiled knots that would send a chiropractor's kid through college.

"How long have you been standing there?" I demanded.

"Just passin' by."

He turned away from the door and disappeared from view. I ran into the hallway and was greeted by a blinding flash. I shot my hands in front of my eyes and blinked at the kaleidoscope of reds, blues, and yellows zooming through my vision. I heard Zach laugh, and his voice trailed off.

"Kate, you better get used to a strobe going off in your face if you're going to marry a model."

I rubbed away the colors and lights from my eyes and focused on the hallway. Zach was gone.

"I'm not marrying any damn model, and you know that," I growled as I stomped down the hallway, poking my head in each doorway in an adrenaline-fed search for my missing photographer. With my handicap of residing in the cottage, I wasn't familiar with the ins and outs of the main house, but I couldn't believe he'd had time to go very far. I even peered outside from a large window near the front door. No sign of Zach. The coat closet was near the door, but I wasn't about to search any tiny, confined spaces.

Instead, I retraced my steps, alternately furious he'd vanished so quickly, and equally uneasy that he was probably hiding somewhere nearby, laughing at my feeble attempt to find him. I felt like I was rushing through some kind of virtual-reality tour of a decorating magazine as I zoomed in and out of each room, pelted on all sides by expensive antiques, designer fabrics, and the fragrance of enough flowers to stock a funeral home.

I almost needed a funeral home after I flew around a corner and came face-to-face with a Ficus, its branches shimmying menacingly. I emitted a less-than-eloquent squeak, and a man emerged from behind the potted tree.

"Boo! Caught you, caught you!" he squealed. "I didn't mean to startle you, but you looked so serious coming down the hall. Is it nerves, dear?"

I chewed at the air as he grabbed my elbow and spirited me into a bright peach drawing room. He was of average height, with a slight, well-dressed build, a chandelier smile, and a narrow, pointed head that was barely carpeted with a baby-fine dusting of orange hair. What hair was missing on his head took up residence in a dense mustache that curled northward on its edges.

He deposited me on a cream silk couch and even went as far as to pat my head. "It's got to be nerves. Look at you, wide-eyed as a frog getting ready to zap a fly. I can always tell the bride. You're all alike—that sweet, pretty innocence, the glow of what's to come, and . . . oh, my mother in heaven!" My tree-dweller sucked in a breath and grabbed my hand. "Just look at that ring. OH . . . MY . . . WORD! What did little Brent do? Rob Tiffany's? Delightful, darling, just delightful."

Suddenly overly protective of my diamond, I politely pulled my hand from his hungry gaze. "I don't believe we've met. You would be?"

The wattage on his smile warmed up to a neon glow, and he clapped his thin hands together, bringing them to rest on his black-and-gold-striped satin vest. "Just where did my manners run to? Indiana? Jane would have my head if she knew I'd slighted you. My deepest apologies, love. I'm Willard Mooney. You know . . . of Willard's Wonderful Wonders?"

Will wonders never cease?

I shook my head slowly. "I'm sorry, I don't—"

He threw his head back in a throaty laugh. "I forgot, sweetie, you're one of those."

"Excuse me?"

His eyes fell on mine, and a mischievous grin slid in place. "You know, one of those outsiders, from another nasty state and all." He leaned forward. "For all these Southern-fried socialites know, I was born and raised in Lexington." His thin voice suddenly deepened. "True son of the South, raised right here on my mama's knee."

He sat back and glanced into the hallway before continuing. "Truth is, I'm about as Southern as the Empire State Building. I hail from Montana, out in Big Sky Country. Bet you'd never guess that, would you?"

"Never," I answered honestly.

Willard's mustache twitched with delight. "There's nothing like a bunch of coffee-table books on the South, mixed with old society clippings from the newspaper morgue, to craft a Wild West boy like me into horse country's most desired caterer, is there?" He didn't wait for my answer. "Oh, and tell me, why on earth do they call the newspaper archives morgues? It's so unpleasant, so . . . I don't know . . . deadly."

My newspaper legacy rose to the surface. "It's not meant to be deadly, it's just that most of the archives were stored in big, cavernous basements."

He waved his hand in the air to interrupt. "No, no, no. No talk of morgues of any kind. We have a party to throw tonight—your party, dear. Time for happy talk. Happy, happy, happy talk."

Personally, I felt Willard was just a little too happy. Maybe he'd been dipping into the bourbon balls or something. Before I could ask him to share the wealth, he leapt to his feet, flittered over to a fresh flower arrangement, and plucked out a peach-colored rose. He dramatically strode over to me and slapped the rose against my cheek. "Oh, no. This won't do, now, will it? No one told me you're a 'winter,' and believe me, I asked. We should have ordered deep red roses and rubrum lilies. You're much more suited to the jewel tones, not these pastels."

His face fell with the rose, which he dropped on a table. "My color scheme is completely off, and that only gives me a few hours to make changes. Oh, I don't know if it will be possible. This will require all my strength and creative juices."

Willard's eyes flared with all the melodrama of an afternoon network soap. "I must go channel some additional energy, and hope I can pull this off." He tapped a long, slender finger to his chin. "That means I'll have to leave Kevvie in charge of the food. Perhaps I can find that nice young thing who does restaurants to help."

Picturing Adam's reaction to being called a "nice young thing," I grinned. "Do you mean my cousin Adam? Have you met?"

"Oh, he's family? Delightful. Yes, we met in the kitchen a short while ago. I have everything under control, but Jane darling likes to put her fifty cents in all the time. I usually just sit there and take it, but your cousin looked positively terrified. I listen, take notes, and kissy-face up to her, then I do whatever I want."

Willard picked up the rose from the table and shoved it back into the flower arrangement. "It usually works, particularly if Jane's taken her happy pills like she should."

He spun back toward me. "I didn't mean for that to sound so bad, but I'm sure you understand. Jane is much easier—I mean, much more pleasant to deal with—when she's . . . um . . . under the influence, so to speak."

"How is she otherwise?"

That put poor Willard in a bad spot. "Well, I don't mean to talk out of school . . . and believe me, you'd be surprised how drugged-up many of these socialites are. It's not foreign to me. I can almost claim a degree in psychology—Dr. Willard, hmm, I like how that sounds. But back to Jane. When she's not taking them, whew, buddy. She can be as mean as a mama tiger whose cubs have been snatched. Violent, too." He shook his head. "I prefer it when my customers are on their medication. It makes my job that much easier. God bless the little Prozac manufacturers. I often say I should buy stock in it, so I can retire early and ingest bottles of it myself."

I didn't doubt Willard's observations, but one comment stood out. "What do you mean when you say Jane gets violent?"

He scanned the hallway again, then joined me on the sofa. In a low, gossipy whisper he began, "Girl, it's nothing for Jane to hurl a vase across a room at you. Once, she threw a kitchen knife at one of my chefs because a soufflé fell at an inopportune moment. And of course, there was the little flambé incident a few years back."

He giggled uneasily at the memory. "I can't believe Brent didn't tell you about it; the story is just legendary in this town. The Golden Horseshoe, one of my competitors, held a huge dinner party here one spring. It was a disaster from the word go. Jane changed her mind several times on the menu and decorations, and simply drove the caterer batty. She was just a major pill, but finally agreed on a proper setup. Well, in trucks a couple dozen of Lexington's finest folks for dinner, and everything went terribly wrong. Things weren't served on time, or to her liking, and everything that *could* go wrong *did*. Anyway, the best part, which is drilled into everyone's memory, came around the time of the main course."

Willard jumped from the couch and built the scene with elaborate gestures. "Murphy's law was in full force by that point, and Jane just went loony tunes. She was so incensed, she grabbed a couple of bottles of wine, doused the dining room table and all the food with the wine, then . . . and then. . . ." He stopped to take a breath. "Then, she got hold of a candelabra and torched the table. With all the alcohol on the tablecloth and such, the place just lit up like Macy's! Not to mention some of the guests' fancy clothes! She practically burned down this entire house, along with half of Lexington's blue bloods!"

He looked at me with wonder. "You've never heard this story? Legendary, I tell you, legendary. Jane went away then, for an extended 'rest.' When she returned to the farm, she was much calmer and, as I said, quite under the influence of some darned strong drugs.

"Oh, but enough about that," he said with a dismissive wave. "You can dig up all the family skeletons after you're married. Tonight is for you and the Brentster. Come with me and see the plans for the hors d'oeuvres and dinner. I think you'll be pleased; it will be just like Cinderella at the ball."

Willard ignored my dumbfounded expression and pulled me off the couch, prepared to make tracks to party central. However, canapés and crystal were the last things on my mind. So Jane had a history of setting fires to make a point. Surely she wouldn't try to harm her own son by setting the cottage on fire or, worse yet, be capable of killing someone and setting that person's car on fire.

I pulled away from Willard. "Thanks so much, but I've got some people to find before lunch. I'm sure you're very busy, and I wouldn't want to delay your work. And besides, I like surprises," I lied, forcing a smile. "I'll wait until tonight to see what you've prepared."

He grinned widely. "You know, you're right. I respect that, and I appreciate your confidence in my work. But if you change your mind, darling, just drop into the kitchen and take a peek." He sashayed to the door. "I bet you'll change your mind. Once we start setting the tables and hanging the pink tulle, you won't be able to resist. Willard knows these things, dear. I'll tell my staff to give you the royal treatment if you come around. Cheer up, Mrs. Almost Brent King, and enjoy the festivities. You're about to be a very rich woman. Enjoy it for the rest of us working stiffs."

He blew me a kiss and left the room. Once he was gone, I belatedly decided I should have followed him to the kitchen, because I had a hunch that Adam was probably being held hostage there by either Jane or Willard's merry band of cooks and party elves. The sooner I could find Adam, the sooner we could go home.

It wasn't Adam I found when I resurfaced in the entry hall, but Detective Rami, sitting midway up the staircase, a newspaper hiding his face. Sensing my presence, he rose and joined me under the balcony that stretched across the expanse of the foyer.

"Well, Kate, hello again. This is about the same spot we met earlier," he observed. "You haven't gone very far this morning. I'm glad to see you're keeping close to home."

I hate to tell you, I wanted to say, *but I'm about as far from my real home as E.T. was from his planet.* "Well," I said, "there's not a lot for me to do this morning."

Nothing to do except hide from an unknown wacko, figure out who my impostor photographer was, find my clothes, collect my cousin, and hightail it home to D.C., where the only things I had to fear were drive-by shootings, terrorist attacks, and corrupt, lewd politicians.

Rami's face crackled into a warm smile. "Too bad, because we have plenty to do. If you're bored, I could use some help."

Before I could reply, Detective Knight appeared in the hallway and dropped her purse at the foot of the steps. "Have you told her our news?"

Rami looked at his partner. "Not yet, thought I'd wait for you." He answered my raised eyebrows. "We've traced the car's registration, but the lab still hasn't identified the body. What does the name Paige Kendall mean to you?"

Returning Rami's stare, I felt the color vaporizing from my cheeks as my eyes grew to gargantuan proportions.

"Know her?" he prodded.

I didn't have a chance to answer.

Knight shouted, "Move! Look out!"

On impulse, Rami body-slammed me to the floor, with a bone-cracking crash, as an oversize vase filled with flowers hurtled toward us from the balcony overhead. Shards of glass flew toward us. Flowers, glass pebbles, and water scattered around, and from somewhere in the midst of the flowers and glass, an old, rusty horseshoe bounced onto the floor near my feet. A piece of water-soaked paper was tied with wire to the horseshoe. Rami rolled off me, and we raised onto our elbows to read the smeared ink.

The message was simple: "Your luck just ran out."

CHAPTER · 12

THE THOUGHT OF a handsome, powerful guy smashing me to the floor in a fit of passion was one fantasy I'd enjoyed more times than I should admit. But actually slamming unexpectedly onto a hardwood floor with a 180-pound detective on top of me didn't feel passionate or exciting.

It hurt. A lot.

It did, however, confirm my suspicion that professional football players who daily indulged in this slam-and-bam were totally nuts and lacked nerve endings in their steroid-enhanced muscles. And in the for-what-it's-worth department, I couldn't recall horseshoe-laden vases of flowers aimed at my head as part of the fantasy.

Detective Rami and I sat stupidly on the floor in our wet pants, staring at the horseshoe and what was left of the vase. Splashed water stains decorated the wall and the polished wood tables. I caught a glimpse of Detective Knight pounding up the staircase, her gun drawn.

"Turn around!" she commanded. "And come over here now!"

Rami leapt to his feet and raced upstairs, leaving me sitting among the flowers and the little minefield of broken glass. Never one to be left out of a party, particularly when I was the star attraction, I scrambled up the steps behind him.

Before I reached the top, a low wail rose from above, blending with the warning of "A gun! She's got a gun! Put that away!"

Mylanta time again—Mother King.

I joined Rami at the top of the stairs as he held out his hand in a soothing manner. "There's no need to get excited, Mrs. King. Just please calm down and come over here slowly so we can talk to you."

Knight holstered her gun, her eyes glued on Jane.

Looking like a poster child for a Boris Karloff movie—pasty-white skin, trembling hand clamped on her neck, eyes as wide as the hallway—Jane scratched at her throat with blood-red manicured nails, but she spoke slowly and with more control than before. "That woman is carrying a gun. If anyone is going to carry a gun in my house, it will be me."

That was a pleasant thought—Calamity Jane packing heat. She might not be bluffing. I figured the detectives concurred, because a round of uneasy glances flew between us.

Knight's hand quivered near her waist, just in case. "Mrs. King, I'm a police officer. I'm sorry if I startled you. Now, can you tell us what you were doing in the hall just now?"

Jane was in no hurry to comply with the polite request. Lumpy streaks of red formed on her neck from continued scratching, and her head developed a noticeable tremor. She blinked several times rapidly and smacked her lips haphazardly, so that splotches of bright red lipstick traveled toward new locations north and south of her lips. Part of me wanted to run from the impending volcanic eruption, but my better part was strangely fascinated with what might come next.

"Mrs. King?" Rami prompted gently yet cautiously.

While the detectives dealt with her delirium, a slight movement just down the hall caught my attention. A closed door edged open a crack. Either the ghost of Bluegrass Winds was paying a visit, or someone was hiding behind the door.

I nudged Detective Rami and silently pointed. His hand brushed under his jacket toward his holster. He quietly slipped past us and plastered himself against the wall.

Jane turned. "Just what do you think you're—"

Before she could blow his cover completely, Rami flung open the door, simultaneously pulling out his gun and pivoting effortlessly in front of the doorway. I rolled my eyes as Brent's hands flew in the air and slammed against a row of bright yellow towels behind his head.

"Don't shoot!" he squealed as a renegade towel flipped over his head and landed gracefully on Rami's pointed gun.

Rami cursed under his breath and lowered his weapon.

Jane snapped back to reality and threw her hands on her hips. "Brent, what on earth are you doing in the linen closet?"

He stepped into the hallway. "I can explain."

Knight shook her head. "This oughta be good."

Brent sneered at her. "I was getting fresh towels, and someone came up behind me, hit me, pushed me in, and slammed the door. The next thing I knew, I heard a crash and Mom yelling about a gun. I didn't think I should come out then."

Good, Brent, I thought. *How kind to leave your helpless mother to fend for herself when someone is pointing a gun at her.*

"And who, pray tell, would shove you inside a closet?" Knight asked. "An amorous chambermaid? I got up here pretty quickly. The only person around was your mother. Is she the one who put you in the dark?"

Jane bristled. "Why would I push my son into a linen closet and slam the door? Do you think I'm crazy?"

She was lucid now. That was a start. However, everyone studiously avoided answering her last question.

We didn't have time anyway, because yet another squeal rose from downstairs. I recognized that one, too.

"Oh, my word," Willard cried. "Who messed up my floor . . . and my lovely flowers?"

Rami's face screwed into a pretzel with extra salt. "Who is that?"

"Showtime," I said, turning down the steps.

Willard, his face as red as his hair, stood among the shards of glass and flowers, waving his arms frantically in the air as if he was shooing away a swarm of bees. Adam was crouched nearby, studying the offensive horseshoe and its cheery warning.

Bits of breath and exasperated spit flew between Willard's teeth. "Just who destroyed my arrangement? Is there no sanctity in this house? Does no one care how much these flowers cost? Or what artistic effort went into designing this piece?"

Our upstairs crew met along the staircase, with Rami right behind my lead.

As Willard's audience grew, his voice ballooned. "For heaven's sake, there were baby-pink tulips and Japanese iris in there! IN NOVEMBER, NO LESS. Do you people have no concept of what is involved in my work? Oh, sure, to you people it's just a bunch of flowers." His voice trembled at a level that made even Jane blink. "MY EVENT IS THIS EVENING! Have you people no shame?"

I reached for his flopping arm and gently eased into my best imitation of a society bride-to-be. "Willard, I'm sure it was a lovely arrangement, and I'm

pleased you worked so hard on it. Irises are my favorite flower, in fact. However, we didn't knock the vase over." I glanced back at my partners on the
steps. So much for the society-bride bit. "Someone, um, pushed the vase
over the landing and tried to hit me with it, but thankfully, their aim was off
a little."

Willard stopped sputtering and paled a few shades, from rich merlot to a
gentle blush. He grabbed my shoulders. "You, darling? Never, no. Who would
do that to you? You're our bride, our leading lady, our princess." He stopped
mid-gush and looked at Jane as if a hundred candelabras lit his brain. He
enunciated very clearly as he stared directly at her, lest she react badly. "Surely,
Kate, you must be mistaken. It had to be an accident. You're just a little
unnerved because of the party, right?"

Rami pushed past us. "No, she's not. I was right here when it happened."

Willard raised an eyebrow and held out his hand. "Oh, really, and who
would you be, beefcake?"

Knight snorted an uncontrolled giggle, and her partner clipped, "I'm the
police."

Willard drew back his hand. "Oh. That's perfectly awful."

Adam rose and joined us. "Well, it's true, it wasn't an accident. Did you see
this note?"

Rami pointed at Adam. "Drop that horseshoe! You're tampering with
evidence."

Adam, always the good guy, immediately obeyed. The horseshoe fell
smack onto Willard's toe.

Willard let out a howl that probably sent dogs, three miles away, scattering
for cover. He danced the entire Nutcracker Suite in fifteen seconds around the
room and finally collapsed onto the steps and whimpered in choked breaths,
"This job . . . is going to . . . kill me yet."

"Be careful what you wish for around here," Knight growled as she stepped
over him and joined us in the hall.

Jane moved in front of the caterer and delivered her own ultimatum. "For
heaven's sake, Willard, you're embarrassing me in front of these people. Get
back to work and clean this mess up. We have a party this evening."

As if we all weren't painfully aware of that fact.

Jane brushed past us and flew down the hall. Knight sputtered a non-
ladylike but very coplike expletive and followed at her heels. As Adam valiantly
helped Willard to his feet, Rami and I counted heads, because our math skills
were sharp enough to notice that Brent had flown the coop once again.

"Now where'd he go?" Rami hissed.

Adam joined us. "He was on the steps when Willard started jumping around."

"I was maimed," Willard corrected feebly as he hobbled past our unsympathetic eyes.

"Geez," Rami snarled. "I didn't know I was going after Houdini." Stomping up the staircase, he pointed down at Adam and me. "You and you. Stay put. I want to talk to you both." He turned away, then looked back at us again. "Be careful, will you? You might be the only two sane ones left, and someone is out to eradicate that."

I swallowed. I appreciated his concern, but I didn't like the way he equated our general well-being to something that could be eradicated. I played with a few more versions in my mind . . . *snuffed out . . . dissolved . . . removed . . . exterminated.* I shivered and swallowed again. All of those words scared me.

"Kate, I don't know what—" Adam began.

It was too late to obey any detective's orders to stay put. I shoved Adam into the nearest room. "Just how close were you and Brent in high school?"

He blinked. "What do you mean? We were soccer teammates, friends. We did lots of stuff together. Why?"

"So, why didn't you tell me what he's really like? I don't remember any of your friends being this neurotic."

As I spoke, I kept poking my finger into Adam's shoulder until he sliced out a disgruntled, "Ouch, Kate, cut it out."

We grumbled, poked, and stewed at each other for a minute or two like a pair of scruffy six-year-olds on a dusty playground.

Adam came to his senses first. He backed off and ran his hands through his dark brown hair. "Kate, what are we doing? What are we—kids? We're adults. We should be above this." He shoved back one final time to prove his point.

I wasn't satisfied. "Answer me, Adam, was he this weird in school?" My voice grew. "Did he always have a penchant for disappearing? And causing all sorts of confusion? Why did I ever let you talk me into this ridiculous weekend?"

He sighed. "I'm sorry, Kate. As for Brent, I don't know . . . we were all weird when we were teenagers. He was a rich kid; people teased him a lot. I felt sorry for him, so I made him a friend." Adam shrugged, coming a bit closer to defeat. "Granted, I hadn't seen him in years, and I did think it was kinda strange that he called out of the blue a couple of days ago, acting like it was just yesterday that we were in school."

That was the first I'd heard of that. Silly me had assumed that Adam and Brent at least kept in touch off and on. "A lot can happen to a person in fifteen or so years," I pointed out.

Adam nodded. "No doubt." He eyed me carefully, then rapidly shook his head. "Brent's a good guy, Kate. Don't think otherwise. He's just as confused as the rest of us with everything going on. We should have stayed away from all of this, but how did we know what was going to happen? He's not some psycho like Ted Bundy."

I raised an eyebrow. "Oh? Are you absolutely sure?"

"Kate, come on, give him a break."

My prickly nature rose to the brim again. "How can I, when he disappears every time something happens?" I came close to stomping my foot, but I refrained. "And that 'something' that makes him turn tail usually involves someone trying their level best to take me out of the equation. If it's not him, it's other creepy people or dead horses piling up all over the place. I'm tired of it, Adam. I want to find out who's doing this."

His eyes narrowed. "Something else is bothering you. What have I missed? What creepy people and what about dead horses? Did another one die?"

"No, as far as I know, there's only one dead horse. But I'm more concerned about other things."

"Like what?"

"Where do I begin? Well, you know about everything that happened last night. Which is plenty. This morning, after I told Detective Rami about it, he started asking questions about Bayou Folly. He wouldn't elaborate, but I think there's more to this horse hitting the glue farm than he's letting out."

Adam made a face. "What's that got to do with the rest of this mess? I don't get it."

"I don't either, right now, but that's secondary. You need to know about my conversation with Alice."

I told him about Zach's dubious identity and waited patiently while he sputtered and fumed.

"But he is a photographer, Kate. I know journalism isn't my field, but he sure as hell acts like one."

"No kidding," I agreed. "All of that has crossed and recrossed my mind. He's disappeared as well. And I'm going to find him. I don't appreciate being lied to."

Adam wagged his finger in my face. "Oh, no you're not. That doesn't sound safe. Maybe he's perfectly innocent, but there's too much going on right now for you to do that. And besides, who's lying to whom? Face it, we're all lying in one way or another. Let's do what we said earlier—let's get our clothes together, call a cab, and get out of here."

Ordinarily, I would have agreed with him, but something held me back. "There's more. Right before I had my little flower shower, our kind detectives asked me if I knew who Paige Kendall was."

Adam went white. "Oh, wow. What did you say?"

"I didn't have time to answer. I'm almost thankful for the flying vase, because I'm not sure what I would have said. The car is registered to her."

Adam closed his eyes. "We're stuck here then, aren't we? If that really is Paige's body, and we take off all of a sudden, you and I could be looking at ten to twenty."

He had a point. Damn. Now I really did have to play the bride for the rest of the weekend. It said a lot about how suspicious we'd appear, but it didn't answer what I'd say about Paige. I still thought that explanation belonged in Brent's court.

If he ever resurfaced.

"You moved when I asked you to remain in the hallway," said Detective Rami from the doorway. "I wish you wouldn't do that."

Adam walked over to him like a guilty child. "Did you find Brent?"

Rami's nose twitched. "No, I didn't. I thought maybe he found you."

The boys could look for Brent. I wanted to find Zach, and I wanted to nose around a little bit about Bayou Folly. If I had to stay, I wanted to at least make it as interesting as possible. Ignoring the look I knew was coming from Adam, I sailed past Detective Rami as if I hadn't a care in the world.

He caught me by the elbow and yanked. "You never answered my question earlier."

I swallowed and gently uncorked my elbow from his grasp. "What question was that?" I said, stalling him.

"Does the name Paige Kendall mean anything to you?"

"Oh, *that* question. That's because I didn't have an answer." *Not a lie*, I argued to myself, *pure truth.* I honestly didn't know how to answer him. Truth-or-dare time, and I was daring him to death.

Rami didn't buy it, and Adam's nervous tics didn't help. "Where do you think you're going?" the detective asked me.

"I have things to do, people to see. It's my party tonight, remember? I have a lot to do and very little time." A lot to do that didn't involve a stupid society party, but I didn't add that. I'm sure he could figure it out on his own.

"Where are you going?" he repeated.

I turned on my heel and quickly strode down the hallway. I summed it up blithely and succinctly. "As my grandmother used to say, I need to see a man about a horse."

I glanced over my shoulder as I practically sprinted out the door. Neither gentleman in my wake was smiling.

CHAPTER · 13

I NEEDED TO WORK ON my dramatic exits. While this one rated a pithy reply, hasty departure, and befuddled audience, the one thing it lacked was a pinch of common sense. As I flew out the front door, I realized two points—I wasn't sure where I was heading, and I failed to snag a coat of any color on the way out to the frozen tundra. I knew, though, that I couldn't turn around and sheepishly sneak back inside. I'd look desperately silly, and I'd have to face Detective Rami. Pausing briefly on the porch, I made an executive decision.

Smoke or no smoke, I knew my coat would be at the cottage. I could grab it, then borrow one of the golf carts and set out on a search for Brent and Zach. The way they'd been disappearing lately, I figured that assignment ought to fill up the rest of my morning, with no problem.

I bundled off the porch and turned onto the gravel drive leading toward the cottage. I made it only a few yards before I heard the voice I was avoiding pound up behind me.

"Pretty chilly out here, don't you think?" asked Rami.

I turned and blinked away the cold breeze stinging my eyes. "I've been warmer."

He'd been smart enough to put on a heavy, dark gray LPD jacket before he set out on his quick apprehension of me. He shrugged out of the coat and dropped it over my shoulders. "Here, with my compliments. Let's take a walk, okay?"

I stared at him. I didn't think much of his suggestion, but I also had a hunch that it was an offer I shouldn't refuse. But I tried anyway. "Don't you think you'll get too cold? You might get sick, then you wouldn't be able to work on this case."

He linked his arm in mine in a pseudo-friendly manner and dragged my feet into action. "The cold weather is good for you; clears your head. Exercise is important, too. Come on, Kate, let's walk and talk. We can head for the cottage."

I stumbled alongside Rami's long-legged stride. "Gee, this is cozy."

He stopped and let go of my arm. "I just thought we could have a nice private talk, outside of the house and away from big ears."

"Whose big ears?"

He shrugged. "All ears are big at this juncture. I'm not pressuring you, Kate. I simply thought we could talk one-on-one. You know, if something came out in casual conversation between us, as just two people walking down this path, that's all it would be. Just a nice bit of information-sharing."

"And if something didn't come out?"

"Well, if I discovered something that could have easily flowed out of this conversation but didn't, I might be pressed to consider it withholding of evidence. And, for that matter, if that something hinders my investigation . . . well, things could get ugly. Bordering on real unfriendly, in fact. You wouldn't want that, would you?"

I walked ahead a few steps. "No, that wouldn't be pleasant."

Rami jogged a few feet to join me. "Good, I'm glad you see things the same way I do." He stared ahead, studying the pattern of the barren tree branches swaying in front of us. "You know, one thing I've noticed is that you tend to avoid answering my questions. I'm really curious, tell me again how you met Brent."

I followed his lead and stared ahead. "Adam introduced us."

He snorted back a laugh; I'd failed to answer properly. "Oh, I see," he replied. "Now, was that before or after Brent returned from Paris?"

Good grief! I squinted into the sunshine and spewed, "Oh, it was after he returned. He had a really successful stint there. I hope we go there on our honeymoon."

Bad choice. *Keep your mouth shut while you can, dummy.*

Rami practically jumped in the air. "Brent was never in Paris." He smiled triumphantly, while I groaned inwardly. "Talk to me, Kate," he said succinctly. "Tell me the truth. Brent isn't really your fiancé, is he?"

I wanted to run away but knew it was fruitless. I was glued to the spot.

The glue felt thicker as he added, "And while we're at it, toss in what you know about Paige Kendall. It's not becoming to pale so badly every time her name is mentioned. You concern me when you do that."

I shook and shuddered for an eternal minute, then rumbled my story to the surface. He would find out eventually, and I was tired of hiding the truth. I knew he was right about the trouble I'd be in if things got worse. My defensive mind argued quickly that I had loyalty to Adam but not to Brent. Why should I possibly jeopardize my career, or even my life, just to help this guy and his family save face?

As I confessed our deception to the detective, my prosecuting mind argued back that a promise was a promise and that I'd assured Brent I'd hold out through the weekend. Surely Rami would understand. He owed me that, I figured.

I studied his dark brown eyes as I wrapped up. "Please, I've been straight with you, so I ask you to grant me a favor."

He made a face.

"Let's keep this info between us for now. I want to stick around and see what happens this weekend, and to do that, we have to keep pretending. You have to honor my request to keep all this a secret."

Rami's eyebrows met across his forehead. "I don't know. So you're saying you're totally innocent throughout all this?"

"Absolutely." I nodded.

"Just caught up in a bad situation?"

"Definitely." I nodded harder. "Hear me out. I'll cooperate with you, if you let me continue to be the bride. Think of me as your eyes and ears," I concluded.

But, my rebellious mind continued, *don't think of me as the mouth just yet.* I'd tell him what I wanted, when I thought it was time. Then, at that point, he could step in and detect away.

"I don't know," he said. "It could be dangerous, and I don't like the idea of amateurs hindering my investigation."

"I respectfully disagree," I countered. "On the contrary, it could make your investigation easier. Look at it this way. The family trusts me, and they operate as a unit. Because of my 'engagement,' I'm being drawn into their circle. They may share things with me that could help you."

We paused and acted innocent, while two horses with unidentified riders thundered past.

When the galloping echo died, I continued. "Look, this family is already a couple of jacks short of a full deck. Don't you think they'll be even more skittish if this engagement business explodes on top of everything else?"

"Maybe," Rami budged.

"Let me nurture their trust while I keep you informed. You'll know every-thing as quickly as I do." *Maybe with just a couple delays here and there.*

We resumed our walk in silence for a few a seconds, before he said, "I don't know. This isn't a game of cat and mouse, Kate. It's a murder investigation."

"I respect that. But how can it be that bad? I have the police on my side."

"I can't be everywhere," he argued. "I'm not Superman. And this is *my* job, not yours. Need I remind you, you're not trained in police work."

Minor detail. How hard could it be?

I was on a roll. "But I'm a reporter. I've covered my share of crimes, courts, and police beats. I know the procedures and I understand your limits. After all, my mom is one of the best investigative reporters around. She taught me all her tricks." I smiled enthusiastically. "Quite frankly, I'm probably as damned close as you'll get without a badge."

That sounded impressive, I thought. Besides, didn't all those TV cops have civilian informants?

Detective Rami wasn't easily swayed. "This isn't how I work. I already have a partner."

I wouldn't give up. "Change is good. I'm as reliable as your partner." *Sorta.* I tried again as shades of Adam's persuasive talents materialized in my words. "Come on, give it a try. You be straight with me; I'll be straight with you. If things get weird, we'll call it off, I'll blow my cover, and then I go home. Story over. You can hang around and catch your killer all by yourself. Deal?"

We reached the cottage steps and stood facing each other as if we were say-ing good-night after a first date. Rami frowned and considered his options. I had all the time in the world and waited patiently for his decision.

Apprehension scraped across his vocal chords. "We'll try it—for now." He threw his finger in the air and cautioned, "But first, I'll talk to my partner. Depending on what we think as a unit, I might change my mind by lunchtime. The decision will be up to me, not you. How's that for a deal?"

It didn't sound as strong a deal as I expected, so I countered just as weakly, "Yeah, well, I guess I can live with that. Whatever you say." I crossed my fin-gers behind my back.

"My first suggestion," Detective Rami said, "is for you to head back to the house and pretend to be interested in this party. That way I know where you are, and you can act as innocent and as much like the bride as you want."

I slipped his coat off my shoulders. "I can give that a shot," I lied.

He took the coat and stepped off the porch. "So, when this is over, what happens to that ring?"

I considered the diamonds crawling toward my knuckle. "You know, I'm not sure. I think by this point I ought to keep it as a souvenir."

He laughed. "You probably deserve at least that. Kate, be careful, will you?"

"Sure," I answered. "Thanks again for the coat. I'll dive through here and see if I can roust up my jacket. Why don't you go look for Brent, and I'll play happy homemaker and clean up around here for a few minutes before I head for the house."

Rami turned around. "I don't believe you."

Smart move, because I had no intention of doing any of that. "I thought we were supposed to trust each other?"

"Supposed to, but don't. Occupational hazard, I guess," he added.

We exchanged glances—mine innocent and sincere, his doubtful and cynical. I stood on the porch and watched him reach the main house and go inside, no doubt to sit on the steps again and wait for my anticipated arrival.

The wait would do him good. I stepped into the chilly cottage. The brisk wind and open windows had worked well in tandem to disperse the overpowering smoky odor, but there was no mistaking the scorched door frame. Someone had heaped our clothes into a neat pile on the couch in a clear indication that they were meant for a good cleaning at the first available pickup date.

I poked at the stack and discovered the complete contents of my suitcase. It bothered me that someone had opted to rifle through my belongings, but I tried to write it off to my overly suspicious mind. It was probably Brent or one of those little old ladies running around the house in their neatly pressed navy-and-white uniforms. I was also uncomfortable with the thought that as soon as the pile headed for the laundry, I was literally left with the clothes on my back. I felt like I'd just lost my luggage at the airport and discovered that my suitcase had wound up in Bora-Bora.

Rummaging through the stack for my coat, I tried to talk myself out of being so jumpy. Clothes were clothes, and obviously, someone was trying to help. I spotted my dress for the party and agreed with Mrs. King that it would be embarrassing to show up at "my" party smelling like a well-used chimney. I found the coat, sniffed it and made a face, and then shook it out for good measure. I pulled it on and buttoned it to the top.

Before setting out on my search for Brent and Zach, I decided to check out my sinister Barbie and Ken once more. I headed upstairs and surveyed the bedroom loft, belatedly realizing that Detective Knight had probably confiscated the dolls when Brent showed them to her. So much for that. Knight had certainly messed with my plans.

Something else messed with my plans as well.

A murky corner of my brain picked up a barely audible creak behind me. In an instant, a big, muscular arm crunched snugly around my neck as a thickly gloved hand clamped firmly over my mouth.

My head snapped back into a dense nylon jacket, and hot breath on my neck issued the same unwelcome invitation that I'd already heard once today.

"Let's take a walk."

CHAPTER · 14

FUNNY HOW QUICKLY my mind flipped through its massive file cabinet of memories, sensations, cheap trivia, useless algebraic equations, and old television theme-song lyrics to locate the basic instinct that told me I was in deep trouble. You know—fight or flight. I instantly remembered that my body was supposed to do one or the other, but the problem was, I wanted to fight *and* fly away.

The reporter's mantra of *who, what, where, when, and why* bounced between my ears in a split second. The *who*, unfortunately, was me. The *when* and *where* were immediate, but the *what* and *why* were distinctly hazy. The zipper on my companion's jacket took clumps of my hair hostage, and his heavy, stained glove shot wafts of dried horse and stale hay up my nostrils. I didn't fret too much about the smell, since the arm across my neck did a pretty decent job of clamping off any airflow from my nose to my lungs.

Tempting fate and the health of my hair, I quickly collapsed in half, spun around, and sent my knee on a mission with a vengeance. I knew contact was secured when his voice shot up several octaves into an anguished wail that men universally acknowledge with a collective wince.

My assailant sank to the floor in a fetal position, and I straightened and tried to collect the breath that he'd squeezed out of my body.

"Why the hell did you do that?" Steve Mathias growled.

I moved menacingly toward him, with every intention of playing Kung Fu master again. His eyes grew, and he scrambled to his full 6-foot-plus height, once again putting me at a disadvantage.

I stopped advancing and tried to maintain my tough-knee facade. "Start talking," I ordered.

Being in an upright position dissipated his agony. He shook out his blond hair, rolled his shoulders, and, in a quick swoop, grabbed my upper arm.

"Let go of me," I squealed in a markedly less threatening voice than my previous order.

"Kate, I don't want to hurt you. I was in the cottage for just a minute." He loosened his grip but still kept hold of my arm. "I know I'm not supposed to be in here, and I certainly didn't want to get caught while you were with the police."

"So it's all right to hide in here and then assault me when I come in?"

I wrenched my arm, but Steve clamped down harder.

"Granted," he said, "I made a mistake. I didn't want you to scream and draw his attention back to the cottage."

"I can still scream—loud enough to break your eardrum."

"Kate, I won't hurt you," he repeated. "I just want to talk."

"Okay, talk," I said. "But let go of me first."

"You won't scream?"

What part didn't he understand? "Let go of me."

He abruptly released me and held his hands up in a conciliatory gesture. "Not here, somewhere else. I'll take you there." Steve held out his hand. "Like I said before, let's go for a walk."

"Okay, fine, let's go," I said.

He gestured for me to head downstairs first, so I flew down and out the door before I could change my mind. He continued past me and crunched on the wintry brown grass behind the cottage. I followed him and paused when I found he was about to head into the woods beyond.

He turned and said, "Kate, are you coming or not?"

Detective Rami knew where I was, I reasoned. Surely, Steve cared enough about his job not to risk it by doing something awful to the Kings' heiress-to-be. Ignoring the melodramatic music swelling in my head, I caught up with him. And his large, four-legged form of transportation.

I was a city girl, whose major interactions with horses had been while seated comfortably in the stands at a race track, contemplating a two-dollar bet based on scientific methods, such as the the horse's name or color. To me, horses looked majestic, graceful, and agile at a distance. Up close, they looked big—really big.

Steve ran a gloved hand along the horse's silky mane and murmured something endearing in its ear. The horse snorted approval and swung its narrow, curious head at me. I eyed it warily and almost missed Steve's edict.

"Go ahead, hop on."

I raised my eyebrows in an arch that managed to shove half my forehead behind my head. "You gotta be kidding me."

He shook his head. "Oh, you're not going to be this way." He grabbed my arm again, and his other arm slid around my waist.

Like a petulant three-year-old, I pulled back. But before I could dig in, I was sailing up and watching the sky spin and the twitching brown muscles grow closer. In an instant I was far off the ground, deposited rather indelicately onto a worn leather saddle, my legs spread wide over the Thoroughbred's rib cage. It was more uncomfortable than a yearly visit to the gynecologist.

My feet were nowhere in the vicinity of the stirrups. Fighting a sneeze, I gripped the saddle for dear life, while Steve effortlessly swung his leg over the horse's rump and landed behind me on the edge of the saddle. His body pressed tightly against mine, and he hunched as he gathered the reins and slapped them gently on the horse's neck.

If I could have moved, I would have run for my life. However, it was too far to the ground. Steve had a crushing, clamping hold on me, and the horse was ready to take off on a much too fast dash through the woods. I eked out a distinctly wimpy yelp as we bounded recklessly between trees that converged on us like the evil forest in the *Wizard of Oz*. What I'd always considered my most padded part was bumped and bashed enough to ensure I wouldn't sit comfortably for the rest of my natural-born life. If I lived that long.

By the time I'd convinced my eyes to slam safely shut, we thundered down a hill that rivaled the state fair's worst coaster, coming to a lurching stop in front of a small ranch house that popped out of the landscape. Steve swooped off the horse and peeled me off the saddle in the most undignified dismount in equine history. Squirrels and birds in the immediate vicinity mocked me with their chattery laughter.

As my legs fought to find their function, Steve steadied my shoulders and asked, "Have fun?"

My expression did the talking.

"Welcome to my humble home. It's not the big house, but that's what you should expect when you're dealing with the hired help."

A narrow concrete porch ran across the front of the unassuming house. Its four simple, heavily curtained windows gave no clue to what lay behind the walls. An ivory-painted door, scuffed with years of boot marks, centered the house and was flanked by weather-beaten Adirondack chairs. A saddle balanced on one armrest, and a huge pair of cowboy boots sat waiting at the foot of the companion chair.

A late-model, black Ford F-150, with the personalized tags "HRSMAN," sat to the right of the house in a gravel drive next to a gleaming motorcycle. Steve transitioned quite nicely from a horse to a hog—a top-of-the-line Harley-Davidson. My attention span for motorcycles was about as long as my enthusiasm for quantum physics, so I shifted my attention to a large barrel planter at the edge of the porch. A dead plant had lost enough leaves that it no longer concealed several empty gas cans stacked clumsily behind the barrel.

I stumbled through the doorway into a room so masculine I could smell the testosterone. His home wasn't decorated in Early American or French Provincial, but in Horse, with maybe a little accessorizing nod to *Guns & Ammo*. The paneled living room held picture after picture of horses—from framed 5x7 winner's circle photos to fairly decent-sized paintings. In between the rows of pictures stood a glass-doored gun cabinet that held enough hardware to outfit a small militia. The burgundy-and-brown-plaid sofa faced a large stone fireplace, and a worn, mushy leather recliner that would make Archie Bunker proud sat across from a makeshift entertainment center holding a television and old VCR.

Steve scooped up a blanket off the couch, and a menacing-looking gun dropped to the floor. He retrieved the weapon and deposited it in the drawer of a small desk nearby. Pretending I hadn't noticed, he asked, "How about a beer?"

I couldn't imagine how he was ready to drink again, after all he'd apparently had the night before. "It's not even noon yet," I pointed out.

He smiled in an oddly charming way. "It's noon somewhere in the world."

It was hard to argue with that kind of logic.

As he headed for the kitchen, he spotted me staring at the gun case and said, "Don't get me wrong, I'm not some Kentucky good old boy."

I took a seat on the gunless couch. "I never said that. Do you know how to use all those?"

Steve considered the collection. "Sure."

"Ever used them?"

His face hardened a shade, and he leveled stare at me. "Only when necessary." He disappeared and soon returned bearing two longneck bottles of Miller. "I hope a bottle's okay," he said. "I'm plumb out of Waterford crystal."

"Do you always sweep girls off their feet this way?"

He sank into the recliner. "Look, I'm sorry about what happened at the cottage. It was an automatic reaction, I guess."

I took a sip of the beer. "So, tell me about yourself, Steve."

After a diffident dismissal that there wasn't much to tell, he proceeded to spill a story that was long on atmosphere but short on details. To hear him tell it, Steve Mathias was destined from childhood to work with horses. He grew up on the outskirts of Louisville and spent more time at Churchill Downs than he did in school. Trainers, both famous and small peanuts, were his teachers and mentors. One trainer took him on as an "assistant to the assistant," which meant Steve cleaned stalls and exercised the horses before dawn. It also was a traveling meal ticket, and soon he found himself on the racing circuit year-round, from Kentucky to California to New York and Florida.

"That's a lot for a kid," I mused. "What about your family?"

He gripped his beer with both hands, then tilted it to the ceiling. "That's not important. Let's just say my family is four-legged."

He paused, visibly uncomfortable with my question, but after a few swigs of beer, he resumed. He was never much for school, since he moved from state to state with such frequency. But, he quickly assured me, that didn't mean he was dumb. He attended school "when it was convenient" and spent hours in public libraries, teaching himself the things he thought necessary.

A crooked smile broke across his face. "When's the last time you quoted a passage from Homer's *Iliad*?"

I squirmed and returned the grin. "Oh, a couple of hours ago."

He aimed the neck of the bottle my way. "My point exactly. I learned the important stuff, then concentrated on the horses. I know more about equine history, racing, training, the whole nine yards than most of those designer-suited guys up at the Keeneland yearly sales will ever know. I have," he added, "what Mr. King calls a gift for training winners."

"Nice compliment," I replied. "How did you wind up here?"

Steve stood and walked over to the fireplace. He stared above the mantel at a painting of Bayou Folly and a jockey in the winner's circle.

"I moved around a lot, track to track, but I always came back to Churchill. I was about nineteen when I met Mr. King. He saw I had talent, and he took me under his wing."

"Mr. King must really like you," I prompted.

"No shit," he snorted. "Yeah, Mr. King's a good man. I'm the son he never had."

Were we missing something here?

"What about Brent?" I asked.

Steve smiled, but it wasn't pleasant. "Oh, I forgot. Model boy."

Even if I wasn't his fiancée, I thought I should defend Brent. "What do you mean by that? That's not very kind."

Another gulp of beer disappeared. "I meant it exactly as I said it. It's not supposed to be nice."

Steve glanced at his empty bottle and slid into the kitchen again, coming back with a fresh beer. "Now Meg—she's another story entirely. You talk about the brains of the family."

"In what way?"

His smile returned, and this time it was genuine. "Man, she is smart. Tough as nails. She can slice you up and spit you out, like one of those salad-shooter things. But you know, that's good. You've got to be that way in this business if you want to survive."

He was quiet for a minute, then mumbled almost to himself, "It's all about survival." He slammed the beer on the mantel, sending a wave of brew sloshing across the wood. His face was red, and his mood dissipated. "That's just it, you know? This freaking family could have it all. But instead, they're letting it go to hell. And it's all their damned fault."

I placed my bottle on a small table and stood. "I don't get it. The Kings seem to have it all. What makes you think anything is different?"

He halfheartedly mopped the beer off the mantel with his sleeve. "Well, sweetheart, things aren't always what they seem, okay?" He wiped his wet sleeve on his jeans. "Just be sure you know what you're getting into if you marry Brent. That's all I have to say."

I played the betrayed, wide-eyed, innocent bride. "You don't like him much, do you?"

Steve answered so quickly that he didn't give me time to bat my eyelashes. "I hate the son of a bitch. He gets in the way, always has. Little Mr. Golden Boy. Dumb as shit, but he looks just perfect. He went to all the best schools, had everything he ever wanted. I might not be some big college graduate, but at least I made an effort to get an education, even if it wasn't in the most traditional way."

Steve joined me by the couch. "And, oh, the women. Women everywhere, from the cheerleaders to the sorority chicks, to the little horse honeys who hang out at the track sniffing for money. They found all they could ever want in Brent."

His face twitched. "Darlin', I hope you don't think you're the first one to capture Brent. You're not the first, believe me. So, how long have you been engaged?"

My stomach burned, and a hot, scratchy tingle inched up my spine. "Not long," I answered truthfully.

Steve snorted and retrieved his beer, downing a good chunk of what didn't slosh out the top. "No kidding. Kate, you sure you know everything about your boyfriend? All the dirty details? For instance, why don't you ask him where he was right before that car was tanked yesterday? I saw him over there."

Now my stomach was really putting on a show. "Was he alone?"

"Not my job to keep track of the golden boy. I really didn't pay that much attention, but the police sure as hell found someone else, didn't they?"

The fiancée in me rose to defend Brent again, even as I pictured him running in that direction after we arrived at the house the day before. Not to mention his sudden interest in something in the distance as we drove up the lane. Everyone had noticed that in the car, but Brent brushed it off. What had he seen? Or who?

"Well, what about you?" I argued. "If you saw him, that means you were there, too. In fact, that's where we met the first time. Remember, you tossed me around that time, too? We have a problem with our meet-and-greets."

Steve's eyes narrowed. "I was working, you were trespassing."

Up to the lips and past the hips went the beer once more, so I filled in the dead space, with the empty gas cans outside planted firmly in my mind. "Yeah, working right next to the car that blew sky high."

He exploded. "Don't try to pin something like that on me. You're crazy. Look, there's a lot of shit going down around here that's eventually going to catch up with everyone, and if you hang around Brent, you'll see it firsthand."

Conscious of how agitated Steve was, I backed up toward the door. A sane person would have dropped the subject; I persisted. "Like what kind of stuff?"

He swung his beer bottle in circles, searching for an answer. "Like a lot of stuff," he sputtered. "Like . . . what do you know about horses? And how you make money with them?"

He had me there. "Honestly, not much, other than it helps to win a lot of races. I know you were upset about Bayou Folly."

Steve shook his head, his anger growing. "Upset doesn't cover it. He was incredible, one of the great horses. But, see, the Kings ruined him. As for winning . . . well, yeah, that helps. But there are other ways to cash in."

I was too worried about my safety to rustle through my trivia book on the horse business. I took another step back; Steve advanced one closer. His breathing was irregular, and he swung the bottle from side to side like the pendulum on a grandfather clock.

"Sex," he said. "Stud fees. The blood of champions. The good horses—they can do it over and over. And they're not cheap dates. Bayou Folly got upwards of two hundred thou for a one-night stand. As far as I'm concerned, there were two murders here yesterday—the chump in the car and Bayou Folly."

I squinted. "Murder? I thought he broke his leg and the vet put him to sleep?"

Steve snorted his disgust and leaned in toward me. "That's what they want you to believe. I know the truth. Bayou Folly was pimped to death. The broken leg . . . I'm sure that was just a . . . what do you call it? An unfortunate accident. A mob hit."

Gimme a break. A dead horse, or at least the upper portion of it, was the mob calling card. But the horse as victim? I shook my head in silent disagreement. Steve was immediately upon me. I backed up against the wall. Picture frames pressed into my back as he leaned so close, his beer-tainted breath mixed with mine.

"You just don't get it, do you, Kate?"

What I got was a very bad feeling.

His voice dropped to a husky gravel. "You need to learn the basics of breeding." He had me cornered like a wild animal.

I stated the obvious. "I need to leave."

Steve laughed softly and traced his finger down my neck and across my collarbone. "Remember, it's not all passion. It's the money. And lots of it. You get the wrong players involved, all hell breaks loose." He leaned back to illustrate with his hands on the neck of the beer bottle. "And then, all of a sudden, craaaack. Bones break at the worst times." His eyes had gone from blue to black.

"You're not making any sense," I said.

A lopsided grin began a slow trek up his cheek. "Sure I am. You're just not willing to listen. It's like your situation—a bride-to-be in a rich family. What's important to you? I know. Money and sex. It's all about power."

I spoke slowly. "I think you're mistaken. You don't know what's important to me."

He laughed again. "Oh, yeah, I know. I see it in all women who are around Brent. The heat, you can almost smell it. And the dollar signs practically reflect in your eyes." He tilted the beer bottle and ran the moist, cool rim from my chin to the hollow of my throat. "What would you do to make sure you won it all? Would you place a bet to win, place, or show? I think you'd place a bet to win, and win big."

The bottle rose and fell with my rapid, choked breaths.

Steve leaned even closer. "But the prize might be more than you can handle, little lady. You could wind up real sorry you ever took the gamble. Bones could crack."

He stared at me a long moment. "Think about it," he breathed.

CHAPTER · 15

THERE WAS NO TIME to think about what Steve said—only time to figure out how to get past him and out the door. I fanned my hands between us, startling him and sending the beer bottle sailing across the room. I doubled down and darted to the left, shoving him aside as I ran to the door. Not looking back, I plunged blindly into the woods and finally found the trail we'd followed before.

Steve ordered me back, but I ignored his shouts. I tore through the woods, trying to remember, in reverse, the direction we came. I kept an ear peeled for Steve to chase thundering after me, but I didn't hear anything. He was bigger, no doubt faster, and obviously more in shape than I was, so I figured if he was after me, he easily would have already caught me. Regardless, I ignored my pained lungs and screaming leg muscles and ran harder and faster than I had in years.

When I came to a fork in the dirt path, I groaned aloud and muttered what I could remember about "two roads diverged in a yellow wood." I swung to the left, hoping I'd made the right choice. I soon stumbled out of the woods into a wide field that did not sit anywhere in my short-term memory. Brilliant—who knew where I was?

I did see a huge barn ahead, one of the "horse hotels" we'd spotted from the car the day before. I ran toward it, eyeing an open door on the side. A dusty, black Lincoln Town Car was parked nearby, so I figured safety—or at least a ride back to the house—was just yards away. I looked over my shoulder at nothing but nature as I slipped through the door.

Once inside, the strong scent of hay assaulted me. My sinuses rebelled, and my eyes flushed with scratchy tears as my springtime allergy kicked in several months off cue. Running my finger under my nose in a futile attempt to ward off a sneeze, I glanced around allergy central.

I was on a narrow walkway that sliced through the center of the barn, neatly separating huge, stark-white stalls that were home to brass nameplates and wrought-iron bars that looked like old-fashioned bank-teller windows. Behind the slotted windows, curious and condescending narrow-nosed horses, named everything from Bold Conquistador to Watchmerun, flipped their flowing manes and snorted their curiosity at their surprise visitor. A quick count up one row found ten such equine residences. Another ten mirrored them across the way.

The barn, equally long and tall, had ceilings soaring several dozen feet. Huge windows flooded the area with sunlight when the multiwatt fixtures above weren't ablaze. This upscale horse house was neat and tidy; there wasn't a renegade scrap of straw messing up the floor. Outside each stall, neatly compacted bales of hay were bound and stacked in tidy towers that looked like they'd been placed there by one of Martha Stewart's elves. Crinkly yellow straw beds cushioned the inside of each stall.

Between the occasional rap of a hoof against the floor, I heard a steady trickle of water somewhere toward the far end of the barn. I headed in that direction, my shoes lightly tapping against the floor. I was about three stalls away from one end when a throaty voice called out of nowhere, "Who's that? Meggie, that you out there?"

The stall door just ahead on the right swung open, and the big ruddy nose of the vet appeared. He shook himself out of the stall, kicking pieces of hay off his pants. The thick, mushy stub of an extinguished cigar dangled between his teeth.

He peered at me with squinted eyes, then gallantly spit out the cigar stub into a small tub outside the stall. "Your feet sounded like Meg." He ran a thick tongue over his front teeth and turned away to spit again. He'd obviously spent a little too much time around his patients and adopted their methods of dental hygiene.

I tried to remember his name by running the Kings' descriptive lists through my head. I recalled "vile man," "asshole," and "jerk." And while they all seemed to fit, none of the names sounded particularly nice with "Dr." before them.

I silently repeated "jerk" a few times until inspiration hit and I said, "Dr. Jer—Gerald, right?"

A slimy smile creased around the overhang he called his nose. "That would

be me, my girl. What brings you my way this morning, darlin'? I, uh, don't
recall what Brent called you last night. What was your name, sweetie?"

I forced a polite smile. "My name is Kate."

Dr. Gerald nodded and peeled off a pair of gloves. "Yeah, yeah, that's it.
If you're looking for the boy, I doubt you'll find him out here. Might get dusty
or muss up his hairdo or something." He belly-laughed at his perceived wit.
"I'm surprised they're letting you wander around alone out here. I thought
crazy Jane would have you trussed up in some fluffy room feeding you bon-
bons and dressing you all up in lace."

His beady eyes ran from my head to my toes. A puff of wintry breath
wheezed between his teeth. "You'll make a pretty bride, I'll say. Hope you wear
something that does justice to that figure of yours and not all that crappy
white crinolines and stuff."

Modesty or disgust—probably the latter—settled over me, and I wrapped
my arms around my waist and pulled my coat snug. "I beg your pardon?"

Dr. Gerald snorted another laugh. "Sorry. That was a compliment, sweetie.
Unfortunately, I haven't spent my medical career looking at bodies under
those toilet-paper-square nighties that don't even cover your ass. Gotta use my
imagination sometime. Crazy me, I look at horses' asses all day."

And I'm looking at one right now, I thought. "How long have you worked
with the Kings' horses?" I asked, trying to ease into another subject.

Dr. Gerald leaned lazily against a stall door. "Oh, years. Long enough.
Why?"

I glanced around, not sure why I asked the question in the first place. "Just
curious, I guess. So, is one of the horses having a problem?"

The belly laughs were history. He stood straighter and ran his words
together quickly. "Why do you say that?"

"Well, you're a vet, you're here. That must mean there's a problem."

Dr. Gerald spun in my direction and pointed a fat index finger my way.
"Look here, missy, I'm a vet. I'm supposed to be here. I'm here most days."

His sputter dissipated, and a perturbed frown shoved his fat cheeks to the
sides of his face. "Look, I'll put it so you can understand it. These here horses
are stars. Stars get constant attention. That's my job. You don't want anything to happen to a star before a show, right? One of these puppies comes
down with an infection or a scratch or bruise that won't heal? That's a pocket
full of cash that doesn't come the Kings' way. Douglas, he's all suave and fancy,
but shit like that just don't go over well when it's his wallet that's pained. So
it's my duty to keep 'em all healthy and frisky. You understand now, darlin'?"

Testy, testy.

"Sure, makes perfect sense." *Except for that pesky little problem yesterday with Bayou Folly.* "I guess you travel with the horses as well," I continued.

Dr. Gerald had moved on to Magnolia Breeze's stall. The horse nuzzled its approval in the vet's neck and was rewarded with a lump of sugar. "Yeah, I'm always busy. Your point?"

I walked over to a bundled stack of hay and took a seat. "I guess you were with Bayou Folly yesterday."

He spun his head. "Yeah, why?"

"I think it's sad, that's all. What happened? Did he get tangled up with some other horses as they came toward the finish line?"

Dr. Gerald's frown deepened. "Bayou Folly wasn't racing. His racing days are—were—over. He was standing stud for a living. You know what that is, honey?"

Did I look as dim as Brent? This was the second time in one day my knowledge of things carnal had been challenged.

"Yeah, I know what it is. For the price he must have pulled, I thought the, um, other horses would come here, and you wouldn't have to travel around."

Dr. Gerald abandoned his tête-à-tête with Magnolia Breeze and considered my query. His chin sunk into his neck and was cushioned with several folds of extra flesh. I blinked away the thought that his face looked like someone had smashed it with a frying pan, causing his expression to simply stick that way.

"Bayou Folly," he stuttered, "he was at Churchill . . . for a reason. Usually . . . he goes . . . I mean, stays . . . here. But we took him with us . . . so one of them Saudi princes could take a look at him and . . . shall we say, place an order?"

"And look what happened." I shook my head. "He broke his leg in the stall?"

"Uh-huh," Dr. Gerald replied evenly.

"Couldn't you do surgery or put a cast on it—something to save him?"

After all, if he wasn't racing, his leg wasn't the part of his anatomy that was necessarily important anymore.

"We started surgery," Dr. Gerald spit back. "And then . . . no, no . . . we couldn't do anything. I had to euthanize him. It was just better that way."

"But how did he break his leg?" I asked. "I mean, I can see running around a field or track or something, tripping over a rock or a divot, or even collid-ing with another horse." I stood on my tiptoes and peered into the nearest stall. "But these are pretty small. How could he break a leg just standing there?"

Dr. Gerald joined me and secured a big hand on my elbow. With an effortless yet powerful twist, he propelled me around toward the door I'd entered when I arrived. "Things happen like that. It just happens, understand?"

We reached the door in record time.

"Look, sweetie," he continued, "I think it's time for you to head back to your party-planning. You just move along that little path there back to where you belong." He gave me a pointed shove out the door and nodded past the car. "The house? It's that way—why don't you go there and, ah, leave me to my work? I'm a little too busy today to spend a lot of time chatting. You move along now, honey, okay?"

As if I had any choice. It certainly didn't look like I was going to get a nice warm ride back to the house either. Acting as if my dismissal had been perfectly normal, I quickly trotted in the direction of Dr. Gerald's succinct orders, while he watched me hoof it down the path.

When the house loomed into view, so did my anticipated Welcome Wagon. I noticed a blob move away from a window. Within seconds, Detective Rami was out the door and on the porch.

"Where have you been?" he demanded, speaking each word with a heavy, accusatory tone.

Wouldn't he love to know? I ignored the lack of concern and overabundance of irritation in his voice.

"Taking a walk?" I tried.

The skin around his eyes squeezed into tight little lines. "I don't think so."

He turned and marched inside. I followed him in and shed my coat. I carefully placed it on a chair and sauntered into the living room as if I hadn't a care in the world. He stewed quietly as I moved to the hearth and warmed my hands over the open fire.

"Kate, we had a bargain. You've already broken it. That doesn't make me happy."

I shook my head and kept my back to him. "No, I didn't break a thing. I told you I'd be back here soon. I just decided to take a walk and clear my head."

In fact, I hadn't had time to break our bargain because I had to take that walk right away, thanks to Steve and his warped method of encouragement.

"Oh, really?" Rami said, unconvinced. "Then why do you have hay sticking on your . . . uh, well, sticking on you? Get attacked by a hay monster on your walk?"

I plucked at the little yellow giveaways. "I didn't break our bargain."

"So, where's Brent?" he asked.

I moved away from the fireplace. "You haven't found him yet? I haven't seen him. I thought he would have surfaced by now."

Rami looked disappointed and embarrassed. He changed the subject. "Detective Knight went back to town to get lab work and positive IDs settled. I thought I'd hang around here for the afternoon. Why don't you keep me company?"

Oh joy, what fun that would be. "Am I under house arrest?"

"Not officially, I just want to keep an eye on you."

"Well, maybe later. I should find Adam and see if he's surviving with the caterer. He didn't know he would be put to work this weekend." I headed nonchalantly to the door. "And I'm getting hungry. Maybe if he's with Willard, I can sample some goodies. I'll track him down, and then maybe the three of us can talk."

"Stay in the house this time," Rami ordered in his polite but not quite chummy manner.

I didn't look back as I slipped into the hall. "Too cold outside to do anything else."

I took a few steps toward the kitchen, then glanced behind me to see if a pair of eyes was following me. I didn't see Rami, but I still didn't rule out some sneaky method of surveillance on his part.

The big problem was that I was developing a nasty habit of lying to the police. I had no intention of finding Adam. I still had to find Brent and Zach, and time was ticking.

I backtracked to the staircase and, for the first time, noticed vestiges of my party. Poofy pink and white tulle had been braided through and up the banister, and someone had attached fresh baby-pink and white roses onto satin ribbons bundled on the tulle at every spindle. A large metal ladder was propped against a wall in the entrance hall, and my eyes rose to the chandelier, which was also bedecked in the pink and white tulle confection. Flushing with a sudden girlish pride at how pretty it looked, I thought how sweet it was that someone had gone to all that trouble to make it look nice for me.

Then my evil twin slapped me out of my Cinderella fantasy and reminded me that this whole affair was bogus and there was a good chance that all of this hard work would go to waste, thanks to a minor thing like a dead body that probably belonged to the real bride.

That kind of thought can really give you the wedding-bell blues.

I sighed and quickly climbed the stairs, trying to focus on the task at hand—finding Brent and Zach. I marched down the hallway, poking my head in assorted doorways, hoping to spot my prey.

I discovered Adam's belongings in one dark bedroom, so I figured I was on the right track. In the room across from his, I spotted two expensive cameras and assorted lenses placed carefully on the dresser. I slipped inside and glanced around.

I noticed Zach's duffel bag on the floor next to the nightstand. It was open, with sweaters and a pair of jeans bubbling up from it like a pot boiling over. I'd say it went against my better judgment to drop to my knees and begin pawing through the bag, but to be perfectly honest, I did just that without a second thought. My high school morality teacher was probably instantly going gray somewhere in the world, and my father would be rolling his eyes, but I just couldn't help myself. Besides, Zach would never know anyway, because nothing in the bag was folded. It was just lumped together in one huge pile.

My clothes search didn't reveal much, other than a love of ragged sweaters, jeans with dubious stains, and a fondness for Gap clothing. His pockets were empty except for forty-three cents and a New York subway ticket. And no name—Zach Tanner or otherwise—was written on the labels the way dry cleaners sometimes do.

I moved to the zippered pockets and discovered packets of film, a rolled up *Sports Illustrated*, and a scribbled piece of notebook paper with our flight information. I found one other piece of paper with a phone number and address scribbled in the same handwriting: 212-555-9824 and 143 Baker Flats, #68.

I sat on my heels and sighed in defeat. My eyes were level with the mattress. Just under the pillow was what I'd been looking for all along—Zach's wallet. Here was my proof. I had this impostor—and maybe a killer—right where I wanted him. My hand shook in anticipation as I grabbed the billfold and flopped it open triumphantly.

I rolled off my heels and landed with a disgusted thump on the burgundy carpet. There, big as day, was his license—picture and all—for Zachary A. Tanner, male, blond hair, blue eyes, 6'1", 185 pounds, DOB 8-2-64, social security number, no visual restrictions, all the usual stuff. What the hell happened to Alice's Zach Tanner? I couldn't imagine there'd be the coincidence of two of them running around, who both happened to be professional photographers. It wasn't like his name was Bill Smith.

I angrily thumbed through the rest of the wallet but didn't find one blessed credit card, debit card, or even a medical insurance card. No traveler's checks, but a wad of $358, mostly twenties. No checkbook or even a stupid library card. I thought it odd that he wasn't traveling with at least a MasterCard, but maybe, I reasoned, he did have those somewhere, under another name. I looked at the driver's license again and pushed the curtain aside and held it up to the window. It looked authentic.

A pair of footsteps outside and the click of the doorknob instantly halted my inspection. Now what? I frantically yanked open the closet door, only to see that Zach hadn't bothered to hang anything up, so there was no opportunity to hide behind a row of clothes. My only escape—other than the window, and I certainly wasn't going to attempt that—was to slide underneath the queen-size four-poster bed.

I flattened myself into a silent lump and watched from the slight opening between the bedspread ruffle and the floor, while jeans and leather work boots clomped into the room. The light remained off and the shades drawn. The shoes walked over to the dresser, opened a drawer, and shut it. The mattress heaved as the person jumped onto the bed and unlaced his boots.

The box springs smashed my hair and threatened to rudely conk me on the head with each bounce from above. The boots came off one at a time and landed haphazardly on the floor in front of my nose. I heard a zipper and the sound of fabric rustling. And then a familiar, multi-pocketed safari jacket fell to the floor in a heap by the boots.

The mattress heaved a couple more times, then the room grew quiet. After a few interminably long minutes, a light, steady snore filtered down to me.

Well, I had found Zach.

C H A P T E R · 16

ZACH'S SNORE TEASED ME into the realization that he wasn't going to be danc-
ing jigs anytime soon. A part of me wanted to roll out from under the bed,
jump up, and screech loud enough to give him heart failure. A juvenile strat-
egy, perhaps, but how many adults hide under beds? I figured once I'd rudely
announced my presence, I could calmly demand to know just who he was. I
toyed with that idea for a minute, then decided the more rational thing to
do was crawl across the floor and sneak out before he found me hiding under
the bed.

With his driver's license still clutched in my hand, I gently swung my
arm across the carpet and shoved the license into my pants pocket. I flexed my
body like an undulating snake and tried to slink out from under the mattress.

My foot hit something solid and pushed it against the wall with a slight
thud. My heart pounded the floor as Zach stirred and flopped over to one
side. The snore returned.

I was perfectly still for a minute, then I rolled to the side and scrunched
into a twisted pretzel of a fetal position to see what my foot had made contact with. In the dark, all I could make out was an object about six or eight
inches long and not very tall. I slid my toes between the object and the wall,
then flicked my foot forward. The object flipped over and landed a few inches
from the wall. My mouth went dry as I realized it was a gun. My brilliant
move paralyzed me when I imagined the barrel aimed right at me as I kicked
it over like an idiot.

What was a gun doing under Zach's bed? Did it belong to him, or did
someone else hide it there?

I figured it had been placed there recently, because I was pretty sure the cleaning staff would have vacuumed the room in preps for a guest. I tried to remember the last time I vacuumed under my bed at home, but came up empty.

I stared at the weapon. I knew nothing about guns, other than they can ruin your day in the worst way if the trigger is pulled. With that in mind, I gently coaxed it toward me until I could reach it with my hand. I pulled my sleeve over my hand and gently grasped the gun, being careful not to get my fingerprints on it. *Detective Rami will be proud of me*, I thought as I scooted slowly out from under the bed. I lay parallel to the bed for a second, and when Zach didn't move, I crept on my hands and knees toward the door. I kept my eyes glued on the gun, its barrel now pointed away from me, as I slid it across the floor.

When I reached the door, I glanced back at Zach, who continued his peaceful repose, his back turned to me and his head buried underneath a feather pillow. I sat on my heels and stared at the gun for a second. Keeping my sleeve pulled over my hand, I gingerly picked up the gun and slipped it into the back of my pants, under my sweater. *Just like all great cops and detectives do*, I thought.

I was packing a piece all right, but it didn't feel snug at all. It felt cold against my skin and undeniably menacing. I didn't enjoy the thought of blowing away my keister and everything south of it, just to prove a point to Rami. I reached for the doorknob and closed my eyes as I slowly turned the knob and gave the door a gentle push. As the door silently gave way, I flopped on my hands and knees again and quickly crawled out of the room, closing the door behind me.

"Thank heavens," I whispered, eyes still shut, the relieved breath flowing freely. I failed to notice, until I opened my eyes, the pair of black patent heels and ankle-length red silk skirt with a peacock feather pattern.

"Just what do you think you're doing?" demanded Jane.

I shot up like the guilty child I was, rather rudely thrusting my chest toward her as the gun sharply poked the small of my back. My unnatural twitch spun a look of horror on her face that probably matched my expression, skin cell for skin cell.

"Why," she said, drawing the word into two syllables, "were you crawling out of that room?" She reached for the door. "Is Brent in there?"

I lunged for the doorknob and ended up grabbing Jane's hand.

Her eyes caught fire. "Let go of me, young lady." The words hissed between clenched teeth.

I did as I was told and babbled, "I'm sorry, Mrs. King. Brent's not in there. I was, um, looking for my cousin's room."

Jane's head shook a bit. "So why were you crawling out of the room? I don't understand."

Just then, Adam turned the corner down the hall. I swallowed and frantically waved my hand and sent it sailing through my hair in a desperate attempt to ward him off. "I thought that was Adam's room," I added in a louder voice. "But . . . um . . . it wasn't. Imagine that."

Adam stopped, a dozen or so feet behind Jane. He wore a most curious expression.

Jane's eyes narrowed. "Is something wrong with your hand?"

"Hmm?" I replied, flicking my hand once more, until Adam quickly backed out of sight. "Uh, no."

Jane, that bastion of peace and tranquillity, shoved a frown across her face. "You need to rest before my guests arrive. Why don't you go back to the cottage and take a nap. It will do us all good to have you out of the house for a while."

"I, um, just might do that," I fibbed.

She leaned in so close, I had a horrible childhood flashback to the scary witch in Snow White. "See that you do, Kathy."

I bit my lip. "Kate. It's Kate, not Kathy."

She gave my shoulder an upper-class poke as she stalked down the hallway and disappeared into another room. I rolled my eyes and briskly headed the opposite direction and found Adam calmly waiting around the corner.

His blue eyes sparkled under raised eyebrows. "You're winning all kinds of popularity contests with the family these days. Hey, Kate, I used to date a divorce lawyer. Want me to call her up and make an early appointment?"

"Very funny." I grabbed his arm and led him down the hall. "Where have you been? Everyone is doing quite a job of disappearing this morning."

"Oh, and you haven't done the same?" Adam spewed. "I've been in kitchen hell with a caterer who can't decide whether to chop vegetables or make me flavor of the month. I hate to disappoint him, but he's not my type. Just because I set up restaurants, people automatically assume—"

I ignored him. "Adam, we have to talk." I dragged him into an empty study. "We've established you're not gay. And I'm not a bride. Okay? We have other things that are more important."

He flopped on the couch and leaned back. "Whatever. While you're at it, explain why you're walking like you've just come from cotillion. Either you're wearing a brace for scoliosis a little late in life, or you've assumed way too much of the model-heiress prance."

He asked for it. I stiffly retreated to the door, checked the hall, then shut the door. I joined Adam by the couch. "I'll tell you why I'm walking this way. Look what I found." With my sleeve pulled over my hand once more, I reached behind my back and pulled out the gun.

That got his attention.

He jumped off the couch. "Kate? Where did you. . . ?"

"Get the gun? Try Zach's room. I also got his driver's license, which says he's Zach Tanner. I was also kidnapped on horseback and accosted in a stable by a lascivious veterinarian. And, oh, yeah, the cops are onto me also, and my mother-in-law hates my guts. So what did you do this morning?"

Adam reached for my wrist and slowly pulled the gun toward the couch. "Is that thing loaded?"

A shiver ran down my back, most notably where the gun had just been. "Um, I don't really know. I didn't check."

Adam frowned. "Put that thing down. You make me nervous swinging it around like that."

I let the gun drop on the cushion. No argument there—it made me nervous too.

Adam's eyes didn't stray far from the gun. "Now, what exactly happened to you?"

I quickly recounted my morning.

"Kate, we can't leave you alone for a minute, can we?" He held out his hand. "Let me see that license."

I dug out Zach's license and said, "It looks real to me. I just don't understand this." I spotted a phone on a nearby table. "I'm going to try Alice again, see if she dug up anything about our photographer."

As I dialed the number, I watched Adam hold the license up to the window, flip it over and over, then scratch at the plastic laminate. He repeated his flip-and-study procedure once more.

"What are you doing?" I asked him, just as Alice answered.

"Well, that's not the typical way I answer my phone," she said. "But then, it's you, and there's nothing typical about the way you do things."

"Hello to you too. I was talking to Adam when you answered."

"Well, regardless," she said, "it's good to hear from you. I hope this means you're calling from a plane on your way back here, safe and sound. I haven't been able to do any work since you called earlier. I can't believe you're in the middle of a murder investigation again. Please tell me you're raking up huge bucks on your calling card as you speak to me from the bat phone that's in the headrest of the seat in front of you. You are at 30,000 feet, right?"

Adam continued his scratch-and-sniff routine by the window.

"What? No, we're still here," I answered. "Wait, hold on just a second." I put the phone on my shoulder and queried Adam again. "What are you doing?"

He squinted at the license. "For someone who gets in as much trouble as you do, you sure don't know how to be sneaky. Didn't you ever have a fake ID before you turned twenty-one?"

"No, did you?"

He glanced at me. "That's irrelevant. My point is, you can take a real license and fake it nicely with a fine cut here or there with a razor blade and a little computer magic to match the wording on the rest of the license. Find yourself a laminating machine at the library, smooth out the rough edges, and *boom!* You're in business."

"Hey! I'm still here!" screeched Alice through the phone, in a voice that probably woke up lawyers in the offices on the floor below Patton Publishing.

I scrambled to get the phone back to my ear. "Don't yell, we're here."

The magic of fiber optics worked wonders several states away. "You never had a fake ID?" Alice asked. "What a loser, we all had those. Whose fake ID are you talking about?"

"Whose do you think?" I said. "I have Zach Tanner's license, which says he's the real McCoy."

"No," she argued. "My guy is the real Zach Tanner. Adam's right, you've probably got a good fake there. And by the way, I don't want to know what you had to do to get his license out of his back pocket. Look, I've talked to my Zach all morning. I think—no, I know—he's legit. I even called a few editor friends from other pubs, and they all told me the same thing. It's like toothpaste and dentists, Kate. Nine out of ten reporters and editors can't be wrong."

I yanked the license out of Adam's hand. "Okay then, find some criss-crosses and look up this address on his license—521 West Riviera Blvd., Washington, D.C. See what you get."

"Nope, sorry," Alice said. "That's the real one's address. I have it right here."

"Well, hell," I stalled. "What was that other address I saw? Try . . . oh, what was it? Baker Flats, something like that, I can't remember the number."

"Never heard of it," she said dismissively.

I held my temper, which was fading fast. "Do you know every street? Can you check? Please? I think the area code was 212."

"Well, in that case, I'm no good to you," Alice answered. "That area code is New York. You should know that."

So I did. Details. "Of course, you're right. But New York? Brent?"

Adam shrugged. We stared at each other, trying to figure out a connection. I shook my head. "I don't know, I just don't know."

"Well," Alice agreed. "Neither do I, but I'll keep trying on this end. In the meantime, there's something else you should know. Remember my friend Robbie? The sports guy? He works for a CBS affiliate in Maryland, covers a lot of horse racing. I gave him a call, offered my sympathies on the passing of Bayou Folly, and got an interesting reply. Word on the street is, there's something weird going on."

My morning conversation with Steve returned to haunt me. "Oh, really? How so?"

Alice continued, not knowing that she was eerily close to the story I'd dismissed as Steve's drunken ramblings. "Pardon my phrasing, but he was apparently as healthy as a horse. Robbie said there was no reason for Bayou Folly to have brittle bones or be overly prone to the kind of injury he sustained. People in the horse business around Maryland also seem to think it's weird Bayou Folly was at Churchill Downs in the middle of November."

"What if I said they moved him there for a special breeding date?" I asked.

"You could say anything. I know squat about that stuff. However, Robbie also told me that scuttlebutt says the horse didn't have a chance."

"Well," I interjected, "I did talk to the vet this morning, and he said there was nothing they could do, that the injury was too bad."

"No, let me finish," Alice said. "Robbie was talking about the vet. These sources say they think the vet in charge acted too quickly in putting Bayou Folly to sleep. Apparently, more could have been done to save him."

I couldn't believe I was defending Dr. Gerald. "But they weren't there to see the extent of the injury."

"True," Alice agreed. "But it sounds like the vet has a bad rep, at least in the Maryland horsey circles."

That wasn't a big surprise. I could vouch for that firsthand. "So are you saying that he killed the horse somehow on purpose? What would that accomplish?"

"You got me," Alice summed up. "I'm just passing along gossip. Do with it what you want. Speaking of gossip, have you by any chance talked to John?"

A rusty window screen caught in the back of my throat. "No, not yet. I've tried several times, but I can't get through."

Alice's voice softened. "He came by here, looking worse than a puppy on death row at the dog pound."

"What was he doing at the office? He knows I'm not there?"

"I think he was looking for a friendly face." Alice chuckled. "And that would be me, believe it or not. We grabbed some coffee, chatted a bit. I tried—I really tried—to convince him there's nothing going on with Brent."

My heart sank past my knees. "What do you mean you tried? He doesn't believe you?"

"The poor guy thinks you dumped him for an underwear model. What would you think if you were in his shoes?" Alice said bluntly.

"I'd believe what I told him," I stumbled. "I mean, I'd understand that this is all a setup, a story, it's not true."

"Well, I think it might take a little more convincing. After all, he knows I'm your best friend and, therefore, would say anything to protect you. He needs to hear it from you."

"But I've called and called him," I groaned.

"In person," she replied. "Come home, get rid of Brent and his goofy family, and come back to that gorgeous doctor who's got the hots for you, before I steal him away. He's a good catch, Kate. Don't screw it up."

"I don't intend to," I replied. "Look, see what else you can find out. In the meantime, I'll try John again, and I'm going to have a talk with Zach—"

I was going to add more, but a resounding explosion somewhere in a not-too-distant area of the house interrupted me. The walls shook, and picture frames in the room tumbled to the floor.

Smoke detectors blared throughout the house.

CHAPTER · 17

RATIONAL PEOPLE, when confronted with a big *ka-boom* and the screech of a smoke detector, would instantly seek the nearest exit. Not Adam or me. *You gotta be kidding* was wordlessly etched across our faces.

I interrupted Alice's tirade of "What in the world was that noise?" with a succinct "Gotta go, call you later," and let the phone drop into its cradle.

No doubt I'd hear about my lack of phone etiquette at a later date.

Adam shrugged. "Let's go."

It didn't take long to figure out where the action was once we got downstairs. A filmy haze filtered down the side hall, and the air was pungent with something that had cooked long beyond its prime.

Detective Rami met us halfway, his gun drawn and ready. He paused long enough to toss out, "Well, at least you're in one piece."

We followed the smell, smoke, and cacophonous shouts until we reached the back of the house. Chaos reigned in the King kitchen. A cloud of smoke lingered overhead, and puffy blobs of white foam from a pair of empty fire extinguishers dotted the walls, stove front, and cabinets like a sea of little meringue puffs. An oozing mound of the foam also covered the inside of the industrial-size stove, not to mention the unfortunate, smoldering remains of what appeared to be a rather large dish of something. My guess was a vegetable soufflé or pastry of some sort, given the assorted stains and renegade pieces of carrots and what appeared to be (my hope at least) pieces of chicken now glued to the ceiling and light fixtures. The stove door, blackened by the blast, swung forlornly from one lone hinge.

I had a feeling lunch would be ordered in for the day.

Rami holstered his gun and sprinted past me to a corner where poor

Willard, face blackened with soot, lay sprawled on the floor. My elusive fiancé knelt by his side, fanning Willard's face with a colander. I didn't bother to mention that the hundreds of little holes in the strainer defeated the noble purpose Brent was attempting.

The weakened but apparently uninjured Willard rose daintily onto his slender elbows and moaned in the direction of the stove, "Oh, my creation. . . ."

Brent increased the velocity of his colander fan. "It was an accident, that's all."

With what energy he had, Willard grabbed Brent's collar. "No, it wasn't. It was meant to ruin things. This whole event is just deteriorating by the minute. I'm ruined. I should have never taken this job. It's jinxed. My reputation is shot."

His grip tightened on Brent into a decidedly nondainty choke hold. With a little assistance from Adam and Detective Rami, Brent managed to pull away. Willard whimpered in a sad little heap while Rami motioned for a couple of Willard's beleaguered kitchen assistants to drop their fire extinguishers and take over baby-sitting their distraught boss.

I reached up to Brent's nose and brushed away a dot of soot. "I know models wear makeup, but this is the second time today you've gotten into the Halloween stuff."

He glanced at me and took over wiping his face with a kitchen towel. "I said it was an accident," he muttered irritably. "I was talking to him, and I guess I leaned on the stove control or something and accidentally turned up the heat too high."

Rami shook his head and checked out the temperature dial. It was at the highest setting, which no doubt turned the pastry puff concoction in the oven into a pastry poof. His tolerance meter inched a degree past overload. "Didn't anyone ever teach you to be careful around stoves?"

Brent tossed his towel into a dissipating mound of foam. "Look, how many times do I have to say it was an acci—"

Above the din of the smoke detector came a horrendous *whap* behind us. Jane stood nearby, her hand clenched in a death grip around a butcher knife that she had successfully plunged into the countertop.

"Stop that infernal beeping!" she screamed.

As Willard cowered in a corner, a pair of workers flew into the hall. On command, the beep died.

Brent flew to Jane's side. "Now, Mom, it's okay, don't overreact. This is just a little mess, nothing to concern yourself with."

He cooed softly around his mother as he tried to pry her hands off the knife. A body tremble rumbled through her thin frame, and tears gathered in the corners of her eyes. Things did not look promising, but I took a couple steps in their direction, in a daughterly attempt to help calm her. Instead, I slipped on foam and lunged for the counter as I performed a pitiful acrobatic routine.

Adam grabbed me from behind. "Bad form. The French judge only gave you a 3.1."

Jane didn't think much of me either. Her twitching eyes narrowed, and she looked like she was going to pick up one of the brass charger plates lying nearby and wing it at me, as if it were an upper-class Frisbee. The fun increased as Meg joined our happy little party.

She swept into the kitchen, her dark eyes growing as she took in the sight. "What is the meaning of this?" she barked. Ignoring everyone else in the room, she zeroed in on me. "You did this, didn't you?"

"Can it, Meg," Brent spit. "Leave her alone. I'm tired of you and your attitude. I'm sorry we're messing with your precious routine, but we'll be gone in a couple of days and you can play with your horsies all you want."

She straightened and pointed her finger at Brent. "You shut up. Don't you have any respect for what your mother is attempting to do for her little baby? Why don't you show a little appreciation around here and help out instead of causing all kinds of trouble?"

She brushed past me and stomped over to Willard. "And you—you're fired. Clean this mess up and get out of here. You'll be paid for your services up until yesterday."

The caterer paled ten shades. "But the party. . . ."

Jane chimed in. "Meg! *You* can't fire him. I hired him, and he has to produce this party tonight, regardless of the mess he's caused. Only then will *I* fire him."

"But," Willard moaned, "I didn't cause. . . ."

Jane and Meg batted the issue back and forth. Brent gave up and stalked out of the kitchen. I wasn't about to let him leave again, so I was hot on his heels, with Adam and Rami right behind us.

I grabbed Brent's sleeve. "Where are you going? I haven't seen you all morning. We've got a lot to discuss."

He took in the troupe gathering. "Look, I want to get a shower, okay? I can't exactly walk around like this the rest of the day. I'll be back shortly. Does everyone want to come? Because frankly, no offense, but Kate is the only one of you guys I'd have join me in the shower." Not waiting for an answer, he turned and headed upstairs.

Upstairs. Oh, geez, the gun. With all the commotion, Adam and I had run out of the room and left the gun on the couch for all to see. In retrospect, not a top-shelf idea.

I poked Adam. "Um, don't you think we should talk with Detective Rami about what we found?"

The realization hit Adam instantly and he grimaced.

Rami, teeth clenched, asked, "Found what? What don't I know about now?"

Adam started upstairs. "We need privacy."

Rami and I followed him up the steps. We reached the room and discovered our worst fear.

"It's gone," Adam breathed.

Steeling myself for Rami's reaction, I explained, "I sorta found a gun . . . and we kinda left it here . . . and now it's gone."

I had a feeling the detective was running every statute and violation he'd learned in the police academy through his head so he could lock us away and never have to worry about us again. "You want to say that one more time, Ms. Kelly?"

Lovely, I was "Ms. Kelly" again and not "Kate" anymore. I was in trouble, no doubt about that.

"It could be nothing," I quietly began. "I . . . um . . . found it in Zach Tanner's room."

Rami blinked. "Where in Tanner's room?"

"Under the bed." Before he could comment, I continued. "I was going to bring it to you, when the kitchen blew."

He rubbed his temples.

I shrugged my shoulders. "I don't know where it went. I wish I did. Maybe it doesn't belong to him. Maybe it's completely harmless."

"Guns are never harmless, particularly when there's a murder investigation involved." Rami's fingers slipped from his temples to swing sleepy circles around his eyes. "Remember when we said there was more than just a burned body out there?"

I followed his train of thought. "Are you saying the cause of death wasn't the fire?"

"Yeah," he said succinctly. "Forensics discovered pretty quickly that the victim had a gunshot wound to the chest. The fire looks like it was just an attempt to dispose of the body. What kind of gun did you find?"

I bit my lip. "I don't know guns."

"It was a .45," Adam stated.

Where had he gleaned that kind of education?

Rami's eyes slammed shut for a few seconds. He sighed and looked at Adam. "You sure about that?"

Adam nodded. "I know enough about guns to say that. What caliber made the wound?"

Rami sighed and tossed his hands in the air. "What do you think? We need to find it now."

"What are we looking for?" asked Brent from the doorway. His shirttail hung lazily over his pants, and he was barefoot. Either he had taken the fastest shower on record, or he'd made it only halfway there. Although his face was scrubbed clean, his hair was dry.

"That was a fast shower," I observed.

He grinned. "Yeah, it doesn't take much."

Who was he kidding? It appeared it didn't take anything.

He ambled into the room and came up behind me and slid his arms around my waist. "So, what are you looking for?" he asked again.

Rami lied. "Nothing important, Mr. King."

Brent playfully rocked me back and forth. "It *must* be important, Detective. You look so serious. But really, do we have to bother Kate? I mean, we're here to celebrate our love this weekend."

I swiveled around and took in his earnest gaze. This make-believe stuff was getting to me. One moment, he would acknowledge the charade, but the next, he seemed to truly believe what he was saying. I knew he was acting, but an uneasy part of me was beginning to wonder if he was that good of an actor or if some part of his brain was misfiring a bit and he really thought we were engaged. I mean, it wasn't that much of a stretch. All you had to do was look at his mother. She was a few beans short of a dip, but at times she appeared completely normal.

Adam looked equally perplexed. "We were just talking, that's all."

"Well," Brent said, "it sounded important to me." He gave me a tight squeeze, and something near his waist poked me.

Would Brent steal the gun? I couldn't think of a polite way to say "drop your pants" in such mixed company.

He pulled away and took my hand. "I have a surprise for you. I've been busy this morning. I thought I'd call in a couple of favors. I've arranged for you and me to have a sauna and massage—the best kind of house call. They should be here by now."

Adam's eyes twitched. "A couples massage?"

Here was a big struggle. I regularly scrimped and saved to treat myself to occasional spa visits at home. Never, and I mean never, had those $70 visits included a nearly nude male model as part of the deal. It sounded wonderful on the surface, but some highly irrational part of me said, *You know, I don't think so.*

Brent grinned. "Some of the best hands in Kentucky." He squeezed my hand, and I flushed. "Besides mine, of course," he added.

My head flipped back and forth, and I heard myself say, "No, I don't think this is a good idea."

Rami completely threw me off base. "Go ahead. It will keep you both occupied for a while."

"See? Now it's an order," Brent said. "Come on Kate, you'll love it. It's just what you need. Just follow me downstairs."

Rami nudged me toward Brent.

I turned around and whispered back frantically, "He's got something hard in his pants."

The detective smiled. "I'm sure he does."

Fine. I stomped over to where Brent waited patiently.

He smiled and led me down a side hallway. "You really need to relax, Kate. You can bank on this: when they're finished with you, you won't know what hit you."

We headed down carpeted steps to a huge party room filled with a big-screen projection system, a pool table, a foosball table, and a polished mahogany bar stocked with enough alcohol to run a successful side business. As Brent took a detour around the bar to grab a bottle of wine and two glasses, I decided that two could play at this game. I planted John firmly in the back corner of my brain, took a deep breath, and reminded myself that I was about to get my second drink of the day before noon. It probably wouldn't hurt.

I followed Brent behind the bar and put on my best pout. "I've been awful, haven't I?"

His eyes crinkled. "I think you've been great, considering everything."

I leaned forward and playfully tugged at his shirttail, hoping that I might expose something underneath. "You're so nice. Thanks for doing so much to make me comfortable." I tried not to gag. "When you were gone all morning, I was worried."

I blinked sweetly and went in for the kill. I slid my arms around his waist, and the mystery object bumped lightly against my arm. I attempted to make out its shape but was foiled when Brent suddenly pushed me away.

"Hey, we'll get through this weekend." His blue eyes dipped toward mine, and the Casanova voice purred, "It'll all be over sooner than you think. Trust me."

That was difficult, because he shoved me away when he noticed that I was zeroing in on his little mystery package. Brent left the wineglasses sitting on the bar and made a point of staying at arm's length as we headed into a full-scale weight room.

Waiting for us by the Nautilus machine were two stony-faced women in white scrubs. The first woman, a pretty, petite blonde who looked like a gymnast, I hated instantly. Her partner I quickly dubbed Bertha. She had her own share of fat cells and most of her buddy's as well. Her dark hair was pulled into a severe bun, making her look like a German prison matron.

The little one spoke. "We're ready when you are, Mr. King."

Brent's magazine smile exploded on his face. "Fantastic. Kate, this is Veronica and her assistant."

"Velma," the muscle woman added, in a voice laden with testosterone.

Brent didn't blink. "Great. Let's get started." He and svelte little Veronica nearly sprinted toward the door. "I'll do the massage first, and, Kate, you take the sauna. It will loosen you up for the massage."

A pang of jealousy, mixed with a healthy dose of fear, slapped me as I stared at the imposing Velma. Why should I get stuck with her, and Brent with the perky little acrobat? I thought this little adventure was supposed to be a couple's thing, but the couple involved seemed to be Brent and Veronica. I wasn't sure if I was more jealous that Brent was with Veronica or more afraid of the very real fact that Velma looked like she'd flip me around on the table like a lump of dough that needed a good pounding.

Velma ushered me into a small changing room and handed me a white towel wrap and a robe. "Take off your clothes. Leave them here. I'll be back in a minute."

So much for small talk.

I stared at the door that shut abruptly in my face. I didn't want to disrobe for her. I wanted to go back upstairs and talk about murder and mayhem. Anything but this. I briefly debated sneaking out of the room, but realized that wasn't an option when, a couple of seconds later, Velma banged on the door and said, "Are you done? I'm coming in."

I squeaked, "Just a second," and frantically shed my clothes and dove into the towel and robe. My solace in my raging fear of the Valkyrie of a woman was that at least the robe was roomy and comfy enough to fit a sumo wrestler.

Velma wrenched open the door and directed me down a narrow hallway to a Spartan room that resembled a large closet with wood walls. No windows, no clock, just a low bench across the far wall. I stood halfway in the door and was suddenly relieved of my robe, thanks to an unceremonious tug by Velma, giving me just an instant to yank the towel back in place before the door slammed shut.

Not quite sure what to do, I found an ounce of bravery and opened the door and peeked into the hallway, but Velma was nowhere in sight. I shut the door again and headed for the bench. I tried to get comfortable, debating briefly the ladylike way to sit there without looking goofy. I gave up when I realized that, since I was alone, what was the point?

I heard a slow hiss, then noticed little curls of steam licking lazily out from the corners. The smoky white trails snaked across the floor like an eerie fog in a cemetery. The room temperature became tropical, and an army of sweat beads popped to attention along my body.

I tried to ignore how hot I was. A massage was one thing, but a sauna? I wasn't too sure.

Ask a roofer laying tar and shingles in New Orleans in July if this heat is his idea of fun and relaxation, I thought, *and I bet his colorful reply would make a minister break out in gales of sweat.*

Hot rolling clouds surrounded me, and my hair exploded into frizzy ringlets. I leaned my head against the wall, shut my eyes, and tried to breathe deeply. *Try to find some enjoyment in this*, was my silent mantra. I even tried humming an accompaniment to the omnipresent hiss.

I'd barely made it to the first verse of my composition when a brisk click snapped on the door. I stared at the door as the hiss magnified into a loud swoosh. Steam poured through the jets, cloaking the room in a thick, milky fog that reduced visibility to the point that I couldn't see my hand in front of my face. The temperature rocketed exponentially, and the searing heat stung my eyes and cooked my skin.

I lunged across the room and fell against the door. Simply staggering four or five steps sapped my energy, making it difficult to breathe. My slippery hands twisted around the doorknob, but the door was bolted shut. It had been unlocked just moments earlier; I had opened it myself.

I pounded on the door and called for help, but the deafening whoosh of the steam drowned out my shouts. Brent was in the next room. Why didn't he hear me?

I screamed and beat both fists against the door so hard that I collapsed in a heap. My knee skidded on a damp, curling piece of paper just under the door. I picked it up and had to hold it close to my nose to read the rapidly smearing ink through the steam.

A straight, bold scrawl read, "Those who can't stand the heat should get out."

My eyes burned so badly, I couldn't tell whether tears or sweat were pouring out of the sockets. Every breath was a struggle, and the heat pricked my skin. As blackness enveloped my vision, I battled to my feet and pounded the door once more.

"Somebody help me!" I cried.

C H A P T E R · 18

AS I WOKE UP, distant faces materialized around me in a fuzzy, speckled blur. Staring at me like I was a specimen in a jar were Detective Rami, his face squeezed into a dried prune, and Adam and Brent. At first, I thought I must have been sacked with a bad case of the flu, because I was alternating between violent hot flashes and bone-racking shivers. Daggers pierced every angle of my head.

As my consciousness gained momentum, I noticed I was soaked to the bone and my skimpy towel clung dangerously to every nook and cranny. Adam was rubbing a cold, wet towel on my legs, and Brent cradled me in his lap. He was rapidly massaging my arms, wringing them out like he was emptying dirty water from a dishcloth.

His rhythm matched a shouted order from a thickly accented voice, which kept repeating, "Get the blood moving, get the blood moving."

Somehow, I didn't think this was a traditional couple's massage.

I knew I was right when the voice materialized as Velma, who appeared from behind and rather rudely tossed a bucket of ice water on me—and no doubt on Brent, who twitched and bounced my aching head up and down on his lap like a Ping-Pong ball.

The ice water brought me back to reality—quickly. I sat up and growled, "Hey! What's the idea?" The room locked into a dizzying swirl, and I sank into Brent's lap with a thud.

"She needs a doctor," Velma decreed, her now empty bucket perched on the ridge of her mountainous hip.

"We're getting one," Brent replied.

I gingerly rested on my elbow. "Would someone please explain what's going on?" I suddenly realized that surrounding me were nothing but men—and Velma, but I wasn't certain exactly where she fit in. "Could I please have a robe or something? And Brent, please, my arms are not bread dough."

Adam smiled. "She's back. She'll be all right."

A few minutes later I removed the wet towel and wrapped myself in a thick, white robe, courtesy of Velma, who nervously reminded me several times, "This wasn't my fault, miss, I didn't do anything wrong."

I felt stronger until I discovered Dr. Gerald, who was bellied up to the bar and waiting for my arrival. That was the best they could do?

Detective Rami read my expression. "He was in the kitchen, looking for something to eat."

I squirmed like a nervous toddler as Dr. Gerald examined me before the gathered throng. I wanted to ask for a dollar a stare, but I refrained. His hands were coarse and fumbling, and his breath was bad.

I gripped the front of the robe in protest and gently shoved his hands away. "I'm all right, really. I just got a little overheated."

Dr. Gerald leered at me at eye level. "You were more than overheated, honey. Just like my horses, getting all sweated up in July in all the heat and humidity. You get whapped that way, and you aren't worth a tick's whisker." He plopped a callused, fat hand on my forehead, then migrated to each cheek. "See here, you're lucky," he slithered. "When the horses do this, I usually stick a thermometer up their ass, but I won't do that to you."

"Do you mind?" Adam asked for me.

Dr. Gerald glanced at Adam and laughed away his valiant protest. He turned back to me. "Little lady, we need to ply you with enough water to make you pee like a racehorse." His greasy smile grew and he winked. "See, there? Now I'm back in my element. How long were you in there, missy? Look at your skin—you were cooking. When your body heats up faster than you can cool it, your temperature skyrockets. It's a good thing Brent found you. A few more minutes and your brain woulda bubbled up and over, and that woulda been it."

Detective Rami moved a step closer. "What do you mean, 'been it'? Been what?"

Dr. Gerald shrugged his lumpy shoulders, stood, and lumbered over to the bar and filled a pitcher with tap water. "I won't cut corners, son, she would have died."

I pulled the robe tighter. "The door was locked; there was nothing I could do. But it was unlocked right before the steam hit. I opened it myself."

Brent walked over to the pool table and rolled a ball into a waiting pocket. "Must have been a malfunctioning valve, I guess."

Velma, who had been hovering quietly in the background, stomped forward. "No, sir. Someone turned it up while I was gone. I never expected anyone could tamper with the controls."

"Who had access to that room?" Detective Rami asked.

Velma frowned. "Mr. King was in the next room for his massage, but there's always the back stairs at the end of the hall. They lead into the kitchen—anyone could have slipped in and out from that direction, and I never would have seen them. I was here, reading a magazine during the sauna. I didn't see anyone come down the main steps. But the back steps. . . ." She shrugged away the rest of her answer.

Dr. Gerald poured a tall tumbler full of water and handed it to me. "Drink this, and we'll refill it."

I noticed for the first time that Brent was still fully dressed, while I had been immediately shoved into the towel and sent off to the ovens. "Brent, had you started your massage yet when this happened?"

"Yes, of course," he said.

But he was simultaneously vetoed by Veronica. "No, not yet." She blushed at his acid glance. "You're mistaken, Mr. King. I was still preparing my oils, and you were . . . well . . . I thought you were in the dressing room. I had the nature CD playing, so I didn't hear anything outside."

Brent dropped his shoulders. "I was ready, just about, so . . . we were more or less . . . getting under way." He sensed his stumbling. "But I heard Kate, and that's what's important, because if we had been in the other room, I never would have heard her."

I couldn't argue with that logic, but Adam tried. "Didn't you think it was weird that the door was locked?"

"I didn't even notice," Brent replied succinctly. "I just unlocked it and went inside."

Dr. Gerald was back with his pitcher of water. I shook my head at the offer of another glass, but he pressed it in my hand. "Drink it, and finish about two more pitchers of this."

I grumpily obeyed with the glass, but unless he thought I was some kind of reservoir, there was no way two more pitchers were going into this body.

He nodded to the group. "I need to get back to the horses; Douglas doesn't pay me to take care of his guests. She should rest for a while, and if anything changes, call a people doctor." Giving me a final glance, he headed up the stairs without saying good-bye.

I was all for that rest. My head still hurt, and my shivers and hot flashes had slowed but not abated. Velma and Veronica helped me dress while Brent secured a golf cart to send me back to the cottage.

He returned, and Adam and Detective Rami accompanied us, like a little security contingent, on the back of the cart and saw me safely deposited inside the cottage. The merry maids had been hard at work. The downstairs was scrubbed clean, and a freshly folded stack of laundry sat in a chair.

I found a pair of jeans, but some of my clothes were still missing, so Brent picked through his pile and pulled out a long-sleeved, white button-down Oxford. "Here—you can wear this. Do you want me to stay? I can bring you some more water."

I accepted the shirt. "No, thanks. I don't need a keeper. I'm just going upstairs to take a nap."

Brent made me nervous, but I actually didn't mind the thought of Adam or Detective Rami hanging out. My macho side had vaporized back at the house, and I was more than a little uneasy about how close I'd come to being a steamed lobster.

Rami agreed—subliminally at least. "You shouldn't be alone, so Adam and Brent will stay downstairs. I'm going back to the house and take a closer look at the steam room." He gave me a wise look. "Have we got a deal?"

His emphasis on the word *deal* struck me as it was intended. I answered, "It's a deal this time."

I stopped off in the bathroom to change and almost collapsed again when I looked in the mirror and saw the rat's nest called my hair and the bright red nuclear glow that still reflected off my skin. I could have given Bride of Frankenstein a run for her money. The boys downstairs were either winning the lifetime achievement award for politeness, or their concern for my well being had rendered them blind.

I crawled under the covers and shut my eyes, but sleep did not come as I expected. Although my body was weakened, my mind was running a marathon. I flopped back and forth, plumped the pillows, discarded the pillows, and then pulled them back under my heavy head.

So much was happening so quickly, it was hard to fathom that we'd been in Lexington for only two days. In that short timespan, someone had tried to kill me—or at least seriously hurt me—three times. And the last time, my foe had come awfully close. I'd also been threatened, spirited off against my will, insulted, and duped. Not my idea of a good time.

I stared at the ceiling and ticked off the list. We had one dead body, who might or might not be Paige. My vote was for Paige, but I couldn't nail down exactly how she ended up shot dead in a car in the middle of a field. Sure, she probably knew where to find Brent, but who, other than Brent, knew her? Could she have arrived and met the wrong person, who then made sure she never got to Brent? But why make such a production disposing of her body? What kind of a killer shouts, "Yoo-hoo? Look over here at this raging inferno! Look what I did!" The farm was big enough to make a single body disappear pretty darn well without a huge effort. Why the big urge to be noticed?

But if that really was Paige, my selfish self argued, why was someone so hell-bent on getting rid of me? I rolled over onto my stomach and studied the intricate iron scrolls of the headboard. Maybe it wasn't Paige. Maybe it was some totally unrelated body, the poor soul. So, someone other than Brent thought I was the real fiancée, and that's why I was the target.

Simple enough. But not definitive.

Who didn't want me around? I started with the head of the family. Douglas King seemed consumed with his horses and business interests and appeared to have a minuscule interest in his children's lives. Why would he care about a fiancée?

The same went for Meg King. She wouldn't win a Miss Congeniality title anytime soon, and her stuffy temperament bordered on mean, but she probably couldn't be bothered to worry about something other than the horses or the farm's finances. Murder wasn't on her agenda.

Jane King, on the other hand, was another story. She was obviously unstable, had a second career as a firebug, and minced no words when it came to her disapproval of little old me. Not only was she the portrait of a prime suspect, she made an easy scapegoat. How hard would it be for a clever killer to pin it on a mentally unbalanced wild card? It was almost too neat. Likely on one hand, but not on the other.

Steve Mathias, another wild card, was a more probable bet. He made no secret of his dislike of Brent, Brent's success with the ladies, and life in general. Jealousy can be a powerful potion, and when it festers over several years, it only grows murkier and more fetid. What better way to sap your rival than to obliterate his love? Plus, if you stripped down his background, Steve was basically a drifter. If he was such a great and respected trainer, he wouldn't be living in a ramshackle ranch house on the edge of the farm. He also wouldn't normally have a stack of empty gas cans as lawn ornaments.

His ramblings about Bayou Folly also disturbed me. What, if anything, did this horse's death have to do with my problems? It certainly was eating away at Steve, and heaven knew, Dr. Gerald got antsy when I talked about it. I rolled over and resumed my study of the ceiling.

Of course—the swampy Dr. Gerald. He had access to the farm and appeared to have free reign over the King household. When you got down to it, the level of care he provided the horses certainly affected the Kings' bottom line. But why would he care about Brent or his fiancée? He had made his share of snide comments about Brent, but was that enough to push a button to murder someone?

And I couldn't ignore that our murderer had a gun, and where did I find a gun? With Zach Tanner—or whoever he was. What was up with that? Why would someone lie about his identity to come on this trip, unless he was connected with Brent or Paige? Brent didn't act as if he knew our mysterious photographer, but then, as Adam had pointed out, most of us were faking relationships of one sort or another at the time. Were they really connected some way? Could Zach be quite literally the "hired gun"?

Ridiculous, Kate, I thought, *you must have fried some brain cells, along with everything else, in that steam room.*

For that matter, if I was willing to make Zach some kind of mob hit man, I ought to go ahead and make poor Willard my killer. I smiled—that was it—Willard tried to cook me like a goose!

But ultimately, Brent's behavior puzzled me the most. Was the dumb-model deal an act? Adam admitted that he hadn't kept in touch; maybe Brent knew exactly what he was doing and wasn't poor, dim-witted Brent. After all, he was smart enough to capitalize on his looks. He commanded adoration almost everywhere he went—except within his family—and he parlayed his innocent fumbles into the image of a charming, likable goof.

Maybe the weekend party was part of some elaborate plan to get rid of Paige yet appear the innocent bystander. But why go to the trouble to look up Adam after so many years? And why would he make it into such a spectacle? Unless, of course, he was also mentally unbalanced? He didn't seem manic-depressive, but maybe there was some delusional disorder I didn't know that would cause him to be a kind of modern-day Jekyll and Hyde.

I sat up and reached for the glass of water on the bedside table, thinking that I should have majored in psychology in college instead of journalism.

Knowing that my nap was never going to materialize, I got up and slid into my jeans. I felt much better and hated to admit that the influx of water appeared to do wonders.

I headed downstairs and found a note waiting for me instead of Adam and

Brent. They had made a quick trip to the house to bring back some lunch, the note said, and I shouldn't go anywhere.

I crumpled the paper and went into the kitchen to find us some plates and glasses. Like a good girl, I downed another glass of water. My headache barely stretched across my forehead, and I still felt a little feverish, but for the most part, I felt normal. I was alive, at least. That cheered me, so I filled the glass with more water and toasted the dish cabinet.

"Oh, excuse me, Kate, I'm sorry. Here I am again."

I dropped the glass in the sink with a clang and spun around to see Steve breaking into the cottage once more.

He tugged at the corners of his jacket. "I didn't mean to startle you. I, uh, heard what happened and was just checking up on how you were doing."

I ran my hand through my hair. "How did you hear? Who told you?"

"Word travels. Look, I know we don't have the best relationship going, but I think you ought to be careful if you're going to stick around. I, uh, was out of line earlier, but I thought you should know things. Whether you want to believe it or not, this family is bad news. I think you should get out while you can."

I eyed the distance between us. "That seems to be the general consensus."

He looked around the room and turned as if to leave. "Well, pay attention to it, then."

"Tell me again why you think Bayou Folly was killed."

Steve hesitated. "Never mind about that. It's not your concern. Forget we discussed it."

He reached in his jacket, and I steeled myself for him to yank out a gun. Instead, he pulled out a yellowed, folded newspaper.

Clutching it in his hand, he tapped it a couple times on the counter, then let it fall open on the countertop. "Make your own choice about Brent, but at least know what you're getting into." He brushed his hand across the paper. "Here, meet *my* bride-to-be." His eyes were cold again, and he bit his lip. He patted the paper a final time and abruptly stalked outside.

I ran to the window and watched him plunging through the grove on his horse. Confused, I returned to the kitchen and picked up the paper. It was dated seven years earlier, but what drew my eye was a black-and-white picture of Brent next to a photograph of a pretty blonde woman astride a horse.

The headline was to the point and sent a chill down my spine: HORSE FARM HEIR IMPLICATED IN LEXINGTON GIRL'S MURDER.

CHAPTER · 19

I'D ALWAYS BEEN A SUCKER for a good story. Without a doubt, the seven-year-old headline certainly roused my interest. I picked up the paper and leaned against the sink, drinking in the words penned by some anonymous staff writer at the *Lexington Herald-Leader*.

The body of Ashley Hannah, age 25, was found in a burning shed on the Bluegrass Winds property the morning of April 3. The cause of death was not the fire, but blunt trauma to the head and chest.

Something in *my* head and chest burned as I read the account. I dropped the paper to my side. Here was another person who just "happened" to die in a fire at Bluegrass Winds. The trend rested uneasy on my mind, while visions of burning cottages and boiling steam rooms flickered through my brain. I certainly didn't want to become the next statistic.

I nervously glanced into the living room. Satisfied I was alone, I resumed reading. Ashley Hannah was described as a champion child equestrian and Lexington native, who was an employee at Bluegrass Winds—a rider and groom for the Kings' "award-winning Thoroughbreds." The fire, at the little-used shed in the "deeper recesses of the farm," was discovered by the deceased's fiancé, trainer Steve Mathias. Police questioned him, but their investigation turned when pictures and rumors of a relationship with Brent King surfaced.

The paper deviated from the traditional AP style and sank into a gossipy section detailing an encounter between Ashley, Steve, and Brent on the night of the murder. Well-heeled "friends" with names like Winkie Rudolph and Bernard Riddlesworth offered eager, dirty quotes about Brent and his "girl groom" going at it behind the stables during races at Keeneland, and how they thought Brent should stay within his "usual realm" of date companions.

I sniffed at the snobby assumptions and discovered the real meat of the story through the next account, from Bobby Joe Harlson, the owner of Lexington's Tequila Sunrise bar. The story described a "very public brawl" between Brent and Steve the night of the murder, resulting in the "intoxicated trio" of Brent, Steve, and Ashley being thrown out before police arrived. Harlson was quoted as saying, "It was just a couple of kids fighting over a girl. It happens all the time here, but when they start breaking stuff and trashing the place, that's when I throw them out on their butts, regardless of who they are."

Once the police discovered this turn of events, not to mention the fact that forensic tests showed "evidence of a recent sexual relationship," Brent was hauled in to the LPD for questioning. I could only imagine how eloquent he must have been under the glare of the police interrogation. Whatever he said, he ended up behind bars under suspicion of first-degree murder.

That was where the story ended. I flipped through the rest of the section, looking for sidebar stories, but came up empty. I couldn't believe that no one had bothered to mention this minor ruffle in Brent's past. Of course, many of Steve's ramblings now made sense, but why hadn't he just told me the whole nasty story up front?

Voices accompanied the sound of the front door scraping open, so I shoved the paper in a drawer near the sink and met the jailbird and Adam in the living room. Brent carried a plate covered in foil, and Adam held a bag of potato chips. Detective Rami slipped through the door a second later, hauling a couple of two-liters of Coke and a bag of ice.

"A picnic indoors," I observed and nodded to the coffee table by the couch. "Why don't you guys unpack over there, while Detective Rami and I fix the drinks in the kitchen?"

Brent laid the plate on the table and immediately unwrapped the foil to reveal cold chicken. "While you're at it, Kate, bring some plates."

What am I, your wife? rose to my lips but hung there silently. Instead, I crooked my finger at Rami and turned for the kitchen.

"You look rested, Kate," Adam noted. "Feeling better?"

"Just peachy." Rested was the last thing I was, but why belabor a point?

Rami followed me into the kitchen. "You do look better," he observed. "I'm glad you got some sleep. I took another look around the steam room but came up empty. Unfortunately, it doesn't take much to lock a door and turn up a thermostat."

I broke open the bag of ice. "Well, sorry my attacker didn't leave a trail of evidence. What about the note?"

Fizzy foam shot out the top of a Coke bottle as Rami twisted it open. "What note? I didn't see any kind of a note down there."

"I hadn't thought of it either, until just now," I admitted. "I found it by the door right before I passed out. It was a bad play on the old 'stay out of the kitchen' saying. I don't know what happened to it."

Rami was not pleased, evident in the way he threw ice cubes into the glasses I'd retrieved from a cabinet.

I opened the side drawer and pulled out the newspaper. "In the big scheme of things, I don't think the note matters much. However, I'd like to know what you think of this."

I handed the newspaper to Rami, and as he scanned the story, I said, "While I was supposed to be under Brent and Adam's watch, Steve Mathias broke into the cottage and dropped this off. He told me to meet his bride-to-be."

Rami nodded and returned the paper. "Yeah. That was big stuff at the time."

"You knew about this? And you never bothered to mention it?" I struggled to keep my voice low. "Don't you think I deserved to know this bit of history? Is this why you don't want me to say anything to Brent?"

He held his finger to his lips and glanced toward the living room. "Kate, I'm aware of the story, yes, but I don't think you need to worry about it. It's ancient history."

"You're setting me up? Unbelievable! You've known it all this time and watched me get into all this trouble? What kind of detective are you?"

Rami frowned. "Kate, calm down. I'm trying to figure out many things on this farm, not the least of which is who is after you. Brent is *here*, isn't he? He's not serving twenty-to-life, so what does that tell you?"

I reached for a stack of plates and tried to ignore my shaking hand. "It tells me he has a hell of a lot of opportunity, albeit a screwy motive. Look, all I have here is a story with a pretty good inkling that Brent violently killed someone. You wanna tell me how it turned out?"

"Hurry up in there, we're thirsty," hollered Brent from the living room.

Rami and I stared at each other.

"We'll be there in a second," Rami yelled back. "We have to rinse some of the plates. Hold your horses."

He moved closer to me, his voice low. "Brent got off. Charges were never formally brought. That's what happens when you're a rich, white, good-looking horse-farm heir in Lexington. He spent a night in a holding cell, managed to get a mug shot that looked like a Benetton ad. While the paper was scrambling to get that story out, the LPD was scrambling to bring him before a judge." He glanced toward the door. "But it's amazing what a big firm of lawyers can accomplish in the wee hours of the morning. Or should I say the law clerks, working overnight. I doubt very seriously the Wellington, Todd and Conleys of the world lost any sleep after the initial frantic phone call from Douglas King. I'm sure they promptly put their clerks to work pulling every string possible to get him out of jail."

Rami screwed the top on the Coke bottle so tight, I didn't think we'd ever drink another drop. "Forgive me if I sound bitter," he went on, "but all too often I see lawyers who think their job is a game—a way to get their client off without regard to justice. Do not pass go, do not go directly to jail, but by all means, collect $200."

"What are you saying? Did Brent kill her?"

He shrugged. "Let's just say the killer was never found—or should I say, convicted. The case is still open. We don't usually like to admit that, unless reporters start sniffing around."

"Duly noted by this reporter. You're taking this personally. Were you involved in the investigation?"

He shook his head. "No, that was before my time. I was walking the beat, barely out of the police academy. Just how old do you think I am?"

He smiled and balanced a couple of glasses on a cutting board masquerading as a tray. He obviously thought the conversation was over, but I reached for his sleeve and almost sent the glasses tumbling to the floor.

"Well, I'm thinking this is an awfully similar situation," I argued. "Do you suspect Brent again? Or is it Steve you're looking at—as some form of revenge? It would make sense to get back a bride for a bride." My momentum was building again. "And have you noticed the gas cans beside Steve's porch? And he keeps showing up around me."

Rami stopped me. "Kate, I suspect *everyone*. I know you're frustrated. And yes, the bride-for-a-bride theory makes sense."

"So you're saying that you've positively ID'd the body as Paige, right? You've known all of this; it makes sense now. When are you planning on telling Brent?"

"No, Kate, I never said that. We have a female who fits the right profile, yes, but I've never glued a name on the victim. You've done that."

"What does that mean?"

Rami pushed the door open with his shoulder. "Take it any way you want. Let's eat lunch."

Why wouldn't he admit the body was Paige? I joined the boys on the floor and dove into chicken, chips, and a refreshing blast of caffeine-filled, sugar-infested Coke. Our meal, even though it was late afternoon, was terribly mundane—not at all what I expected from a country estate. Where was the delicate china the thinness of rose petals, and tea and crumpets, and all that mess? I wiped chicken crud off my diamond with a cheap paper napkin. I'd always wondered what crumpets were—I thought for sure I'd learn this weekend.

I didn't learn much of anything during lunch. Rami kept an eye on me and steered the conversation to the weather and University of Kentucky basketball. The former was freezing cold and the latter was expected to be red hot. Something in the male chromosome section took hold, and Brent, Rami, and Adam chatted like old college roommates. I mostly crunched more potato chips than my arteries should allow.

We were cleaning up the gnawed chicken bones when Zach appeared in the doorway, bearing his huge bag of camera gear.

"There you are," he grumbled, half friendly, half perturbed. "I couldn't get anyone at the house to tell me where everyone was. You guys partying without me? That's not fair." Dropping his bag on the floor, he snatched the chips from Adam's hands and shoved a handful into his mouth. "I thought we'd shoot the happy couple now. It's getting late. You've got an article to write; I've got a bride and groom to photograph. Come on, folks, the camera calls."

One half of the happy couple looked at the other half. Brent flipped his eyebrows and turned to Zach. "Look, maybe now isn't the best time. We're not exactly ready for a full-fledged shoot. Just snap away later, at the party."

Zach's cheeks turned red. "I'm here to work. I'm not here for my health—I'm being paid to do a job. Now, are we gonna do this or not?"

Oh, yeah. He was here for some reason, but for what, I couldn't decide. I'd like to see Alice pay him in this lifetime, now that she knew he was an impostor. I wanted to know why there was a gun under his bed. And I needed it known that I didn't want my picture taken.

"Brent's right," I agreed. "Just shoot us later at the party, all gussied up. I'm hardly dressed for a photo."

Besides, he knew we weren't really engaged, so what was the big hurry? I wasn't a betting woman, but the odds were pretty good that this story would never hit print. Meaning, of course, that there was no need for glamorous (or otherwise) pictures.

Zach would have none of it. "Sure, you're dressed. All you need is a little lipstick, and you're good to go. I like your messy hair and the big, sloppy shirt. It's the natural look, very chic, very now. All the great heiresses are slumming it these days. Power to the people. All that good stuff to make the readers think the rich folks have the same boring lives we all do."

That was the most polite way anyone has ever told me I looked awful. But, hey, most heiresses weren't running for their lives all day either. Besides, I wasn't really an heiress, and he knew that. Big shirt and messy hair. I started to suggest a pair of garden shears and a Bic razor for Zach's dead-straw coif and mangy beard.

Instead, I stomped upstairs to brush my hair and glop on makeup, while Zach took solo pictures of Brent. Our studious photographer, after awakening from his nap, apparently had selected a spot near the house to shoot us. As I slathered on eye shadow and blush, I wrinkled my nose at the mirror. Since the gun was now missing, I certainly hoped the only thing he planned to shoot us with was a camera.

The way Brent could saunter under the eye of the lens without as much as a dust of powder was disturbing, but he did it for a living and didn't need cosmetic help like the rest of us mere mortals. I thought about changing clothes, but I was too comfortable in my fashion statement "sloppy" shirt and jeans.

Despite the afternoon sun and only a few scattered clouds, Zach had rigged three light stands around a pair of trees, just to the left of the house. Sheets of what looked like tissue paper were clipped over the lights, and Adam held a big, flexible circle of reflective foil at Brent's side as Zach snapped photos. Detective Rami had disappeared.

I watched as Brent fell naturally in step with the camera. He leaned casually against a tree, his head cocked seductively, jaw firm, eyes brooding and sexy. The camera was a tonic for Brent, who seamlessly morphed into a practiced model whose relationship with the camera bordered on erotic.

I wasn't a picture person. Once a camera lens turned my direction, I adopted a frozen smile that was about as natural as a Hell's Angel biker singing lead at the Metropolitan Opera. Occasionally, if I was having a great time or I wasn't fully aware of the camera's lens, my picture would turn out halfway decent. However, I was afraid my picture wouldn't pass muster for the side of a milk carton after this photo session.

Brent spotted me and held out his arms. "There you are. Come on over here and be my bride." He winked as if we were sharing some naughty little secret.

I reluctantly joined him under the tree, and he immediately yanked off my coat.

"What are you doing? It's freezing out here!"

He looked surprised. "No one knows that. You can't wear that bulky coat. Just smile and pretend it's 70 degrees and sunny. It's all part of the job. Get used to it."

I looked to Zach for help, but he nodded. "No coat. Snuggle up to Brent if you want to get warm."

Before I could complain again, Brent draped his arms over my shoulders and pulled me against him. He bent his head next to mine and grinned. "Smile, Kate, this is our engagement photo."

Buzz, buzz. Whir, whir. Just how many shots could those fancy cameras do in a couple of seconds?

Brent spun me around like a tiddlywink and posed us in various states of attraction for several minutes while Zach snapped away. I tried to pretend I was a supermodel, making millions with each click of the shutter, but that didn't diminish the jangled thoughts in my head. A vivid image of John flashed before my eyes when Brent suddenly ran his hands through my hair and cupped my chin into his hands. He dropped his face just a hair from mine and froze. His breath brushed over my nose, but we never locked lips.

After several frames and zero passion, Brent dropped his hands. "There's the money shot. That one always draws a reader. The 'almost kiss'—it's a classic. You fill in your own fantasy before the lips ever touch." He smiled broadly. "This is fun stuff, huh, Kate?"

Oh yeah. Great fun. I was freezing. I was staring at a possible murderer. I wasn't an heiress, and I certainly wasn't a fashion model. And someone wanted me dead. I could think of many more fun ways to spend an afternoon. I looked to Adam for help.

He put the foil reflector down. "How about some shots of Kate by herself? Surely you've got enough couple poses."

Zach shrugged at Adam's unsolicited advice. "Whatever. Brent, step aside."

This was not the help I had in mind. Now I was truly on the spot. Solo portraits of me. Egad.

Zach reached for my arm. "Sit in the grass here. Bend your leg up and lean on your knee." The ground was cold and hard. Eminently comfortable. He crossed my arms around the front of my leg and looked me in the eye. "Having fun yet?"

"This isn't necessary and you know it," I clipped. "Why the sudden urge to take all these pictures?"

He shrugged. "Maybe I'm making a collection for my scrapbook. This is more interesting than any vacation I've been on recently."

While Zach fiddled with lenses, Adam joined us and asked him, "Just where do you usually work?"

Good question.

Zach shot a look between Adam and me and replied, "Here, there, wherever the money takes me. I do well—lots of D.C. stuff and a couple of times a year in New York. Depends where my clients want me. My office is my car."

"So you do a lot of fashion shoots?" I prodded.

He held the camera to his face. "I shoot lots of things. Now, smile."

I tried smiling, but what a waste of time. It slid right off my face. "Have you ever worked with Brent in New York?"

Brent turned around and looked at me, and Zach dropped the camera to his side and said, "Kate I'm trying to get some work done here, and I can't do it if you keep talking." He glanced at Brent. "Models don't pay any attention to photographers, even though, if it wasn't for us, they'd be nowhere."

Brent's face hardened, but he kept quiet.

Zach stared at him. "He wouldn't remember it if we'd met."

There was definitely some kind of electricity between Brent and Zach—and not the kind that warms you on a cold night. More like the kind that you're warned to avoid during storms and around downed power lines.

"Brent, you'd remember Zach, wouldn't you?" I asked.

"There are lots of photogs I work with, and most of the time, our shoots are very hectic."

Zach snapped a couple of pictures, then reached for my knee. "Will you please cooperate, Kate? Sit Indian-style now, and lean back. It's time for that come-hither look." He messed with my hair. "See? What did I tell you? No respect from the talent, none at all." He shook his head and continued shooting.

Now that the lens was on me, Brent had lost interest in the photos. He slumped against the tree and bundled up in a thick coat. Meanwhile, I slowly froze to death.

Another layer of chill draped the air moments later when Meg trotted by on horseback. She dismounted. "What's all this?"

Brotherly love kicked in. "Do you need glasses?"

Her face tightened as if she'd just opened a carton of cottage cheese covered in fuzzy green mold. She slid her gaze down her narrow nose at me. "Are you trying not to make the social pages on purpose? What an interesting look. Brent, not that I'm ever sure what you're thinking, but I can tell you how Mother will react to pictures like this."

He jumped to his feet and zipped his coat. "You're just jealous because you'll never make Miss Lilly's column."

I didn't know who Miss Lilly was, but I had a hunch she wouldn't find the siblings' trench warfare suitably upper-crusty either.

Meg seethed. "I appear where it counts—on the sports pages, with our winners. I don't have a juvenile need to fill my ego with pointless parties and contrived romances."

Brent rolled his shoulders. "Yeah, well, that's where you belong, with all the jocks and animals."

Brent and Meg snorted back and forth at each other like a couple of six-year-olds and never noticed Zach snapping photo after photo. Meanwhile, my mind focused on her comment about contrived romances.

I stood, grabbed my coat, and dared to join the sniping duo. Just to add fuel to the fire, I slipped my arm through Brent's. "Excuse me, Meg, but what do you mean by contrived romances?"

From her expression, you would have thought I'd slapped her. "You just don't get it, do you? You're not the first, and you won't be the last." She tugged on the bridle and stalked away, but not before her horse left a testament in support of his mistress. A very smelly pile of testaments, in fact.

Meg glanced at the little fertilizer gift and actually smiled, before mounting the horse and galloping away in a cloud of dust and dead grass.

I couldn't think of a better incentive to end our photo session, but we had to contend with one more distraction. As Meg departed in one direction, a golf cart driven by an ancient blue-haired maid bumped up to our group from the opposite side. She was hell on wheels, with all 15 m.p.h. of the engine puttering at full tilt. She gingerly alighted from the cart after a grinding pull on the brake, then marched up to me and handed over a cell phone.

"Miss Kate?" she said, her blue hair matching her blue, veiny fingers. "You've had several calls from a Miss Alice Donard. We've tried to take messages, but she's quite insistent. This last time, she said it was urgent and I must find you at all costs." She shyly handed me the phone.

I glanced at the others. I trusted Alice with my life and knew she meant business when she stooped to harassing a little old lady into risking pneumonia for the sake of a phone call.

"This will only take a second." I immediately dialed Alice's number, even though I knew we probably needed privacy. Two rings later, she answered.

"Hey, it's me," was all I managed.

"First off," she commanded, "don't ever hang up on me again—especially when there's a noise like that in the background and your butt is in a sling to start."

I winced. In my mind's eye, I could see the cigarette swinging wildly around the room as she paced the floor. "Sorry," I said sheepishly, "but I had to go. It turned out to be nothing."

"How was I supposed to know that?" Alice boomed. "I had all kinds of visions of pieces of you flying all over the place. It was not pretty, believe me."

No kidding. I took a few steps away from Brent and Zach. "Look, there's more to tell you, but I can't talk right now. I'm sort of having my photo made."

"Well, la-di-da. Don't forget, your damn photographer isn't even legit. You need to talk to me instead. This is more important."

Zach, Brent, and Adam all managed a superior staring contest in my direction. I turned my back to them and scooted around the tree trunk. "Look, can't this wait a few minutes?"

Alice exhaled, and I blinked away the imagined smoke spewing from the receiver. She spoke quickly. "No, it can't. You stand there, doing whatever it is you're doing, and you listen to me and smile real pretty at everyone looking at you. Are you doing that?"

I bent around the trunk and obediently shot the guys a smile. "Done. Talk."

"Okay," Alice said. "I called Robbie back and nosed around some more. I also did a clip search and found this article about Brent and a woman named Ashley Hannah. He was arrested for her murder, Kate. The—"

"Yeah, I'm a step ahead of you," I interrupted. "I just found out about that. I don't know what to think, but others know. It's apparently no big deal."

"Others? Like who? The police?" she asked.

Brent came around the tree. "Kate, we need to wrap this up. Can't you call her later?"

I nodded and made noises into the phone. "Mmm-hmm. Yeah. That's right. Thanks, appreciate it."

Alice sighed. "Okay, obviously you can't talk right now."

"Mmmm-hmmm." Deadly eloquence. That was me.

Brent locked eyes with me and waited.

"Like I said," Alice continued, "I called my friend Robbie and asked very pointed questions. He called me back and gave me quite a story. That horse farm you're on is in serious trouble. It's not the cash cow it was in the '90s. Very few winners and even fewer dollars coming in from stud fees. What income that's there heads directly to pay off the debt column. That farm is drying up faster than the two-minute Kentucky Derby. Robbie said Bayou Folly was one of its last hopes. But now the horse is nothing more than a bottle of Elmer's glue on the shelf at the corner drugstore."

Brent's hand wrapped around mine and tugged at the phone as Alice added, "Bag this fiancé and story, Kate. You'll be lucky if they pay your plane ticket home. At this rate, Brent won't inherit a rusty horseshoe, and all you'll inherit is grief."

C H A P T E R · 2 0

"SAY GOOD-BYE."

I sure hoped Brent meant say good-bye to Alice and not adios to my life. So I was a sensitive soul. A girl could get that way. A bad part of me glanced down at his other hand, just to make sure there wasn't a gun involved in his order.

He dislodged the phone from my hand and clicked off the call. Great, Alice would just love being disconnected a second time. I'd be safer on the farm now than I would be going home to a furious friend.

"That was very rude. We weren't finished talking yet."

Brent slipped the phone into his pocket and started to walk away. "I decided you were finished. Now come on, let's get this done so we can go back to the house."

I was a Southern girl, but not a pushover. I didn't take kindly to receiving ultimatums like that. As the song said, "I am woman, hear me roar." And I did.

"Don't order me around, Brent. Your explanations tonight will be on your own. Adam and I are leaving."

He spun around and grabbed my shoulder. "No, you're staying right here. You can't leave now. Everything is in place and has to go as planned."

In my estimation, nothing had gone as planned, including the next thing that slid out of my mouth. "Did you grab Ashley Hannah this way, too?"

Brent's eyes overtook his face in a bloodless coup. His hand fell from my shoulder, and he stumbled back a few steps. His words fell just as awkwardly. "You just said . . . what?"

Well, that sealed it. The honeymoon was over before it began.

"I know about Ashley, Brent."

Adam moved closer, and Zach stopped digging in his camera bag. "Who's Ashley?" Adam asked.

"No one," Brent snapped. "It's not important."

"It was important when they found her murdered on the farm, wasn't it?"

Brent looked ill. His face was a floured cake pan, and his lips moved in odd, jerky motions. "That was a long time ago. I don't want to talk about it."

Zach tried again where Adam failed. "Who's Ashley?"

I answered, "You want to tell them, Brent, or should I?"

He went for the abridged version. "She was a friend—a farm employee—who died here. A long time ago."

I'd had enough. "She was a lot more than a friend to you, Brent. Don't forget to tell them about the way she died and how you wound up behind bars for her murder."

I sure knew how to charm my beloved. No wonder I was still single. I might not keep my man, but my little outburst grabbed the attention of Zach and Adam. They showed me all kinds of interest. Plenty, in fact, as if I'd just announced where to find a million dollars.

Brent stared at me. "That was a mistake, Kate. Get your facts straight. I had nothing—*nothing*—to do with Ashley's death. Why don't you talk to Mathias about this, if you want to throw around old theories? I'm sure he'd like nothing more than to pin it on me." His eyes narrowed. "I thought you were a friend, Kate. Why are doing this?"

Adam moved between us protectively. "We're all friends here, Brent. It's just been a rough couple of days. You can't deny that."

Zach busied himself taking down the lights, since it was pretty obvious the romance was gone from the photo shoot. Still, he managed to stick close enough to catch the conversation without missing a beat. What was that old saying about curiosity and the cat?

"I thought I could trust you, Kate," Brent said.

"It's hard to trust anyone at this juncture, don't you think?" I replied. "I think it's time we all stopped pretending. There's no need to take these pictures, there's no need to hide my identity." I caught Zach's eyes. "Or anyone else's identity, for that matter."

Zach's face was as blank as the white sheet that filtered his light. He looked impassively at me and resumed packing his equipment. Not a twitch, a blink, a frown, or anything that said, *Oh, no, I'm caught*. Adam's disappointed face told me Zach's lack of concern gave him the same indigestion I had.

Zach zipped his bag and pulled up his hood. "Don't stress him out, Kate.

Models don't take pressure well. You wouldn't want him to walk out on this and disrupt everyone. Doesn't matter whether it's a private matter or a New York shoot, it's bad news for everyone when the talent balks."

Brent's face glowed. "The thing in New York was diff—" He stopped abruptly and stared at Zach. His eyes narrowed to slits, and his jaw clicked like there was a timepiece under his gums. "You're full of shit. And you're fired. I'm calling the shots this time."

Adam jumped into the fray. "You can't fire him, Brent, but if he goes, we go."

Bravo, Adam. The chorus from that old '80s ditty "Should I Stay or Should I Go" had played frantically in my mind all day, and I was back on the swing of wanting to stay. After all, now we had Zach's broad hint that he and Brent shared more than a love for the camera—even if it was for different reasons. The incident in New York was a fresh lead, but to what destination?

I tried Adam and Zach's earlier attempt at information-gathering. "What happened in New York?"

Unfortunately, I was now on the receiving end and was brushed off just as rudely.

"Nothing happened," Brent clipped. "He doesn't know what he's talking about." As he had successfully done so many times before, Brent decided to solve his problem by disappearing. He leaned toward Zach in a menacing enough manner that Zach backed up, then Brent jerked away and stomped toward the house.

His triumphant exit was blocked by Detective Knight, who plowed through the front door and met him on the porch steps. "You seem to be in a hurry," she observed.

Brent flipped up the hood on his jacket. "You could say that." Instead of going up the steps, he turned and headed around the side of the house.

We'd lost Zach's interest, as well. He took Brent's lead and hauled his gear in Brent's direction. "Gonna shoot some of the party setup and stuff."

Knight watched their departures with a raised eyebrow. "Hope they're not leaving the scene of a crime."

"Be careful what you wish for," Adam mumbled.

That got her full attention. "Oh? Anything I should know?"

When we didn't respond, she nodded my way. "I hear you've had quite a day. You holding up okay?"

"More or less," I sighed. "But at the moment, less."

She grinned. "Well, that's what you get for playing detective without a license. I'm not much on having extra help, but Detective Rami says you and he have an arrangement that I'll have to live with for a while."

Whatever. He could have the arrangement for all I cared.

She ran her hand through her long, rusty curls. "Save your energy, Kate. From what I've seen going on inside there, you're in for quite a shindig tonight. Too bad it's not legit. I wouldn't mind someone throwing me a party like that."

Oh, brother, the party. I squinted at the hazy sky, in a futile throwback to Girl Scout days, and tried to place the sun's position, but my kemosabe clock was definitely rusty. There was not a globe of fire anywhere in sight. Instead, all I saw was a flat, gray-white sheet of clouds, with a flicker of light embedded somewhere in its folds. So much for telling time the old-fashioned way. I knew it was afternoon, which was bad enough, because that meant the night wasn't that far behind.

The longer I could avoid the party, the better off I'd be. "I'm not much in the party mood right now," I said. "Other things interest me instead. For instance, what do you know about the horse business?"

"Well, about as much as any Kentuckian, I guess. I go to the track a few times a year, am impressed with the beauty of the horses, and I lose a lot of money. I invite out-of-town friends and then spend the day pretending I know what I'm doing, when what I'm really doing is betting on the color of the jockey's silks because it matches the paint in my bathroom. Why do you ask?"

At least she was honest. I liked Detective Knight. Too bad we weren't working together on a more pleasant matter, where we could meet for a beer on a Friday night and grouse about men, work, why we still have panty hose, and why there are still "Partridge Family" reruns on TV. Adam seemed to be enchanted with her, too, though his reasons were probably more hormonal than mine were.

I would have answered her question, but we were interrupted by a loud scuffle coming from the backyard. Our trio investigated, and we discovered Brent and Steve ripping each other to shreds, in a pretty fair imitation of a middleweight bout. Knight jumped in between them and yanked the two apart. She shoved Brent against the house with one hand and clutched Steve's collar with her other.

Tooling down a Madison Avenue runway apparently didn't match the brawn used in breaking in horses and hauling hay around barns. Brent nursed a drip of blood oozing out of his right nostril, and Steve, his face on fire and sweaty, fluffed his shoulders several times like a rooster strutting his stuff around the barnyard.

Steve looked at me. "Didn't anything I told you matter, Kate?"

Brent answered for me. "It's all lies. Why don't you try the truth next time and see how your story turns out?"

"Hey, both of you—zip it," Detective Knight ordered.

Steve ignored her and yanked out of her grip. He pointed an accusing finger at Brent. "My fiancée is dead because of you. I thought your fiancée should know that."

Brent lunged for Steve again, but this time Knight ran interference. "I told you to break it up," she yelled. "Now, go to your corners, boys, wherever that is, but make it away from here. I don't want to see the two of you together the rest of the night. And if I do, it'll be because you're both cuffed and in the backseat of my car. Understand?"

Not a lot to argue with there.

"Do you understand?" Knight shouted.

Steve backed away first. "Don't say you haven't been warned—all of you. History is just repeating itself. You'll be sorry—especially you, Kate. Just watch."

Knight issued her own demand. "You watch the threats."

Steve ignored her and stalked off toward the tree line.

Knight turned to Brent. "Mr. King?"

He stared at us, then brushed past us as if he were a naughty little boy being sent to his room. He strode around the far side of the house, through the backyard, and in the general direction of the cottage.

Knight's friendly attitude left with them. "What was he talking about? What did he warn you about before?"

I didn't have time to answer this question, thanks to a *pop, pop, pop* that whizzed past us. It took a split second to determine the origin of the sound, but we had a little help when the pops turned into whumps, and bullets splintered the side of the house. Adam and I dove to the ground and rolled into a prickly bush.

Detective Knight didn't make it that far. She crouched, her face scanning the backyard. She whipped out her gun and aimed into the open yard, firing off a few shots of her own. She took off running into the yard, but not before ordering us to stay down.

No problem there. Adam and I crawled as far into the bush as we could without scratching ourselves to death.

"This is ridiculous, just insane," Adam hissed. "Do you hear anything? I think they stopped shooting."

I looked at my older and wiser cousin. "You go first."

The Kings' family-affection affliction had rubbed off on Adam. "Uh-uh. They were shooting at you. You go first. I'm an innocent bystander."

So there we sat.

"Is this like when we were kids?" Adam asked.

I looked at him and nearly had my eye poked out by an errant branch. "I don't recall growing up in a war zone and being shot at daily."

"No, no. I mean playing hide-and-seek. And, Kate, I wouldn't exactly call this a war zone."

"Are we having this conversation?" I asked. "Or am I just in some kind of delirium from being shot at? Is that what it is?"

My answer was another round going off in the distance.

We scrunched as close to the ground as we could, and Adam wrapped his arms around me and said, "I don't like this."

"Me neither," I mumbled into his jacket.

The silence that followed, in reality, lasted only a few seconds, but it was like waiting for those last minutes to tick off the classroom clock on the final day of school. An eternity. A lifetime. The worst human punishment, short of declaring chocolate a poison.

Knight's voice rattled on the air in broken, indecipherable chunks. Finally, the wind carried it clearly to our bush. "Kate. Over here. It's safe."

Adam and I waited for one more call from her until we convinced ourselves that it was worth crawling out from our bushy haven. Adam pulled me out, and we took turns dusting each other off while casting wary glances all around. We found the detective near a bunch of trees.

She was not alone. Her gun was aimed squarely at her subject. His hands were up in the air. Another gun lay in the grass at his feet. I was not so much concerned with the gun in the grass as I was with the alleged perp's face.

"Holy shit," Adam breathed.

I couldn't move. "Holy shit with sprinkles on it."

My darling Dr. John Donovan shrugged his shoulders, his hands still held high in the air. "Hi, sweetie. How's it going?"

CHAPTER · 21

TO SPARE THE GORY DETAILS of the ensuing few minutes, which were surreal at best, suffice it to say that we combined the best of all the old game shows, including "I've Got a Secret," "Jeopardy," "Family Feud," and "What's My Line?" in the most elaborate "He said, she said" tourney around. I was amazed that Detective Knight didn't shoot us on sight.

At least, after much discussion, she put her gun down.

Despite the way things looked, the gun did not belong to John. He insisted that he'd arrived at Bluegrass Winds in a rush and, faced with the enormity of the farm, wasn't sure how to find me. According to John, he was getting a bird's-eye view of the house when he heard the gunshots and spotted a person in a hooded, bulky coat running into the woods.

"Male or female?" Knight snapped.

John's face colored. "I'm not sure. I only saw the person's back, and the coat was pretty androgynous. Besides, I wasn't sure what was going on, so I wasn't looking for anything or anyone—except Kate."

Not a winning answer in any of our eyes, but it was nice to hear that he still cared where I was.

He had no reason to follow the person, but his curiosity sent him in the direction of the elusive runner. That led him to his present spot, gun in hand.

"Do you have a habit of picking up guns like that?" Knight asked.

"Not particularly," John answered. "I figured this wasn't something normally lying here, and given what I've heard about Kate lately. . . ." As his voice trailed off, concerned but accusing brown eyes landed on me.

I was at once heartened to see him, yet deeply curious how he found me and just what he'd heard about my recent exploits. The uncomfortable part was that if Alice was his mole, he hadn't heard the half of it. I didn't look forward to that conversation.

As if he were just shooting the breeze, Adam asked, "So, what brings you here, John?"

"I'm taking Kate home."

He caught both looks from the female contingent, and while Detective Knight could deduct whatever she wanted, I brushed aside the comment. John Donovan was the last person I knew who'd stake a claim on "his woman." Yet, given the day I'd had, I was ready to whip my hair into a ponytail and let him drag his cavegirl wherever he chose.

John made a face. "I assume you know that Kate isn't really—"

"She knows," I interrupted.

"Good. Then, you don't need to pretend anymore. Come home with me."

Knight cleared her throat. "I'd like nothing more than for all of us to go home right now, but it's not possible." She retrieved the gun from the grass. "I have work to do. You folks need to get him hidden somewhere before this entire thing falls apart."

"Hidden?" John said. "I'm not hiding anywhere. I'm taking Kate home."

"Not right now," Knight replied. "Take him to the cottage and stay there. And be aware of your surroundings, all right?"

Knight noticed John's set jaw. "To the cottage. This isn't a joke."

Adam stepped up and waved his arm toward John. "Come on, John, I'll fill you in on stuff."

They took off in a reluctant walk, but Knight landed a hand on my arm. "Your priorities are really screwed up. I should call in an MIW on you."

I scratched my news-reporter memory for the acronym's match.

"Mental inquest warrant," she explained. "Seventy-two hours of forced reflection in a happy farm. If I had that guy in my bed, I sure wouldn't leave it for Brent King—regardless of his runway look and portfolio."

"You know better," I replied. "I think I'm the last person around here who should get hauled downtown for that. In fact, I could probably make a pretty good list, and my name wouldn't be anywhere near the top. I don't think there are enough beds in the ward for this family."

We exchanged a smile, and I asked, "Are you married, detective?"

Her smile dissolved and her freckles twitched. "Was—past tense. Tried it on for size, but it turned out to be a real bikini. You know what I mean?"

"Not really. Want to explain?"

"Nothing ever fit right, and all the parts you want hidden are out in the open. It was better left to someone who knew how to fill out the requirements properly in public. It just wasn't my style. And . . . there's something about a redhead hauling a gun and a badge around that tends to intimidate most men."

I grinned. "Can't imagine why."

She nodded toward John and Adam. "You better join them, Kate. I have a shooter in a generic hooded coat to find, and the sun is fading fast. Stay out of trouble."

I spotted them near the cottage porch. I wasn't sure how much Adam had told John, but the look I got upon arrival almost made me call for Knight.

Adam stepped off the porch. "Well, then. Three's a crowd, and you have a lot of catching up to do. I'm gonna head for the showers and force myself into the monkey suit before the party starts." He squeezed my elbow. "I'm outta here. Have fun with the storytelling."

John watched him walk away. "What's this place?"

"It's where you'll hide for a while until we can figure out what to do." I pulled him into the cottage, shut the door behind us, and grabbed his collar. I kissed him long and hard, like I meant it. And I certainly did.

"With that kind of greeting," he said, "I should have let you go another couple days."

I kept hold on his collar. "Watch the smart talk, or I'll do it again."

So I did.

I had a lock on his affections, but the rest of him was restless.

"Kate, Adam told me things."

"Things that upset you, I'm sure," I finished for him. "I really don't want to talk about it now, John. Just know I'm in one piece and glad you're speaking to me."

He looked around the room. "Thank Alice for that. She should win the friendship award for badgering me to death."

"Until you believed that I wasn't involved with Brent?"

His eyes caught mine. "Can you blame me for wondering? It all happened very quickly. He was there in your apartment, and you didn't exactly act innocent."

"I didn't act innocent because I was too busy worrying that you thought something was going on—as you obviously did."

I bit my lip to quell my urge to argue. *Don't screw this up, Kate.*

John had followed me to Kentucky, for goodness' sake. No one had ever done that for me before, and I was willing to blow it for a stupid argument?

I spoke quietly. "I'm sorry this got off to a bad start. Believe me, it hasn't improved. I assume, between Adam and Alice, you know what's going on around here?"

He wandered around the room, inspecting items on the tables, checking out the kitchenette, then gazing up the stairs. "I know enough to be worried, enough to wonder what the hell you're still doing here, and enough to know you need to come home with me—now."

"Wouldn't I love to?" I replied. "But your timing is off—I have to play the bride for Brent tonight." I immediately marked that down in the back of my mind under the section of what not to say to a boyfriend.

John made a wicked face. "Where *is* the groom, by the way?"

I studied the floor. "He's actually one of the hooded-jacket guys Detective Knight is on the prowl for."

"Oh, that's just great. That eases my mind, Kate." He shook his head. "You have no obligation to this family. But you've got an obligation to me."

I raised my eyebrows. "I do?"

"Yeah. I kind of want you around for a while, and I don't like someone trying to hunt you down. Come home with me, Kate."

He didn't realize how much I wanted that. "It's not that simple, John. Later, we'll talk for hours about what's happened, but I've got to do this tonight. I can't get this far and let it all fall apart. Yes, this family is weird. Yes, Brent scares me. And yes, someone doesn't want me around. But you know me, John. I can't let this go unsolved."

"Need I remind you what happened the last time you got involved with a murder investigation?" he pleaded.

That wasn't necessary. My memory was clear on that one. A lot of bad stuff happened, I was almost arrested several times, and I ended up in the hospital. But, for all the problems it caused, there was a pleasant outcome.

I grinned sweetly. "Yeah, I remember—I met you."

He sank onto the steps. "Kate, you're going to make me an old, old man." He sighed through to his toes. "All right, tell me the rest."

I slid beside him and gave him a quick update.

"I don't get it," John said as I finished. "Identification of the body should have been done and filed away a long time ago."

"The body was badly burned," I offered.

Doctor John disagreed. "Dental records. You think you know the person. Make a few phone calls. Collect a few faxes. Compare here, compare there. It's done. Why the holdup?"

A nagging thought surfaced. "Because it's not Paige's body?"

"Possibly." He shrugged. "But why all the secrecy? Tell everyone it's not her, move on to finding out who it is. And if it isn't her, why isn't she down here raising all kinds of hell about you?"

I nodded. "Good point."

He wasn't done yet. "But what if it *is* Paige? Where's her grieving family? Why aren't they here, looking for answers, pointing fingers?"

Good questions. Uncomfortable questions.

John was on a roll. "And what about Brent's mom? She sounds like a classic schizophrenic. What medication is she taking? Zyprexa? Risperdal?"

How should I know? My priority was avoiding Jane King, not rummaging around in her medicine cabinets. "Beats me."

"What I'm saying is," my good doctor continued, "if she doesn't take her antipsychotics regularly, the situation could go downhill pretty fast. It all depends on how severe her condition is. Now, I'm not labeling her a murderer, but if her medication isn't under control and she's in an advanced schizophrenic state, there's no telling what she might do." His voice grew excited. "You know, that could be it. It might allow for her confusion about you."

"You lost me," I said.

John leaned in to explain. "Say she killed Brent's real girlfriend and she's not on her medication. She's not in control; she's not thinking clearly."

I snorted. "Well, there's an understatement."

"No, I'm serious," he said. "In her mind, she thought she removed the obstacle, the threat to her perceived security—her control over Brent. But now she has to deal with you. She thought she eliminated the girlfriend, but here you are. You're perfectly innocent, but in her mind, she could hallucinate that you're another threat. Maybe she hears voices telling her that you're a threat that has to be destroyed.

"These voices are real, Kate," he continued. "A schizophrenic hears them all the time, over and over, bombarded with whispers, or screams. They constantly repeat commands, or insults, or orders. It's hard for most of us to comprehend. If her medication isn't controlled, she might not even realize she's stalking you. Is there a way to find out if she's taking her meds?"

I stood and leaned against the banister. "I don't know how we could do it without causing a ruckus. I know she's had something, because Brent called it a 'snack,' and everyone knew immediately what he meant."

"Okay, she had one pill that you know of, but is she taking it regularly? That's what we need to know."

"I don't know. I can't ask Brent or, especially, Mrs. King. What do you suggest?" I asked.

John stood. "How about a maid? They see everything. You could ask as a concerned daughter-in-law-to-be—pretend you're worried she'll forget with the excitement around this party."

I nodded. "That might work."

He started up the steps. "What's up here?" He stopped when he realized it was only one bedroom. "Kate, where do you—"

"I sleep upstairs. Brent was on the couch."

John twitched his eyebrows. "I want to go to the party tonight. I want to make sure you . . . I want to see what happens."

You want to prove to yourself that I'm not really enamored of Brent, I finished to myself. "You can't. You don't have a tux."

"Sure I can. I'll be one of Brent's rude friends from out of town, make a lot of noise about the casual look being 'in' these days. I don't care if these people think I'm rude or a bore. I'll never see them again. Besides, that way, I can be Prince Charming and sweep Cinderella out of the ball before the clock strikes twelve or someone tries to kill her."

That stung. "Gee, John, thanks for couching that in such gentle terms."

"If you won't leave with me now, at least give me the option of calling it like I see it," he said.

"Detective Knight won't approve."

"Doesn't bother me. Besides, won't there be gangs of drunken socialites swarming through the place? She'll be so busy keeping an eye out for DUIs, she'll never see me milling around. If you're staying, those are my rules. I've played by yours. It's your turn."

He was being a good sport, that was true, and heaven knew I wanted to be around him a lot longer than I'd ever see Brent. I'd always dreamed about Prince Charming sweeping me off my feet, and here he was with the offer on the table. I'd be a fool not to take it.

"Fine, but I think we should at least warn Brent that you're here, or else he'll blow a gasket and screw it all up." I walked to the bathroom. "Look, I need to get ready for this mess. The bride can't show up at her own party looking like she's had the day I've experienced."

"Oh, I don't know," John corrected. "It shows you have guts, tenacity, and aren't willing to give in to tradition." He moved closer to me. "And quit calling yourself a bride."

I smiled. "I don't think Brent's mom or her guests would see it that way."

He shrugged his shoulders. "I told you before, I really don't care what they think."

"Bear with me, Doc, okay? A few more hours are all I need. But right now, I'll just jump in the shower."

John stepped into the tiny bathroom with me. "Last one in is a rotten egg."

CHAPTER · 22

"YOU DIDN'T BUY that dress for him, did you?"

I yanked the dress off the hanger and slid it over my head. My still-damp curls tangled briefly in the zipper, but one tug later, the black crepe dropped in place on my shoulders. "No, why?"

John bundled a pillow into his lap. "It's nice, and I wondered why I'd never seen it before."

I grinned. "Not too many occasions on my social calendar say 'come in sequins.' You know me, I'd rather be in jeans on your couch." *I'd rather be in jeans on anyone's couch right now,* I thought.

I glanced in the mirror behind the door. I didn't look too shabby. The hemline was just above my knees, and the bodice had an overlay of sheer black fabric, with black, silver, and white sequins and bugle beads arranged in a delicate flower pattern. Pair it with black hose, black heels, and a pair of cubic zirconium earrings I'd worn in a distant incarnation as a bridesmaid, and I would be all set.

No one had to know I'd bought the dress off an after-season clearance rack for $39.95 about three years earlier. It was a whim, done in a weak moment on a lunch hour, right after I'd read a *Cosmo* article that berated anyone who didn't have a kicky black cocktail dress waiting in the closet for all those glamorous social events a single gal attended. Regrettably, given my exciting social life, the closet was exactly where it stayed until I dragged it out at Christmas eleven months earlier and then again for the weekend charade. It was a miracle it still fit.

"Well, I guess I feel better about things," John said. "Because no one in their right mind would try to harm someone who looks as good as you do.

Especially Brent. I know we haven't become fraternity brothers or anything, but from what I've seen and heard, I don't think he's got enough brain cells to plot a murder."

I put in my earrings. "I hope you're right. I don't know who to trust these days."

"You better be careful about me, too. I could be dangerous. I could be the wolf in sheep's clothing."

I rather liked John's clothing choice—which wasn't much. "The wolf's going to freeze to death if that's all he's wearing."

John crawled across the bed. He reached for my zipper and gave it a yank. "Oh, the wolf is plenty warm."

Our animal instincts were surfacing, but our sixth sense missed the visitor clomping up the staircase.

"Kate, are you ready?" Brent paused on the top step. His face darkened to nearly match his outfit. "Kate, what the hell?"

I found the grace to blush. "Brent, hi. You remember John, don't you?"

Brent's hurt fury both amused and scared me. "What are you doing here?" he asked John. "I mean, it's obvious what you're doing here, but it's with Kate, and . . . and she's with me, and it's our engagement party. You can't be here, doing what it is I think you've . . . um . . . done."

John stood behind me, but I couldn't decide whether to interpret his move as stalwart support or as a somewhat futile attempt to hide his boxers when faced with a model in a tux. "Don't tell me I have no right to be here. You're the one who shouldn't be standing in Kate's bedroom."

Brent moved closer. "It's my damn bedroom, in my house. You were not invited."

This was not a good start to the evening's chatter. I handed John his pants and a shirt. "Let's be grown-ups, shall we? Brent, we're not going to have this conversation right now. John is my guest, and I'm glad he's here. Yes, I'm ready as I'll ever be tonight, so let's go to the house and behave like civilized adults."

"He's not coming," Brent said.

"I am too," John replied as he pulled on his pants. "You got a problem with that?"

"Yeah, I do," Brent snapped.

"Well, I don't," I interjected. "And the bride gets what she wants. We're all going. And don't worry, Brent, I'll be your bride tonight. We had a deal. I don't break deals . . . do you?"

My conversations lately seemed to border on the surreal. The weird thing was, what I'd said made sense to me.

When I didn't get an answer, I grabbed Brent's hand and pulled him down the steps. John stumbled behind, seconds later. I reached in the closet for my coat, but it still reeked of smoke.

"Awful," I mumbled, dropping it onto the closet floor. "Let's hurry up before I freeze."

John dropped his coat over my shoulders, but Brent snorted and pulled it off. He slipped out of his jacket and firmly anchored it on my shoulders. He looked darkly at John. "She's *my* date."

Before we could fight that one out, the phone rang. I took a step toward answering it, but Brent clamped a hand on my arm. "Leave it. Let's go."

"But shouldn't we—" I started.

"No," Brent clipped. "It's not important. Let's go."

John wasn't interested in the phone either. He was on our heels going out the door. Brent and John anchored hands on my elbows, both of them staking a claim and practically carrying me across the yard. If that was the worst thing I had to face at the party, I could live with it.

Maybe, maybe not. It hit us the second we ascended the porch steps lined with Japanese lanterns. Once inside, we saw that the pink fairy had thrown up over the entire interior. I liked pink, but in the race for sheer quantity over quality, the color scheme made me feel like I was swimming in a bottle of Pepto-Bismol.

"Oh, this is awful!" Brent summed up for all of us.

Pink ribbon laced through yards of sheer net, on a twisting excursion along the banister of the grand staircase. Clouds of matching netting and ribbon were bunched over each doorway down the hall. Riots of pink roses, pink daisies, and ruby-throated lilies drenched every tabletop. And at the foot of the staircase was a waist-high black-and-gold urn filled with an eruption of flowers and greenery spilling off the sides like wax dripping from a candle.

I was glad that wasn't the arrangement that had fallen on me earlier. If that had been the case, all anyone would have needed to do was pick up one of the lilies off the floor and stick it in my folded hands. Case closed.

Delicate strings from a quartet in a distant room floated down the hall, and staff in black uniforms scurried noiselessly past, hauling trays of canapés and cocktails to the gathering guests, whose polite, muffled laughter hummed just a room away.

My chest constricted. Could I pull this off? It was showtime, and despite everything, I had promised to be the bride to a room full of strangers who expected a polished, charming socialite desperately in love with the Crown Prince. My ankle twitched in my high-heel shoe and swayed inward. I reached for John's sleeve.

"You all right?" he asked.

"Not really."

Brent retrieved his coat and cleared his throat. "I need a drink. I'll be back. What do you want?"

"Anything alcoholic," I answered. "Shouldn't I stay with you?"

I caught John's frown.

Brent did too. "No, I'll be right back. You stay here with him," he ordered as he went down the hall.

"I have a name," John mumbled.

"And it's one I love to hear," I whispered back.

"How long do we have to stay?" He sounded like a kid waiting to have a tooth pulled.

I felt the need for novocaine as well. "Till the bitter end, I suppose."

John fell into the swing of the ruse. "Can't you and Brent have some kind of big fight? You could cause a scene and storm out in tears. Then I can be the mysterious stranger in cheap clothes who rescues you."

I grinned. "Works for me."

We crossed the hall and discovered Adam sitting at a piano bench in the front parlor. He excused himself from his conversation with a small clump of early arrival blue bloods and motioned for us to meet him near the corner bookcase.

"You look like a mobster in that tux," I said.

"Thanks, but I'm afraid I left my machine gun in my violin case upstairs." He tugged at my dress. "Katester, you look lovely. John, you look, uh. . . ."

John smiled. "Shut up, Adam, while you're ahead."

Adam laughed, then dropped his voice. "No problem. Look, this is important. I just took a call from Alice a few minutes ago. She said she rang the cottage, but no one answered. Where were you?"

I looked at John. "Told you we should have answered the phone."

Adam waved his hand. "Anyway, before Brent comes back, listen up. Try this name on our friend Zach—Jack Hepburn."

I made a face. "Jack and Zach. Cute. Who is he?"

"Apparently, the discovery of his true identity resulted from a strenuous grilling Alice gave the real Zach Tanner. She went to his office and wouldn't

leave until they figured out who our guy is. Seems he now remembers returning from lunch a few days ago to find Jack Hepburn hanging out in his office.
He's a photographer, but he hasn't worked with the real Zach in years."

Adam slid a look around the room. "Zach #1 apparently taught our guy
some tricks of the trade, then Jack went off to make his millions in New York.
However, he didn't do too well in the Big Apple. Zach told Alice that Jack was
scouting for a job, said New York was overrated, and he wanted a fresh start."

"That still doesn't explain how he ended up here, calling himself Zach
Tanner," John said.

Adam nodded. "Granted, but Jack's description fits our Zach. That doesn't
tell us much about winding up with us, but it's a pretty good start."

"It's more than we had before," I observed. "And that might explain some
of his comments about working with models."

The model I was considering returned with two champagne flutes in his
hands and cast a pall on our conversation.

John's eyebrows twitched. "Adam, you think we should hit the bar?"

"Sounds perfect to me."

It sounded awful to me, since that left me alone with Brent and our adoring fans, who were rapidly filling the room. As I watched my cheering section disappear, I desperately wished I could accompany them.

Brent handed me the glass. "I thought we started this with a bottle of
champagne, so we may as well end it with one."

I stared at him, not sure how to take his comment about "ending it." I
swirled the bubbles in the glass. "All's well that ends well, I hope."

He frowned. "Huh?"

"Never mind."

"By the way," Brent added. "We're in trouble with Mom. We weren't properly introduced, to her liking. She didn't know we were here yet, and she
didn't get to make a grand entrance with us."

He downed his champagne in one long gulp and set the glass on the piano.
"Don't worry about it. She'll be in party mode soon." He glanced at me.
"Did I tell you that you look really hot?"

"No, but thanks. You look pretty good yourself." And the truth was, he
did. Brent King wore a tux like it was a second skin. He could probably wear
one on a beach and still look sharp.

The model charm kicked in gear. He shot a look toward the guests, then
scooped up my hand and kissed it a little too passionately. He followed that
by pulling me close and playfully toying with my hair. I was seventeen shades

of crimson, and every hair on my neck could feel the ogles from everyone. I hoped John was off somewhere, drinking himself into a stupor, so he didn't have to witness this.

Brent unlocked himself and spun around to address the crowd. "Excuse me, but if you can keep a big secret from my mother, I'll give you a sneak peak of the coming attraction." His smile lit up the room. "I know Mom will want to formally introduce us later, but I just can't wait for you to meet my special, special Kate—who's somehow agreed to honor me by becoming my wife."

The room erupted in applause, and I had a terrible flashback to the little restaurant where this all began. I was rushed by a stampeding horde of well-wishers, whose drawling tones and penchant for polysyllabic attempts at saying "Dah-ar-a-lin'" smothered any real attempt at conversation. I mostly smiled and flashed my ring as much as possible.

Brent enjoyed the attention, but he got a little possessive when the questions flew in my direction. He tried to steer the conversation toward his career several times and was a little put out when one society creature brushed him aside and said, "Yes, dear, we all know you take good photos."

I pried myself away from the circle with the feeble excuse that I needed to search for the little girls' room. I didn't make it very far. I crossed into the hall and was caught by a gaggle of clotheshorses in eye-popping dresses and jewelry. Suddenly, my dress felt every bit of $39.95. At least I was able to make up some ground with the ring.

Even though I was dying inside, the business of mixing and mingling really wasn't that hard. I discovered this crew was so intent on impressing each other with their tales and trials that all I really had to do was feign interest and insert a few well-placed phrases, such as "Oh, really?" and "How fascinating!" I was drawn into a lecture on what to expect not only from Brent, but from my second, and probably third, husband.

A woman with shocking red hair leaned in close. "Remember, dear, if at first you don't succeed, try, try again. The men sure do!"

"Keeps you in the lifestyle you deserve, honey," mused another.

I stared at them. What a nice sentiment for a bride-to-be to note in her memory book. I was warned also to avoid decorating tastes in the Martha Stewart realm.

I heard how, while shopping in the Hamptons recently, one of the ladies in my group ran into a horrible woman in ratty clothes and no makeup, who was screaming bloody murder at a store clerk. It was none other than MS herself.

The point to her story was succinct. "Why, after all, you should only treat the help that way at home, not in a store!"

The dresses broke into tittering laughter, and I grabbed that opportunity to vamoose. I didn't think it could get much worse, but as I trudged down the hall, a hand emerged from a doorway and yanked me into the butler's pantry between the kitchen and dining room.

Jane, dripping in sapphires, demanded, "Don't you have any manners?"

I could have argued the point with the woman who'd pulled me out of the hall as if I were a sack of potatoes, but I passed.

I noted how large her pupils were. "Is there a problem, Mrs. King?"

"You are taking over my party. I am the hostess, not you. Don't you have any respect for this production I've arranged on your behalf? You didn't wait for introductions, you have ignored me completely, and, no doubt, you're probably offending my guests. We won't even discuss your outfit."

I bit my lip and counted to ten.

She wasn't interested in a reply. "Remember this, dear. I created Brent. I made him what he is. You will not take him away from me. Other girls have tried, and I put a stop to it, so don't think I won't do it again. You are not the right person for my son."

I agreed with her, but I kept my mouth shut. No sense in disturbing her further.

Her voice lowered. "We'll get through tonight, and then we'll talk. I'm sure my husband will arrange something to send you on your way quietly." She grabbed my wrist and slowly squeezed all feeling from my hand. "And if you persist, I'll make you so unhappy that you'll bolt out of here—just like the others." Her eyes were coated in a sticky glaze. "And then, I'll have to take care of my little boy, my hurt little boy. Everyone will feel sorry for me. I put together all this work for nothing, thanks to a mealy little wench like you."

She let go of my hand and shoved me into the dining room. A couple sampling a cheese tray looked up, considered Jane's friendly appearance, then quickly backed out of the room. I moved around a small table for protection. A flowered candelabra with five tapers separated us, so I figured I could flash the candles at her the way they used to ward off evil spirits in old movies. Maybe that would make her disappear.

Jane leaned over the table. Her black eyes flickered in the flame. "Believe me, Kate, this will be a night you won't soon forget."

Pass the Cheez Whiz. We've got ourselves a party.

C H A P ✝ E R · 23

IN A HOUSE FULL OF PEOPLE HAVING FUN, I felt entirely alone. Winging cheese cubes or kiwi pieces at Jane as I fled the room wasn't correct protocol, but it might hold her at bay. Where were the cops when you needed them? I had a homicidal mother-in-law on my hands, and she had a big-time reverse Oedipal complex. There was no time to wonder where my good detectives Rami and Knight were. I needed Superman.

I settled for Willard.

He popped into the room, nearly blinding me with his gold lamé vest and red tux. He stared at me for a split second, then flew to my side. "Dearest angel, there you are. And don't you look yummy?" He smiled sweetly at Jane. "And Janey, I simply must have you taste something—you are the master at selecting the best. Please, my dear hostess, find your way to the kitchen. It's imperative you go."

Duty called. Jane silently brushed past and disappeared toward the kitchen.

Willard took my arm. "Get thee as far away from that loony woman as you can. When you see her enter a room, you leave. I know this is your night, but for everyone concerned, especially you, stay this side of Texas out of her sight. What you do in the future is your call, love, but I'd grab the Brentster and only come back here for holidays and funerals. Capiche?"

"Got it. By the way, thanks for all your work. It's certainly, um, fluffy."

Willard beamed and winked. "Only the best for you, sweetie. I better slide over to the kitchen now and figure out something for Janey to taste. You, dear, depart."

Fine. As long as I didn't become one of the dearly departed. Instead, I ambled into another room full of guests and was promptly tagged by a sharply pointed ruby fingertip. I turned and was engulfed by a spray of white ostrich feathers molting on a black-sequined gown.

"Darling. You must be little, uh, Katherine. Patsy Tucker . . . of Winchester. How on earth did someone like you capture Brent?"

That was a slam from Patsy Tucker of Winchester. For one thing, she broke my cardinal rule and called me Katherine. Only my parents managed to call me that, and usually only when matched with my middle name in the midst of an announcement that I was in big trouble.

I smiled politely. "No one was as surprised as I was." I poked my head around the feathers. "Oh, look, isn't that George Clooney over there? He's from Kentucky, isn't he?"

George Clooney was nowhere, except in my imagination, but Patsy Tucker abandoned me with the speed of a mosquito flocking to sweaty skin.

I searched the room for an escape route and realized it wouldn't come easily if I was looking for pleasant conversation. There was so much evidence of plastic surgery around me that Mattel could have whipped up a year's supply of Barbie dolls. However, I consoled myself that if I looked closely at most of the women, they weren't as young as they seemed at a distance. Their skin, tucked into neat little nips at their ears, was so tight that their lips were permanently pulled into a fake country-club smile.

I wasn't the only plastic-surgery virgin. My eyes landed on Meg across the room. She was glumly talking with her father, who looked as bored as she did. Meg apparently missed the "formal dress" memo, because she wore a simple black pantsuit and no makeup or jewelry. Her black hair was smoothed tightly behind her ears, and if I shut my eyes and pictured bright red lipstick and lots of expensive jewelry, I'd swear I was looking at a younger Jane.

I debated joining them, but I stopped when Dr. Gerald lumbered into their corner. The trio exchanged hushed comments, then Meg and the veterinarian slipped out of sight. Douglas caught me staring at them and merely nodded, before pasting on his own fake smile and strolling into a clump of guests.

"There you are." Brent's voice was less than friendly. "I've been looking for you. You're my date, remember? From now on, you're with me, understand?"

I looked at his tired and pained eyes. Little lines gathered at the corners and sank into his tanned skin.

"I'm your hostage," I said.

"Sweet, Kate. Real sweet."

Another interminable group of nosy guests saved further endearing comments. Brent rose to the occasion, prattling on as if he hadn't a care in the world. I was sucked into the vortex and practiced more smiling.

"So," said a tall man with an embarrassingly large bush of hair growing out each ear, "I guess you two will get an early Christmas present, with all that extra cash, huh? That insurance money should only take about a month before it's paid out, right? That's what happened when my Foolish Spring bought it. Tidy little sum there for an engagement present. How many mil is it?"

The woman to his right slapped his hand. "That's not proper conversation for a party. Save it for the backside."

He shook his head. "You know we're all curious. Such a tragedy to lose such a great horse. If I were your father, Brent, I'd question Gerald about how hastily he put Bayou down. My vet said the horse could have been saved. Almost looks like it was done on purpose."

Brent shifted his weight. "I really don't know a lot about that. It was a great loss to our family."

The man leaned toward me. "You're not family yet. Tell them to be careful about having Larry Gerald around their bank box. It's too bad you had to come in on the middle of all this mess, but in retrospect, I wouldn't be bothered. The insurance money ought to give you one helluva honeymoon. Come on, Brent, how much are y'all cashing?"

His wife sucked in a lungful of breath and dragged him away, leaving us alone.

Brent rolled his eyes. "They're all vultures. They don't want to be here. They just want gossip."

The vulture in the $39.95 black dress was intrigued. "How much *will* you get from insurance, Brent?" I asked.

"I don't know. That's not my department." He surveyed the crowd. "I don't bank it, I just spend it."

A camera flashed, and a black suit headed in our direction. Zach was neatly shaved, and his ponytail was tucked discreetly in his collar. At first glance, he looked as white-bread as the rest of the guests.

"These people sure love to have their pictures taken," he stated. "I've had a little harem following me all night long. But, in all that time, this is the first picture I've snapped of the happy couple." He reached for a glass of wine from a passing tray and tipped it back. "Trouble is, the couple doesn't *look* too happy."

"Save it, will you?" Brent said. He stomped away, apparently forgetting his edict that I accompany him everywhere.

"He needs another drink," Zach observed.

"It probably wouldn't hurt all of us," I answered. "Look, Zach, we need to talk."

"No time for talkin', darlin', I have pictures to shoot."

Figuring there was safety in numbers, I grabbed his sleeve. "No, you don't. You're done." I took a breath. "There is no article. No need for pictures. Your work is finished . . . Jack."

His chin shot in the air like a rocket off a launching pad. "Zach," he corrected. "You've apparently had a little too much already."

I lowered my voice. "I know you're not Zach Tanner. Let's try Jack Hepburn. Why are you here, Jack? Why don't you tell me now, before I make it known to everyone else?"

He dropped the camera to his side and grabbed my elbow. "You don't know anything."

"I know enough. Why are you here?"

His eyes flew over my shoulder, and he paled to match the carpet.

Detective Rami appeared casually at our side. "Good evening," he said.

"One that I hope is almost over," I answered.

The photographer dropped his hand from my elbow.

Rami smiled at me. "Impressive look you have going there. Seems like you're fitting in nicely."

"Thanks, I appreciate it. I personally feel a little underdressed."

He pulled at his tie. "No kidding. You pass it off well. Enjoying yourself tonight?"

I glanced at "Zach." The polite chitchat had given birth to little beads of sweat that rolled down his freshly shaven face.

"Not really," I said, probably for both of us.

"Well, I'm afraid things won't improve much."

Zach and I exchanged glances.

"Why don't you join me in the other room for a minute, where we can talk? I have some news to share with you."

"Me too?" Zach asked.

Rami nodded. "Most definitely. Detective Knight is gathering who she can find."

We followed Rami into the parlor across the hall. It was filled with people, and in one corner, Adam and John patiently waited.

Seconds later, Knight dragged Brent in. "This is the only crew I could manage at the moment," she said in greeting.

Brent was antsy. "What is this? A game of Clue? Some kind of bad joke? We don't have time for this. We're in the middle of a party—my party. Whatever this is can wait."

Knight shook her head. "No, it can't. We have some news. News I think you'll find particularly interesting, Mr. King." She didn't waste any time. "We have a positive ID on the body found in the burned car." She paused for effect and watched our reactions. "It's not Paige Kendall, Mr. King."

Brent paled to match his white vest. "I don't know what you mean. I . . . I mean, I'm glad. I mean, I don't . . . um . . . know anyone named Paige Kendall. How can you be sure? I thought you'd decided—"

Nothing had been decided. He caught himself and dropped the sentence.

Knight zeroed in on Brent. "I thought you'd be more relieved than this. And, Mr. King, we know you know Paige. Don't get me wrong. Ms. Kendall is still considered missing."

"Oh, okay then." Brent relaxed, but that still wasn't the correct reaction.

Adam interrupted. "So, who is the body?"

Rami took up the story. "Martina Sloan. That name ring a bell?"

Brent's head jerked. "That's Paige's roommate. How . . . why did she end up here?"

Rami shrugged. "We were hoping you could shed some light on that."

"Ms. Sloan's work and family reported her as missing," Knight began. "Quite frankly, it doesn't matter whether it's police in Kentucky or New York, it doesn't take much detecting to figure out you've got twice the problem when both inhabitants of a small apartment disappear at approximately the same time. We checked the dental records of both women to our victim, and boom—we had a match, but it wasn't what we expected."

We played a silent game of shooting bewildered looks at each other. John broke the uneasy silence. "So, where do we find Paige Kendall?"

"That's our next priority," Knight said.

Tax dollars would be saved for the Lexington Police Department. Brent's eyes grew large, and he stepped clumsily into a potted tree adorned with twinkle lights. Zach scooted out of the room, his camera smashed against his face like he was running and photographing a herd of animals. The rest of us turned to see a young woman, in a filmy purple dress and carrying a monster macrame handbag, burst into our little circle.

"Brent King, what on earth are you trying to pull?"

It appeared we'd found the one and only Paige Kendall. Very much alive. Very much furious.

"Brent, what is Jack doing here?" she demanded. "What's going on?"

I slid between Adam and John, but Paige's finger pointed my direction. "And who the hell is she?"

Brent's breathing was labored, and his face was green. He reached for her hand. "Paige, I thought you were—"

"I was gone." She wouldn't pass Jane King's politeness test. "Yeah. I needed time." She spoke loudly. "WHO IS THIS WOMAN?"

Knight stepped in, and I realized the detectives were as surprised as the rest of us. "I recommend you don't create a scene, Ms. Kendall. Where have you been the last few weeks?"

"Who wants to know?"

Knight flashed her badge. "We do. Answer the question, please."

Paige flushed. "The Iron Curtain fell a while back. I have every right to take off for a few days. I wasn't running away from anything." She looked at Brent and added, "Or anyone. And look, this is Kentucky, not New York. I only grow it for medicinal purposes, and I'm not carrying, so you don't have any jurisdiction—"

Brent silenced her by wrenching her wrist. "Paige. Stop."

Fire shot from her eyes, but fire of another kind glinted up into my eyes. Paige wore a diamond ring just as large, just as stunning as the one on my finger. I calculated Brent's monthly payments for both rings and nearly fainted.

"Not here, not now." Brent glanced nervously at Rami and turned back to Paige. "We need to go somewhere and talk. Now. I can explain everything."

"You better start talking, because this is supposed to be my party, and you obviously started without me." She considered me. "I don't know who you are, but don't even look in his direction."

Curious heads were navigating our way. Like everyone else, I was intent on hearing the story and figuring out how Jack fit in, but that wasn't in Paige's grand scheme.

Brent's chin shook. "Please. Excuse us. We need to talk alone for a few minutes. We can't do it here."

Rami nodded. "Don't go far. You have ten minutes. There's a lot our little group needs to discuss."

Brent grabbed my hand. "You come, too."

Oh, brother. Brent managed to wear a smile as he hustled us past the guests and down the hall toward the kitchen. The busy kitchen, besides being the home of many knives, didn't suit us well for a big explanation. Brent muttered under his breath and pulled us out the back door, into a tent extension holding the catering trucks and equipment.

"What is going on?" Tears formed in Paige's eyes. "You will not humiliate me this way, Brent. We've been down this road before. I will not tolerate you cheating on me."

Two men in little white coats broke between us, carrying tubs of ice.

Paige ran her hand through her hair. "For heaven's sake, Brent, we're getting married. When are you going to grow up?"

He stepped back and bumped into another server hauling a large soup tureen. "I am not cheating on you. And you have a lot of room to talk." Three more servers bustled through the tent, all casting looks that said we were very much in their way. "Where have you been, Paige? You disappeared. What was I supposed to think?"

She wasn't interested in debating her travel schedule. "Why is *she* here? Are you going to tell me who she is?" Her eyes landed on my hand, and she gasped. "My ring. She's wearing my ring. Brent, no!" She pitched an angry swing at him and bolted out of the tent.

He ran after her, and I followed. Paige leaned against the wall of the small office attached to the barn. I could hear her sobs yards away. Brent reached her, but she was in no mood for a reconciliation hug. Instead, she pummeled her fists on his chest and heaved angry sobs into his shirt. This was no place for me. I noticed the door to the equine office open a crack, so I slipped inside, where I could stay warm until Brent and Paige got over the hysterics.

The office was a large, open room, home to five desks, lots of computers, and a mishmash of horse equipment, from saddles placed on chairs to trophies and racing cups decorating various makeshift bookcases. So this was the heart of Bluegrass Winds. I had never pictured an office setting, preferring instead a glamorized image of life on the farm that wasn't so coldly technical.

Since I had nothing better to do, I surveyed the room and casually glanced across the desktops. A computer on the corner desk hummed, so I took a look. A spreadsheet chart glowed on the screen, with a cursor pausing on a column of dates. Even I could detect that it was a breeding record for one of the horses. I scrolled the page up, and Bayou Folly's name flashed before me. I saw what Steve Mathias meant when he said the Thoroughbred had been pimped to death.

An impressive list of breeding dates and outrageous payments filled the columns. A one-time romantic encounter with Bayou Folly, regardless of whether the match provided offspring, netted a cool $200,000. The date columns showed also that payment in full was due well in advance of the actual meeting. I scrolled down to the end of the column and saw a total of just over $18 million for the year.

I could see why the Kings were so devastated at the loss, but what I hadn't considered was the insurance payment. My eyes scanned the desk, and with little effort, I found a folder marked "Ins. Bayou Folly." On top was a form insuring the horse for $70 million.

Bayou Folly was a great roll in the hay, but in the end, he was worth more dead than alive.

A toilet flushed behind a door a couple feet away, and in a panic, I closed the folder, dropped under the next desk to the right, and pulled its chair in front of me. Dr. Gerald ambled out from the small bathroom and came immediately to the desk. He tapped on the computer keyboard a couple times, then dialed the phone.

"It's me. You got your end straightened out?" He grunted. "Well, hell, you should hear the talk up here. There are so many jaws flappin' hot air that the breeze picked up about ten knots. All I care is that the check, as they say, is in the mail." He paused. "No, no, I'll handle this end, you stay out of it."

His brief conversation merited a second phone call. "It's about time. Are you walking around there with your pocket ringing?" His voice was urgent. "Listen . . . Mathias needs to be handled. Those liquor lips of his are making too much noise in the wrong places. He's not as dumb as you think. He knows horses, he knows the score."

Dr. Gerald was silent but agitated. He paced some more, then landed his ample behind on top of my desk. His fat leg swung in front of the chair. "You just remember, it's my ass in a sling right now. Too many people are talking. What guarantee do I have that I'll get what's coming? I've risked everything so you can pay your bills. I want to make sure I can pay my bills for a long time. Understand?"

Whoever was on the other end raised Dr. Gerald's blood pressure. "A break is a break, whether it's a clean one or a shattered one. Hell, yes, I know the difference. I didn't have a lot of time—I just got the job done for you. That horse is long gone; I saw to it that he was shipped out immediately. No one is going to pay attention to what the break looked like. It's all supposition, a bunch of talk. Accidents happen. I was there, remember? It's my word, as a respected authority, against theirs. We need to move on and cash those checks."

After another irritating comment, he slid off the desk, shoving the chair farther under the desk. I bit my lip as the chair slammed into my knee.

"Well, if you don't want to talk there, meet me out here now. I'll see you in a few minutes. Let's settle this once and for all."

He slammed the phone down, and I watched his feet clomp through the door, which closed softly. I waited a couple of minutes, then emerged from my cocoon and tiptoed to the door. I leaned against the wall and looked out the window but didn't see Dr. Gerald or his phone buddy.

I unlocked the door and slipped through. The cold air sliced past my shivering sequins, but even so, I was sweating like I'd run a marathon. So Bayou Folly was a maxed-out credit card and Dr. Gerald offed him for a cut of the insurance money. Steve's ramblings about a mob hit suddenly made sense.

I eased around the side of the barn, expecting to find Brent and Paige. The plethora of tears and shouts were lost to the night, which turned up my thermostat even higher. Never let them see you sweat. Too late.

A blast ripped through the air.

My heart flew to my throat. The once-darkened barn was now ablaze in lights. Had they moved inside where it was warm? Paige had been carrying a huge handbag, large enough for a gun. But if she had fired a gun, I was probably the last person she'd want to see.

So I ran straight for the barn. I had officially gone mad.

I picked at the beads on my dress as I hesitated just outside. Buckets clanging and liquid splashing gave me a reassuring hint that someone was working inside. Maybe I'd mistaken the noise for an innocent bucket slamming against a stall. But, in that case, where had Brent and Paige gone? I pushed open the barn door.

I found Brent. He was lying on the floor, face bathed in sweat. A nasty red stain spread across his shirt. Horses in their stalls stomped out their displeasure at the turn of events.

I ran into the barn and slid on the wet floor, which was soaked in pools of gasoline.

Brent stretched out his hand. "Kate . . . behind. . . ." He didn't have a chance to finish. A rake whapped me across the back and sent me to my knees.

"Are you ready to die, Kate?"

I turned around and managed to stand. Meg faced me, just a few feet away. The rake, now at her feet, had been replaced with a much more potent gun in her hands.

"This is all your fault," she began. "Everything was perfect until you came along."

"Meg, please put the gun down." I knew it was a futile request, but it certainly was earnest.

She ignored me. "These horses . . . this farm . . . it's my life. It's all I have. And now, just when I have the money to make it work again, make it the success it should be, you show up."

I glanced at Brent behind me, and Meg waved the gun. "You can blame it on Brent. He's always, *always* had the attention. It's my turn now, and nothing will stop it." Her eyes squeezed shut and then flew open wide. "I went to New York. I saw you there."

"Meg, I was never in New York," I protested.

She shook her head and continued with her New York hallucination. "You said you weren't his girlfriend, but I knew it was a lie. Everyone has always lied to me—told me I'd be the success and I'd have everything, not Brent. But no, he gets paid for smiling at a camera. Do you know what I do? How many hours I spend out here, trying to make ends meet? Trying to keep this farm profitable? Hours. Hours!"

Her eyes glowed. "I've worked so hard, for so long. It's not my fault things got out of control. You can't blame me for trying to fix it. The last thing we needed was the expense of a wedding and everyone gushing over Brent. I had a solution, it's going to work, and the farm will be okay. That's why I went to New York for you. You weren't going to ruin my spotlight."

"It wasn't me. I wasn't in New York." I didn't know why I was arguing the point, but at least it kept her talking.

Her mother's child surfaced, and she talked as if I weren't there. "I took care of her. It was easy. I put her in her car and brought her here—just like Ashley. Just like it happened back then." She looked down at Brent. "They'd catch him this time; he'd get what he deserved. And there I'd be—the good one, the successful one."

She lowered the gun and unlocked the stall next to her. The frightened Thoroughbred bolted out and effortlessly sailed over Brent's body, then ran wildly into the night. She raised the gun again and held it steady as she let the next horse loose. It reared out of its stall, and I jumped to the side and let it pass, wishing desperately that I were riding it.

She took a step toward me. "But then you showed up here. How, why, I don't know. You just keep coming back. You're always here. But I've got you now—both of you. I won't have to worry. You're both right where I want you."

I wanted out in the worst way.

"Murder-suicide is such a tragic thing, especially when you thought the couple would marry." She fired the gun in my direction, and I flew behind a support beam. Meg mistook that for a direct hit. I cowered behind the beam and watched in horror as she pulled a lighter out of her pocket, lit it, and tossed it on the ground. A ferocious wall of flames erupted and raced along the walls, fueled by the combination of gasoline, hay, and wood.

Meg fired another shot blindly and let the next horse go free. The frantic animal knocked her to the side, and the gun flew from her hand and slid across the floor.

I tried to pick up Brent, but he was dead weight. Burning clumps of hay floated around us, like eerily horrific falling stars. I swatted at them wildly, trying to keep them away from Brent.

Thick black smoke rolled through the air and darkened the room to a nightmarish haze. A crossbeam gave way and tumbled to the ground, splintering off burning sections, one of which slammed close to Brent. I pulled at his shoulders and tried to move him away from the flames. He moaned loudly.

"I'm sorry, I'm sorry," I cried, momentarily letting my guard down.

Meg charged at me with a shovel in her hands. She swung and hit me broadside with it, and I slammed against a stall and knocked over a stack of hay, which promptly ignited. That was inspiration enough for me to leap forward. I barreled straight at her like a linebacker and sent her to the floor. She grabbed for my skirt, ripping the side seam. I kicked her away and almost stumbled into a burning beam.

She bounced up, ready once again for action. Her face was nearly black from the soot and smoke. Add that to her black pantsuit, dark hair, and the envelope of obsidian smoke around us, and she merged into every monster that ever hid under my bed.

We spotted the gun lying nearby. I was closer and dove for it, but Meg had the advantage of athletic leg muscles, which she used to kick me like a soccer ball. She hit me squarely in the chest. Meg finished the play with an illegal use of hands as she shoved me into a stall filled with the acrid smoke. I landed hard against the wall and slid into the corner. It was so hot, I felt like my skin was melting off the bone. It would have been hard to breathe normally after a fight like this, much less one done in a cocktail dress in a burning building. My lungs were ready to call a time-out.

I rolled over and looked up through the smoke. Meg stood in the doorway of the stall, coughing violently and leveling the gun in her trembling hands.

She stared at me with empty black eyes.

With the icy calm of an Olympic marksman, she aimed the gun and fired.

C H A P  E R · 24

I SCREAMED AND rolled to the side. Something hot and stinging sliced my sleeve in half and thumped into the wall behind me. Splinters of wood showered my hair, and I lay frozen with fear, waiting for the next shot. Meg didn't hang around for a verdict. She slammed the stall door shut and slid the bolt with triumphant finality.

My upper left arm sizzled with the sting of a dozen rabid bees, and I felt something moist pulling what was left of my sleeve to my skin like a sticky adhesive. *Oh, God, I've been shot,* I thought. *I'm a travel reporter. Travel reporters don't get shot—policemen do, criminals do, drug dealers do. Not nice girls like me, wearing diamonds and what's left of a once-nice dress.*

Shock paralyzed me, and the smoke ate at my reasoning skills. Tears gushed down my face as I curled into a ball, coughing and crying. I heard a shout and another struggle outside the stall. Forcing myself to stand, I shoved my good shoulder against the stall door. It wouldn't give way. Another gunshot exploded, and I sank against the wall once more, terrified that Meg was shooting at the door.

Dots danced in my vision. This was not a good sign. Meg or no Meg, I screamed as loudly as I could over the fire's roar. Within seconds, someone on the other side unbolted the door, and a large, looming figure scooped me up and tossed me over his shoulders. The fire swirled around us as he dodged burning beams and clumps of burning hay. I shut my eyes against the searing heat and soon felt a rush of cold air and heard a chorus of shouts.

I was tossed backward, over to another set of hands, which brought me gently to the ground. I opened my eyes to see Steve, my hulking rescuer, running back into the barn as voices implored him to stop. I was outside, safe in John's arms. I looked up to see Adam and a host of faces that meant nothing to me.

I couldn't comprehend much that was said, particularly since everyone was talking at once. The barn was completely engulfed in bright orange and gold flames that licked the sky like the devil's tongue tempting the heavens. Invisible heat rolled across the lawn, giving the appearance of an old television receiver flipping wildly and distorting the picture.

Emergency vehicles abounded and were peppered on all sides by party guests in their finery, holding their drinks and watching the sideshow. I spotted Meg at a distance. She was sitting on the ground near the barn, her face draped with an oxygen mask. Detective Knight and a uniformed officer, neither of whom seemed particularly concerned with Meg's comfort or health, stood over her.

Blankets were tossed on me, and from somewhere behind me, an oxygen mask dropped over my face. The cold, fresh air was welcome, but it stung my lungs and brought tears to my eyes. I focused on John, who looked frantic. It was all a haze, until he ripped off the rest of my sleeve, causing the pain in my arm to whip me back to reality.

I cried out a wimpy protest, and he purred comforting things that were lost to me, thanks to an uproar of shouts that erupted by the barn. Steve emerged again, this time accompanied by a firefighter helping him haul out Brent. Emergency workers grabbed Brent, and Steve collapsed on the ground. John instinctively took off toward them, along with several other guests. There were quite a few doctors in the house that evening.

A scream pierced the cacophony, and I watched Paige break through a cluster of people and rush to Brent's side. *Show's over,* I thought. *She can have him.* Still, I was worried about Brent. I never managed to see exactly where he was shot, but his lack of movement, and the handicap of lying in the middle of a raging fire, didn't bode well for his general health.

I wanted to stay around for the finale, but instead, my compatriots and I were hauled off to a nearby emergency room, where I traded my ripped and ruined pseudo-designer gown for a fashionable hospital ensemble (sexy open back included). I had enough oxygen pumped into me to launch a hot-air balloon. I was relieved to discover I hadn't been seriously injured. The bullet had grazed my arm, leaving me with a nasty scrape that could have come from falling off a bike onto a gravel road.

At least I qualified for a pretty impressive bandage.

Detective Rami dropped in as much as the nurses did. Between his quick visits, I managed to explain the night's events, apparently to his satisfaction, since his third visit was the final one.

In the meantime, John sat with me in our little curtained cubicle. "We've got to stop meeting this way," he said.

"I'll do anything to date a doctor," I answered.

"Quiet now, I think you still have some smoky, dead brain cells up there. Remember, I'm off duty right now. Tonight I'm just the wildly concerned boyfriend who wants you to get better."

"I'm working on it. How's Brent?" I cringed when John's jaw twitched. "Be honest, John."

"Last I heard, he was in surgery. The guy who carried you out is in pretty bad shape, too. We'll know more in the morning about his prognosis."

Not good news.

I shifted around, trying to get comfortable. "The last I saw of Meg, she was trussed up on a gurney like I was. Where is she now?"

"Don't know, and I really don't care," John said. "It's late. Why don't you try to sleep a little, and I'll convince them to spring you from here under my care. Adam went back to the farm to collect your stuff. We're not going back there. We'll get a hotel suite somewhere for the rest of the night."

He kissed me lightly, and I obeyed his request.

At some point in the wee hours, I awoke and stumbled into a welcome pair of jeans and a sweater provided by Adam. We drove to the promised hotel, and I slept soundly through to the early afternoon.

The Marriott folks pampered me more than the mansion ever did. A nice hot bath helped me soak out the smoke and stiffness from my prizefighter encounter with Meg. My arm throbbed, and I sported a lovely preseason sunburn from my time in the Easy-Bake Oven, but at least I survived my engagement party.

I emerged to find football on the TV and John and Adam feasting on a huge room-service spread. John had sprung for a suite with a little sitting room, so I joined them by the couch and enthusiastically dived into the assorted goodies.

I looked up at their amused faces. "What? I didn't have dinner last night, remember? I'm hungry, get over it."

John pulled out a package of Snickers bars from a bag on the floor. My hero. "Here's your dessert, when the rest of it is gone."

I reached for some fries from Adam's plate. "So, any word on Brent?"

"I called this morning," John said. "He got through surgery all right;

there shouldn't be any major complications from the gunshot wound. He has some burns and smoke inhalation, but nothing that won't heal in time. All in all, he was pretty lucky."

Adam pulled his plate of fries away from me. "He won't be jumping on any runways for a while, but he'll be back to charming the masses soon enough."

"What about Steve? And Meg?"

"They're watching Steve for a couple of days, but he should be okay. He was pretty strong to begin with, so that will help with his recovery," John said. "I think they released Meg around the same time we brought you here, but I'd assume her accommodations are not quite as nice as these."

Adam handed me a soda. "You literally cracked the scam about Bayou Folly out in the open. A lot of the office was damaged in the fire, but they can examine the computer hard drives and ask a lot of questions. Dr. Gerald squealed like a pig when he realized what happened. I guess he figured since he didn't have cash in hand yet, he was safer blowing the whistle on Meg. He killed the horse, under Meg's instructions, so they could collect the insurance. From what I heard, the money was flowing quickly. I imagine the insurance adjuster will be getting a visit today from the police.

"As for the horse," he continued, "even if it had actually caught its leg in a stall, the break would have been a clean snap, they would have casted it, and Bayou Folly could have survived. But in this case, Dr. Gerald hit it with a blunt object and shattered the bone. Before any other vets could look at the radiographs, Dr. Gerald had the horse put down immediately. He then had it shipped to a place you don't want to know about. Let's just say there's nothing left to investigate."

That certainly put the farm in jeopardy. If the insurance company denied the claim and accused Meg of insurance fraud on top of everything else, the future of Bluegrass Winds was in dire peril. Having its heiress charged with murder wouldn't help either.

We finished our late lunch and packed up for a quick visit to the hospital before catching our flight home. When I asked how Jane was handling things, John answered, "Remember that song 'I Wanna Be Sedated'? Take it from there."

Adam nodded. "No kidding. The party sure went down in local lore, at least."

Alice had been right about Zach's true identity. Once everyone learned the photographer was Jack, the story came out, much less sinister than what I'd concocted. Paige and Jack had a fling on a job in New York at the time Brent came along and swept her off her feet. With Brent's perpetual lack of focus, he simply ignored Jack and never actually made the connection at first when Zach Tanner appeared. Jack's masquerade as Zach was a fluke. He'd been in the real Zach Tanner's office when Alice left her initial message. He recognized Brent's name and thought he'd have a little fun revenge on his ex and her new boyfriend. He just didn't bargain for Paige's disappearance and my substitution.

We arrived at the hospital and promptly ran into Detective Rami.

"You look good today. Feeling better?" he asked.

"Much," I answered. "You look like you've had a long day, though."

He nodded. "Comes with the territory. I'll walk you to Brent's room. It's under guard, so I'll make sure you get through. Ms. Kendall's there. He's in and out of it, but he ought to be okay eventually."

"What about the other King sibling?" I asked. "Looks like Meg has some of her mom's problems, huh?"

"That's the least of her troubles," Rami said as we got into the elevator. "She's admitted to all the assault attempts on you and Brent. She also confessed to killing Ms. Sloan, thinking she was Brent's fiancée, and then driving her body back here in Ms. Kendall's car. I'm not up-to-date on my delusional homework, but I think it had a lot to do with her determination to get rid of a fiancée, whoever she might be."

"You hit that one square," John supplied.

"When we were in the barn," I said, "she mentioned Ashley Hannah. Do you think she killed her, too?"

Rami led us off the elevator and turned down a hall. "We're not quite clear on that one yet. The investigation remains very much open now."

"What about the gun Meg had in the barn?" I asked. "Was that the missing murder weapon?"

He shook his head. "No. After Meg shot Ms. Sloan, she hid the gun under Zach's—er, Jack's—bed. When she went to retrieve it and it was gone, she had to use a different one. I suspect you'll find some missing pieces in Douglas King's gun collection. We confiscated the gun she used in the yard yesterday. The murder weapon was found stashed in a basket full of towels in the massage room." He smiled slightly. "I guess you were right about Brent's, uh, pants."

I smiled back, in spite of myself. John's brain kicked into gear, and I got another one of his looks. I'd have to explain that one later. "But why did Brent hide it in the first place?"

The detective shrugged. "A misguided attempt at helping out, perhaps?

Except he didn't bother to show it to me. He decided, instead, to hide it in the towels when you were attacked in the sauna, lest he be suspected of hurting you. And, of course, I suppose we've all learned about his short-term memory problem."

We reached Brent's room, and Rami said, "I need to run, but I wanted to thank you for your help, even if it was unsolicited many times. I guess you've had your fill of Kentucky hospitality. Why don't you come back when it's on better terms?"

I shook his hand. "You can count on it, Detective."

I poked my head in Brent's room.

Paige stood. "Look, we were never formally introduced or anything, but thanks. I wasn't very nice to you last night. I . . . uh . . . I tend to run away from uncomfortable things. Brent and I have our problems, but I hope we can work them out. I couldn't handle it last night. I was confused. We were talking, and his sister came in the barn. I was embarrassed and just ran outside. I had no idea what was about to happen. If you hadn't come into the barn, I don't know what. . . ." She wiped her eyes and squeezed my hand. "Thank you." She glanced at Adam and John, then sprinted out the door.

Even though Brent was tied to every device known to medical science, he still managed to look like a soap star following a perilous encounter with a dastardly nemesis. He was groggy but conscious. "Kate, I'm sorry all this happened. If I'd known. . . ." He reached for my hand and held it tightly. "You didn't deserve it."

"Neither did you," I said.

He stopped squeezing my hand and held it softly, stroking my finger. "Kate, keep the ring."

"You're kidding, Brent. That's the painkillers talking."

He smiled weakly. "No, really. You should have it."

What on earth would I do with a ring like that? My evil side surfaced for a second, and visions of pawnshops and trips to the beach with cold hard cash danced in my eyes. "No, no, Brent. It wouldn't be right."

"Please, take it. Enjoy it," he said. "Besides, it's not real. The stones are fake."

So I kept the ring. I placed it in my jewelry box, but I never brought myself to wear it again. I thought I'd wait until the real thing came along. And if it never did, well, I could always pull out Brent's ring. Who'd know the difference?

A few weeks after we returned home, John and I were locked in our idea of domestic bliss—a Saturday night, burning logs on the fireplace, basketball on TV, cold beer on ice, and a box of Chicago-style pizza on the coffee table.

"Kate? Let's not get engaged."

The pizza slice, half in and half out of my mouth, was no doubt an attractive sight. "Excuse me?"

He handed me a napkin. "Not now. Not yet. Engagement stuff is too much to deal with, and all we'd ever think about was what happened in Kentucky."

John was wonderful in every way, but the "E" word had yet to cross my mind with him. This was certainly the first time he'd ever mentioned the subject. I wasn't quite sure what to say.

"Um, okay, that's fine."

He smiled and went back to his pizza. "Good. Great. Good idea. Not yet, anyway."

Not yet?